THE LAST POST

Written

Rhys Evans / De

Prologue:

Rhys Evans an ex-British soldier who was still classed as absent without leave after many years,

Now hiding in a farm in Northern Ireland close to the coast with two good friends and a young girl,

The farm was owned by an old man who owed Rhys a big favour for saving his son's life a while ago on another adventure,

The other people hiding at the farm with Rhys was: Duncan and Moose, close palls to Rhys.

They all served together in the Special Forces, with multiple operations in hostile environments,

The girl was the girlfriend of Duncan who was rescued from the Amazon jungle in Brazil,

She was a lot younger than Dunc but was a good girl,

They all respected her from what she had been through getting them of the jungle and escaping across Peru to cross the seas and get to Ireland,

There should have been another girl,

Rhys's girl, Carmem.

There was an accident whilst they were all crossing the Atlantic ocean in the boat they had high jacked from a group of people who were going to double cross them and take the emeralds that Rhys and his pals had found in the Amazon Jungle,

The boat had stalled for some reason in the middle of the Atlantic Ocean at night in bad weather,

They were being thrown around in very large waves and heavy winds, everyone on board was working hard to sort things out, when there was a scream.

Carmem disappeared into the water into the night,

There was nothing they could do,

They were all lucky to survive that bad night.

Rhys was devastated and heart broken, he blamed himself for not making sure Carmem was wearing a life jacket.

He hit the bottle for a few days and just stayed in his cabin,

It was a long journey to the coast of Ireland,

Rhys sorted himself out and came to terms with the loss of his Carmem.

Rhys called his old friend called: Dan in Ireland, he used a secure line and arranged to hide the boat in a hidden cove.

Rhys told Dan what they had been through, he was the only person he could trust.

They would hide on Dan's farm that was well out of the way from prying eyes.

Old Dan was a good friend to Rhys with a long past,

Dan was a commander in the IRA long time ago,

His son was murdered in Bosnia by a sniper,

Dan knew Rhys had saved his son's life on many occasions when his son was serving in the Irish rangers unit.

The old man knew ways to get rid of the emeralds, he had black market connections,

Old Dan had dodgy connections that were linked with the IRA, the Irish republican army, He was the IRA, a long time ago.

CHAPTERS:

1: The farm:

2: IRA:

3: Lucky or unlucky encounter:

4: Voyage to Asia:

5: Cyprus scandal:

6: Blind affair:

7: Thai tragedy:

8: Carmem:

CHAPTER 1:

THE FARM:

Dan's farm on the border of Ireland and Northern Ireland.

"Are you's going to get your ugly British arse's up or what,
I've been up since the crack of dawn attending my stock and cooked ya all breakie, so I have" came a loud call in a strong Northern Irish accent!
I could smell bacon cooking, my head was cloudy,
"Taff, why is Moose snuggled up to my missis before he gets a dig" Duncan bellowed!
I looked across the room to where Dunc was shouting from,
I saw Dunc sat up with his young girlfriend next to him and Moose was on the other side of her snoring away!
There was a thump on the floor as Moose landed heavily,
"What in the hell is going on" Moose growled!
"And you call me the pervert" Dunc announced!
"What you waling about now Dunc! Moose asked?
"Why are you in my bed Moose" Duncan asked"?

"You see, here's a funny thing,
I went to the carzy late last night, still out of it and that's all I remember, sorry mate, I'd rather cuddle you, she's all bone" Moose threw back, "don't you dare" Duncan growled!
"Ok folks let's get downstairs, Dan has cooked us breakfast and we must of drunk all his booze last night" I announced!
We all made it downstairs and sat round the big wooden table in the room next to the kitchen,
Old Dan was cursing in the kitchen,
"bloody English here, causing me stress at my old age thanks to my no good son" he moaned,
"Top of the morning Granddad, tis a fine day, so it is" Moose called out in a false Irish accent!
Dan looked in from the kitchen,
"Less of the pretend Irish you drunken git you" old Dan yelled!
Dan brought plates through and plonked them on the table, Duncan's girl got up and went through to the kitchen, "that's grand young lady" old Dan said,

Dunc's girl came through to us carrying a tray with cups and a jug of coffee,
She went back out to the kitchen,
Dunc's girl's name was hard to pronounce in English as it was a native tribal name: Teeneratulia, Dunc and the rest of us called her Tina, she liked it too!
Dan and Tina brought all the food in and sat down,
"Smells good Dan, thanks again" I said,
"Eye lad, we need to talk later, these emeralds are pretty hot so they be, getting hard to pass them on, so it is,
I know someone else but the trouble is now is that too many people know about some emeralds for sale that have a dirty past, however no one knows where they are, that's for sure,
I know how to hide a trail, so I do, been playing this game for over fifty years, so I have, your safe here lads and lasses until I can cash up the emeralds for you, then see you on your way to better water's so to speak" Dan waffled on,

"you saved my son many times Rhys in the past whilst he was with you, the daft boy, anyway I'll see you right, so I will, my sons gone now, god rest his soul, stupid boy, anyway as you know my place is your place so just sit tight for a few days or so and I'll get things sorted" old Dan exclaimed!

I nodded and so did Dunc and Moose, we had respect for the old man, we also missed his son Billy too, he had been a god friend and soldier, was easily lead though,

He got out of the army and came back to Northern Ireland, got mixed up with the wrong crowd and was murdered over some drugs deal that went wrong.

"Now then I need to go to town again for supplies, Tina can come again, and most folk are used to seeing her with me now" Dan told us,

Tina was fine with this,

Dan had told his friends in the local town that the young girl was his dead son's girlfriend and she had nowhere else to go, the story had stuck and was believed by the locals,

We had been at the farm for over five weeks now, old Dan's farm wasn't too big but he had a lot of land and wild stock, cows and sheep mainly,

There was two farm hands Dan employed that were actually on the run from the Irish police for being involved with the IRA in the past.

Dan in his younger days was a commander in the Provisional IRA, most people knew this and respected him,

He was ashamed of his son joining the Irish rangers when he was a teenager then transferring to my outfit in the British army many years ago, another story!

I knew old Dan when his son and I was on leave from the army, I decided to go with him over to Northern Ireland for two weeks as he kept boasting how pretty and easy the Irish women were!

I helped Dan on the farm and we became good friends over the years as I kept visiting Dan, I helped out financially when Dan was in a bit of trouble too,

Dan and I respected each other and there was real trust there, he used to tell me: "once in never out, were both soldiers here, so we are"
I knew about his dealings with the IRA whilst I was still serving in the British army doing sneaky jobs with the recce platoon also called cop platoon:
Close observation platoon,
We used to watch suspected IRA operatives and send all information back to the big guys at HQ,
I actually had to watch Dan for a while, nothing came of it, and my lips were sealed!
Dan's son, Jimmy was really lucky to get into the Irish rangers as he had a bad upbringing and befriended lads who had dealings with the other gangs in Northern Ireland.
Billy was a good mate and soldier shot down by a sniper in Bosnia

CHAPTER 2:
The IRA:

Northern Ireland came into existence with the British Government of Ireland Act (1920) which divided Ireland into two areas: The Irish Free State, made up of the 26 southern counties, and Northern Ireland - comprising of the counties of Antrim,

Down, Armagh, Londonderry, Tyrone and Fermanagh.

Roman Catholics, who made up around one-third of the population of Northern Ireland, were largely opposed to the partition.

On 19 July 1997, the IRA declared a cease-fire, effective July 20.

At the end of August, the Secretary of State for Northern Ireland announced her finding that the cease-fire was being observed, allowing Sinn Fein,

The political party closely identified with the IRA, entry into negotiations on Northern Ireland's political future.

The July 20 cease-fire ended a 17-month terrorism campaign and led to the opening of inclusive political talks in September.

Following the cease-fire there was a marked decrease--although not a total cessation--of sectarian violence. Police believe that paramilitary groups in Northern Ireland were responsible for 22 deaths, 251 shootings, and 78 bombings during 1997.

Both republican and loyalist paramilitary groups continued to engage in vigilante "punishment" attacks, although there was a decrease in the number of such incidents even before the July cease-fire.

Despite the lowering of the overall unemployment rate in Northern Ireland in December 1997 to 7.8 per cent, the unemployment rate for Catholic men in Northern Ireland remained twice that for Protestant men. Sinn Féin is the oldest political party in Ireland, named from the Irish Gaelic expression for ``We Ourselves".

Since being founded in 1905 it has worked for the right of Irish people as a whole to attain national self-determination, and has elected representatives in every major Irish town and city.

Description

Formed in 1969 as the clandestine armed wing of the political movement Sinn Fein, the IRA is devoted both to removing British forces from Northern Ireland and to unifying Ireland.

The IRA conducted attacks until its cease-fire in 1997 and agreed to disarm as a part of the 1998 Belfast Agreement, which established the basis for peace in Northern Ireland.

Dissension within the IRA over support for the Northern Ireland peace process resulted in the formation of two more radical splinter groups: Continuity IRA (CIRA), and the Real IRA (RIRA) in mid to late 1990s.

The IRA, sometimes referred to as the PIRA to distinguish it from RIRA and CIRA, is organized into small, tightly-knit cells under the leadership of the Army Council.

Activities

Traditional IRA activities have included bombings, assassinations, kidnappings, punishment beatings, extortion, smuggling, and robberies.

Before the cease-fire in 1997,

The group had conducted bombing campaigns on various targets in Northern Ireland and Great Britain, including senior British Government officials, civilians, police, and British military targets.

The group's refusal in late 2004 to allow photographic documentation of its decommissioning process was an obstacle to progress in implementing the Belfast Agreement and stalled talks.

The group previously had disposed of light, medium, and heavy weapons,

Ammunition, and explosives in three rounds of decommissioning.

However, the IRA is believed to retain the ability to conduct paramilitary operations.

The group's extensive criminal activities reportedly provide the IRA and the political party Sinn Fein with millions of dollars each year; the IRA was implicated in two significant robberies in 2004, one involving almost $50 million.

The breakfast was great, as usual, plenty of smoked bacon, fried Irish bread, mushrooms, sausages and beans, lots of toast and a big pot of coffee,
"Dan, once again breakfast is great my friend" I commented,
"Maybe one morning one of you's can make it, so they can, if it wouldn't be a burden" Dan put in,
"I would love to cook for you all" Tina announced!
"You doo lass, you help me with too much around here anyways, Tina, let these lazy buggers pull their fingers out! Old Dan growled!
"ok we get the message, trouble is you told us to keep low key here, so any chance we can stretch our legs and stuff" I asked
Dan gave me a hard stare!
"Well that all Depends on what you mean and stuff boy so it does" Dan growled back!
I nodded and smiled at Dan.

"maybe we can go out and do a spot of wild foul shooting with the nice shot guns you keep locked in the cabinet, help out about outside, get some exercise and that, we've been hiding in here for weeks now, getting lazy" I said!

"And what's wrong with being lazy for a while, considering what we've been through" Moose put in!

"look lads, I've told you, your all over the international news, you've seen the tv, Brazil and England are at logger heads with you lot disgracing some old monastery, killing an endangered spices of monkeys, murdering some forgotten Indian tribe and kidnapping the tribes chief's young daughter and lots more, all these sacred emeralds you have stolen, and there's more like MI6 agents killed by you lot" Dan exclaimed!

"Ye, what a crock of shit that is and you know it" Duncan growled!

"I know it, you know it, at the end of the day there will be a cover up story of some sort and both countries will come to an understanding with some dirty money to fill the fat cats pockets, it will be an old story in time until then you lot need to be out of the way until I can get rid of the emeralds and get you on your way, so help me god I will" old Dan said sternly!

"Ok boys, my farm hands know you're here, they haven't said a word and will not so they won't!

You can get out and about, do some shooting but you don't go to the village, I know your like, a few beers in the local and all hell will break loose, can't have this, I've got a reputation here, if the locals ever thought I was hiding missing British soldiers in my place, they'd have me hung, drawn and quartered! This is an IRA supported area, most common expressions here are: Bloody British empire" Dan added!

"Got the message boss" Moose announced! We all helped to clean up and put the breakfast plates and stuff away,

I asked Dan if me and Moose could go out for a jog, Dunc wanted to stay and help the farm hands,
Dan was ok with it,
Dan and Tina left in his land rover and headed to the local village,
Me and Moose got changed and went out for a jog around the close area,
Duncan borrowed some wellies and helped out with the two farm hands.
"Slow down boyo, you trying to kill me" Moose called out!
I stopped and Moose caught up with me,
"Hang fire mate, got a stitch that would drop a camel" Moose coughed out!
I laughed and walked on, we weren't too far from the farm when moose clicked his fingers, and I knew this was a warning sign,
Moose pointed to a vehicle up ahead in the tree line, there was something shining,
"bino's mate, someone looking for something" he whispered,
"Come on" I said and ran into the trees and took cover,

"Don't have my pager on me, you got yours" I asked Moose? "no mate, I am disgusted, we all agreed that whatever the circumstance was we would always carry Sarge's pagers at all costs so we can call for help, bollocks mate" Moose whispered,
"Ok it's probably nothing, but Dan did say no one comes out here as the area is often flooded, sometimes you get a lost tourist but very rarely, let's check it out"
I whispered back to him,
Me an Moose made our way through the thick trees and got as close to the vehicle as possible,
We listened for a few minutes, there was no one around, and we got closer and listened again,
I moved then Moose moved, we got to the back of the vehicle, there was no sign of anyone,
"She's still warm mate" Moose whispered, so she hadn't been there to long I thought to myself,
We checked the doors to the Land rover, all secured,

I did notice inside on the back seats: a hand held radio, Motorola, usually used by the security forces, there was an ear piece attached to it, also Moose saw in the front that there was sat nav sucker markings on the windscreen,

We sat behind the vehicle for a few seconds then went further in to the trees to observe,

"Ok mate could be nothing, could be something, lets skirt around quietly and find them ye" I whispered,

Moose gave me the thumbs up and followed as I set off!

We both walked slowly through the trees, Moose pulled my arm and tugged me down, he gave me a hand signal: enemy listen in,

I heard nothing, "what's up Moose" I asked quietly!

"Not too sure mate, heard something" Moose whispered back, we squatted there and listened,

There was a rustling noise from ahead of us, We listened!

"Tango two alpha roger that, we have movement at the target, three unknowns in the grounds, observing" over,

Moose looked at me and gave me the thumbs down sign which meant bad guys, "ok roger that, clear eyes on the target and logging movement's, no sign of whiskey one or two over" we heard someone talk softly,
"Roger out" we both heard,
Moose looked at me,
That's not civi talk mate, that's army talk, we got professionals at work here" Moose whispered!
I nodded to him,
"Ok let's get closer" I whispered,
We crawled slowly to where we heard the talking come from,
"Tango two alpha to control have positive siting of whisky 3 have positive shot await your orders over" came a voice,
Moose looked at me,
What the fuck is going on mate, Dan's farm is over there" Moose whispered to me,
"Dave this is so shit, what bollocks job are we on here, looking for AWOL soldiers mixed up with this Brazil mercenary emerald storey" another crock of shit job" one of the men whispered.

"Moose I think were in the shit again" I whispered,
"Send you message over" came a quiet voice from ahead of us,
We both listened!
"Roger that, I confirm I have visual of whisky three and have a clear shot over"
"Whiskey one and two we have no visual, do we take whiskey one over" we heard again,
"Roger that" came the same voice,
Me and Moose heard the bolt action of a rifle loading a bullet into the chamber of a weapon,
"That's a Barrett sniper rifle, mate, we need to do something fast" Moose whispered,
"Ok moose play with me, drunk as a skunk ye, you know the story" I whispered,
Moose got up and so did I.
"Where the fuck are you mate" Moose slurred loudly!
I stumbled forward, "ye fucking idiot, you sure you dropped it here mate, I slurred loudly and stumbled forward,

I could hear Moose laughing out loud in front of me,
"Where are you mate," I growled!
"sorry fella's, didn't mean to disturb like this, whatever you's two are doing is nothing to me, by the way, I lost my phone around here somewhere, you carry on with your gay stuff and mind me" Moose slurred, I heard him fall over,
"Bollocks, can you believe that, messed my best jeans up, fuck it" Moose slurred again, I tried not to laugh!
"Hey nobber, where the hell are you" I shouted in an Irish accent! And stumbled forward,
I fell through the bushes as a man in camouflaged overalls stood up,
I saw Moose to my right fighting with a bush and cursing!
"I think you two gentlemen should leave his location as soon as possible before you get hurt" came a voice from the ground, I looked down and saw a well camouflaged man lying in front of a large sniper rifle,

"Oo, look at you's two playing soldiers, here, Moose come look at these two woofters" I slurred,

The man who stood up took a swing at me, I saw it coming and blocked it with my arm, I threw two quick hard punches into the man's ribs, I felt the crack, he went down, at the same time was on top of the other man who was behind the rifle, I heard a crack and looked at Moose,

Moose nodded to me,

The other man was on the floor trying to get to the radio that he dropped, I stamped on his fingers and kicked him in the face!

"Who the fuck are you's" I growled in an Irish accent!

"Listen soldier blue, tell all here or you end up like your mate here" Moose spoke out in a false Irish accent!

"Ok, ok, you win" the man I put to the ground moaned! "We work for a private company who's interested in the farm over there and certain people who are staying there" he added,

"What's with the shooter mate", Moose put in!

The man on the floor thrust his hand into his pocket and pulled out a hand gun, I pre saw this and kicked out striking his wrist, the hand gun flew out of his hand,
He dived for the rifle on the ground that his mate was laid behind,
I dived to and landed on top of him as he swung the sniper rifle around and fired,
Moose hit the deck as I snapped the man's neck with ease,
I quickly picked up the ear piece from the radio and listened!
"Tango two alpha send sitrep over" the ear peace sounded! I looked at Moose, "there calling mate what the fuck do I say" I growled!
Moose grabbed the ear piece from me, I saw him push in the talk button on the radio,
"Tango two alpha roger that, target quiet am observing over" Moose said in a funny northern accent,
"Roger that, keep us informed out" came the reply from the radio ear piece,
"Ok we bought us some time here, need to get rid of these two idiots" I told Moose.

"I have an idea" Moose whispered, and started to search the bodies, "bingo, back in a jiffy mate" Moose added! And ran off towards where the land rover was hidden under the trees,
I heard the vehicle start up and Moose drove it as close to me as possible,
Moose jumped out,
"Ok let's get those stiff's in the boot and get back to the farm mate" Moose growled!
"Yes sir" I commented,
We plonked the two bodies into the boot of the land rover with their equipment and drove to the farm that was only five minutes away down the track across the field,
I called Dunc on one of the secure mobile phones Dan had got for us, I explained what happened, "wow leave you two alone for one minute and look what happen" he growled!
"Duncan start to pack things up pronto" I ordered!
I rang Old Dan and told him what had happened.

He told me he was finalising a deal to get rid of the emeralds, I told him just get what you can, we need to get out of here as soon as possible,
Dan agreed and hung up.
We got to the farm and ran into the house, "Dunc" I shouted!
Dunc came down the stairs with a full holdall,
"Ok, what now" Dunc groaned!
I filled him in with exactly what happened, "I called Tina, she said Dan was with some strong men with funny accent, he is in the pub upstairs I wait in jeep, she told me, I told her to get to the farm as soon as possible" Dunc announced!
 "ok troops, we wait till old Dan gets back with Tina, doesn't matter how much he got for the emeralds, we offer to take Dan with us, if he agrees we torch the farm and the nob heads that were watching us and get the hell out of here on the boat" I growled!
 Moose and Dunc nodded their heads at me and went to pack stuff up,
I went out to the land drover and opened the boot,

I took out the sniper rifle and other stuff that was with the nobs that were sent by who knows to take us out!
We waited in the farm for a good hour, I tried to call Tina and old Dan a few times, and the mobiles went straight to voice mail, The farm hands came in looking worried, "everything ok" one of the lads asked?
I knew we could trust them, as Dan had told to us their stories and how they were hiding out on the farm for their own goods, they had joined us on many a night for evening meals and drinks, we knew their story and trusted them, they were interested in the emeralds too,
I promised them they would get a good split if they helped out with things!
The two lads just carried on as normal tending to the farm and sleeping in an annex next to the barn.
We all looked at each other.
"We have a problem" I said to everyone, "Dan and Tina are not answering their mobiles, there at the pub in the village doing some deal with the emeralds, something not right! I announced,

I looked at the two young farm hands, "listen guys we need your help, we need a diversion when we go into the pub and find out what's happened to Dan and Tina, maybe you two go in as usual, you well known in there, start an argument and get your selves thrown out, me and Dunc will do the rest, Moose will be cover with that monster gun" I threw to them!
Both of the young lads nodded, "Old Dan's been like a father to us, we won't let you down, we are not too fond of the IRA and how they do things, my sister had her head shaved, covered in tar and covered in feathers, left taped to lamp post all night long for all to see as warning to others, no girl is to see anyone from the British Army, we had heard the stories before whilst we ate at dinner and drank afterwards,
We could trust the boys!
"Something's up boys, we either go to town or fuck off on the boat" I said,
Moose and Dunc knew what I was talking about!
"Let's go bro, there in the shit, I know it" Moose announced!

"Duncan get the shotguns out of the cabinet, were going to town lads" I growled! We jumped into the land rover with the two young farm hands and headed off to the local town!

It didn't take too long to get there, we pulled up and stopped next to the post office, it was starting to get dark now,

"I think we hide the land rover and go in by foot ye" Moose exclaimed!

"Good idea" I answered back,

We drove off and parked behind some garages and got out,

"ok lads, the pub is just round the corner, Moose you take the sniper rifle and get to high ground and watch the pub, me and Dunc will recce the pub and let you know what's going on" I put in,

"Roger that mate" Moose agreed!

Ok lads you go in and have a drink as normal, you got my number, text if you see anything, all the best, see you later, plenty of room on the boat lads" I told them, they both gave me the thumbs up, "see you's soon captain, so we will" came the reply,

Me and Duncan made our way round to the back of the pub, there was only one pub in the village.
We found a few jeeps and two range rovers parked in the rear car park, there was three men talking in Irish accents and smoking next to the vehicles,

We quietly went round the side of the pub and found a fire escape ladder,
We went up in silence.

We crept onto a balcony and listened, all we could hear was the music from down below in the pub,
Me and Dunc pulled open a fire door on the top floor and moved in slowly,
We crept down the corridor, there was doors to rooms but it was quiet, we found the main staircase and went down a floor, I could hear someone arguing in a strong Irish accent!
"That old fool and his young whore are a joke, he's old school IRA, and boss will rid of them the hard way, the old man no longer rules here" we heard someone say down the corridor,
"ye and those emeralds will see us right my friend, so they will" another person said, we heard two guys laughing!
"There was a scream!
"That's Tina mate" Dunc whispered, Duncan looked at me sternly, "I love that girl mate" he whispered,
"Start a fire upstairs Dunc quickly I whispered to him, Dunc nodded and went back up the stairs,

I was just round the corner listening to the two Irish men talking, I smelt the smoke, "Something burning around here mate" I heard one of the Irishmen say, "that's the chef burning the food in this shit hole" the other guy announced!
The smoke came down the stairs and into the corridor where the two Irish men were, "I think we got a fire here, so we have" one of them say!
I heard one of the men bang on a door, "boss we got a problem out here" one of them shouted!
"Sort it out then, were nearly done here, so we are" someone shouted in a strong Irish accent!
There was another scream from a woman! My mobile phone buzzed in my pocket, I looked at it,
: Rhys what do you want us to do, was the message,
I replied: cause a fire and get out ASAP!
The smoke was getting bad now, I could hear Dunc coughing up stairs,
I moved down the corridor where the two Irishmen were, they were coughing too,

"Shamus we need to get out of here now" I heard one of them call out!

"Boss we got a fire out here" the other man shouted, they were both coughing!

They saw me, "you shouldn't be up here pal" I heard them say!

I was coughing! "Just been with a whore upstairs and pretty good too, we got a fire up there somewhere, how the hell you get out of this place" I shouted in a false Irish accent!

"That way, move your ass" one of them shouted!

As I passed them both I swung out with the shot gun that was under my jacket and caught one of them in the belly, he buckled over, the other guy was too slow as Dunc was on him, I heard a snap!

I grabbed the other guy and landed him onto my knee, I felt a break in his back and put him to the floor,

A door was opened,

"What the fuck is going on here" came a strong Irish accent!

 I saw a hand gun poke out of the opened door,

Dunc was there in an instant and grabbed the hand holding the gun, he pulled the man out of the room and fought with him on the floor,
I dived into the room and saw two men holding guns,
"Who the fuck ae you's" I heard!
I let off two shots from the shot gun I was carrying and the two men fell silent!
"Rhys you crazy sun of a bitch" I heard someone call out!
It was Dan's voice, I turned around to see Dan tied up on a bed, Tina was next to him tied up too, I got up and started to untie them both,
"Double crossing bastards they are" Dan growled!
"Nice to see you too" I announced!
Dunc dived in through the door, "he's history pall" he announced, looking very mean!
"Duncan" Tina shouted!, Dunc went to her and gave her a big hug and got her untied, I could hear a lot of shouting from outside the back of the pub, where we saw three large guys minding the new range rovers,

Smoke was getting pretty thick now, we were all coughing,
"Time we got out of here, Dunc grab the bags and help old Dan there" I put in,
"Less of the old Dan I'll be telling you, yes get those bags and the case over there" Dan shouted! And pointed to a black briefcase sitting on the table,
"Pass me that hand gun too and check the other one for a piece" Dan added,
I grabbed the case and it was quite heavy too,
Duncan grabbed the hand gun and checked the other body, Dunc threw Dan a hand gun,
We all got out of the room and dashed down the corridor to the stairs, there was a lot of commotion at the back of the pub, I guessed it was the two young farm hands we brought with us,
The down stairs bar was empty, and the fire alarm was sounding loudly,
"Anyone for a quick one" Dunk said,
"Dunk sometimes I don't believe you" I replied!

Tina slapped Dunc on the back, "you big fool" she told him,
We could hear a lot of shouting out the back of the pub, there was a lot of people out the front too,
"So where to now" Dunc asked?
The smoke billowed into the bar and something went bang upstairs, windows smashed!
"Dunc when I said start a little fire to cause a bit of smoke, didn't mean burn us all mate" I cussed!
"You know me mate" Dunc answered!
A door was pushed open,
"Who are you's" someone shouted! We turned to see two large men standing there with pistols,
"Can I get you two a drink lads" Dunc shouted! And threw a large bottle of booze at them,
The bottle smashed!
Two shots went off and a third one!
The two men who came through the door were now on the floor, "your all dead men, so you are" one of them moaned, I fired twice and finished them off!

Tina screamed!

There was a shot from outside!

I quickly called Moose, "need cover mate, coming out the back where the range rovers are, there's one more out there mate" I told him, "roger that, the two young farm hands started to fight each other, and the bid lad by the range rovers took one out, the other lad has scarpered! I got him, I heard a shot!

We all piled out of the side door into the rear car park, two bodies were lying on the ground and not moving,

"Well take these range rovers, find the keys Dunc" I ordered!

Moose called me on the mobile, "on my way mate, pick me up on the way out, I'll be by the phone box we passed coming here" Moose told me,

Dunc got the keys and we jumped into the Range rover, Dan was lagging behind, "you ok mate" I called to him, we could here sirens going off from the fire brigade wagons that had arrived out the front,

"We need to vanish pronto folks" Dunc called,

"Dan you ok" I called again!

Old Dan slumped to the floor, I went to him, "you catch a bullet mate" I said to him! "can you bloody believe it, I'm finished here my friend, so you are, you saved my son and I think I've repaid my dept to you, get out of here Rhys, the boats got plenty of fuel and supplies on board like you asked, take young Luke with you, he will see you right, I didn't tell you the whole truth, he's a nephew, he's run off somewhere now, don't argue with me, just get out while you can son" Dan coughed!
He fell to the ground!
"Bollocks" I shouted!
"Rhys you coming or what" Dunc shouted out of the window of the Range rover!
I patted Dan on the shoulder and picked him up with the bag he was carrying and got in to the vehicle,
"Get us out of here Dunc" I insisted!
We pulled off with speed and passed all the people who came out of the pub,
There was two fire engines starting to sort things out,
We drove up the road and saw Moose standing next to a phone box.

Dunc stopped the Range rover, "room for a little one" moose asked!
"Get in, good shot by the way" I said to him, "where's Dan" Moose asked?
I told him what happened!
Moose sat in silence as we drove off,
We were driving down the track to the farm, "someone's running there mate" Dunc called out!
We slowed down and caught the running lad up, "you need a lift young man" Moose called out of the window!
The young lad stopped and got his breath back, "there is a god, so there is, I thought you lot had bought it, I nearly did back there, Tommie got shot, I got out of there" the young lad said, "inn you get boy, old Dan has gone, he's asked us to take care of you, so we will" I told him and dragged him into the vehicle and we pulled off,
We got to the farm very quickly, Dunc skiddered to a stop outside,
"Ok as I've already told you all, this needs to be quick and slick! You know your jobs, now let's get to it! I ordered!

Everyone got out of the Range rover and did what they had to do,
The young farm hand: Luke came out from the barn carrying a black holdall,
"Rhys, Dan would of wanted you to have this, there is more in there, and he has a secret storage place, under the barn, top secret, weapons hid for the IRA if needed and loads of cash, he took me and Tommy in years ago,
He told us all the stories and promised when his time was up, me and Tommy will be sorted out for the rest of our lives' as long as we left Ireland" Luke whispered!
Luke put the holdall bag down and opened it,
It was full of cash,
"Dan you will always amaze me" I said, and smiled,
"show me what else we have here Luke" I asked him, Luke smiled, "ye, come on"
Luke announced, we will need some more hands to get the other stuff if you want it Rhys" Luke added!

I called to Moose and Dunc, they came straight out!
"What's up mate, were busy packing stuff up in there" Moose threw at me!
I showed him what was in the holdall, Moose's eyes became very wide,
"You won the lottery mate" Dunc exclaimed!
"A present from old Dan, if Luke wasn't here we would never know about it" I told them,
"Well done young man, well look after you, just you keep your eyes off my missis" Dunc growled!
Luke lead us into the barn, he had moved bales of hay out of the way,
There was a trap door open with light coming out,
We moved closer and looked down the whole and down the steel ladder,
"Police and other people been round here in the past, never found this place though" Luke announced and climbed down the ladder.

"steep ladder and mind ya head" Luke added and went down.
We followed Luke down the ladder which lead into a ship container with lights and a ventilation system, "it's a bloody IRA hide, we've seen this before, Dan you bad bugger" Moose exclaimed!

"Take a look at this lot" Dunc called out! Shelves of rifles and ammunition, some serious weapons in there too, boxes of grenades and a lot more.
"Was he waiting for world war three" Moose commented!

Luke brought another black hold all bag over,
"There's another one over there, its bad money so it is" Luke announced!
"It's here on hold until the Provo's require it,
Provo's slang word for the IRA,
Luke told us they know it's here but don't know where exactly!
"Ok let's get as much of the weapons as we can out and the holdalls, plenty of ammo here two,
I want to be down with the boat in the next half hour before we get some company of some sort" I ordered!
"When we leave we torch the place and the rover with the bodies in, need to burn it well ok" I added,
"I'll take care of that with Tina" Dunc announced and went to it,
We loaded up the range rover we took from the pub, Moose and I drove off to where the boat was hidden.

Luke, Dunc and Tina got the rest of what we needed and took it all outside ready for when me and Moose returned!

We drove up a steep hill and parked the rover next to an old pill box that was used in world war two as a sentry post to watch out to sea.

The bunker had steel reinforced locked steel doors.

Dan had bought this part of the land years ago, and the Irish police had demanded to look in there ages ago, suspecting an IRA hide, nothing was found!
Luke gave me the key back at the farm to the door and I unlocked the outer door,
Me and Moose started to get our stuff inside the bunker at the back,
There was a toilet area, with a false wall that could be pulled out,
It lead to a tunnel that went deep down into the side of the cove and down to the sea level,
Stories say that in the past this cove was used by smugglers transporting anything in and out from the sea,

We made our way down to the boat, there she was, looking like the way we had left it when we had arrived here months ago,

Dan had told us he had looked after it and some moderations had been made by trusted people who he knew, he never told us what had been done to the boat, just it would be a surprise when we needed her!
"Looks good, nice new coat of paint I see" Moose exclaimed!
"Look at the name mate" I said to Moose, Irish Dan was painted on the front of the boat.
"Nice" I said, "ok Moose let's get loaded and get back to the farm" I ordered!
There was a hanging tarpaulin in front of the boat painted like the sides of the walls of the cove, the boat was well camouflaged,

Dan had made sure that if someone found their way in here from the sea by accident or something, it was very unlikely as the surf was bad and there was torturous rocks to navigate through, I remember Moose trying to get in here, a night mare, the boat was bashed around too much, all repairs had been done thanks to old Dan.
We loaded the boat up as fast as we could and went back to the farm.
It was dark now,
From the farm we could see the pub in the local village on fire and flashing blue lights from the fire brigade,
"Ok troops load up, Dan comes with us and we bury him at sea, burn the place Dunc" I ordered!
"When this place goes' it's going to look like the fourth of July mate with all the ammo and kerosene and stuff around here" Dunc exclaimed!
"Do it" I told him.
Dunc went over to the barn and started the fires,
Dunc climbed into the rover and we set off!

"bon voyage" Tina said,
"So where are we going boss" Dunc put in,
"not too sure yet, I want to get as far away from Ireland as we can and let Dan go to the sea, he was a merchant seaman most of his life, he told me where he wanted to go if his time come and we were around, so be it, Moose will study the charts and use the sat nav to get us out of here my friends" I announced!
We got to the bunker and loaded all the stuff on the boat, I locked the door to the pill box bunker from outside and climbed down the rock face and jumped into the sea, none of the camouflage was left, so when we left there would be no evidence of a boat being there,
I was waiting in the water and the boat came out with a struggle, I had to swim like mad to get clear from the rocks, I heard the boat bang the rocks a few times,
Dunc pulled me in,
"You mad bastard" he growled!
"Fucking nightmare getting out of here, lucky I didn't mow you down you nutter" Moose shouted out!

I got inside,
"Shit I nearly drowned out there, what took you so long" I growled!
"Tide coming in boss, not easy getting out, ya mad man" Moose exclaimed!
Tina slapped me on the head, "stupid" she growled!
"Anyone else want a dig" I groaned,
"A man to be careful of, so you are" Luke, put in,
"Ok Moose, you know what to do" I growled!
"Eye eye captain" Moose bellowed back, the nose of the boat lifted into the air and off we went,
"Where we heading boss" Dunc called out!
"Not too sure yet, keep heading North West for a while Moose, I need a good drink" I exclaimed!
"eye eye Captain, get me one too" Moose put in!
We all went below and left Moose in control, Dunc passed me a bottle of whiskey, "Bush mills, oooh" I commented!
"That's a grand malt, that is" Luke announced,

Tina went to the galley to sort things out,
Me Dunc and Luke took a some good swigs from the bottle,
"Put hairs on your chest young man that will" Dunc commented,
"Hair doesn't grow on muscle big man" Luke announced!
Me and Dunc looked at Luke and laughed,
"Don't forget me up here ya bastards! Moose bellowed!
Luke took the bottle up to Moose,
"So mate, where the fuck are we going" Dunc asked!
"To tell you the truth old pall,
I have no idea after the mess we just left back there, those monkeys observing us,
Ira, my Carmem lost to the sea,
I feel really old all of a sudden mate" I told him,
Dunc stared at me.
"Hey, you know me, I'm not soft with words,
We all know you hurt like mad inside Rhys, were with you pall" Dunc replied,
The boat bounced around and Moose was laughing!

"Pack it in Moose" we all shouted!
"ar Jim lad, yo ho ho and a bottle of rum"
Moose growled and the boat steadied,
Dunc got up and patted me on the back and went into the galley were Tina was,
I sat there just staring out of the window,
Looking out to see, and thinking of Carmem.
That night we all got a bit drunk, we counted the money that was in the holdalls, there was: three quarters of a million pounds in there,
We bought on board some nice weapons too from Dan's hidden arsenal:

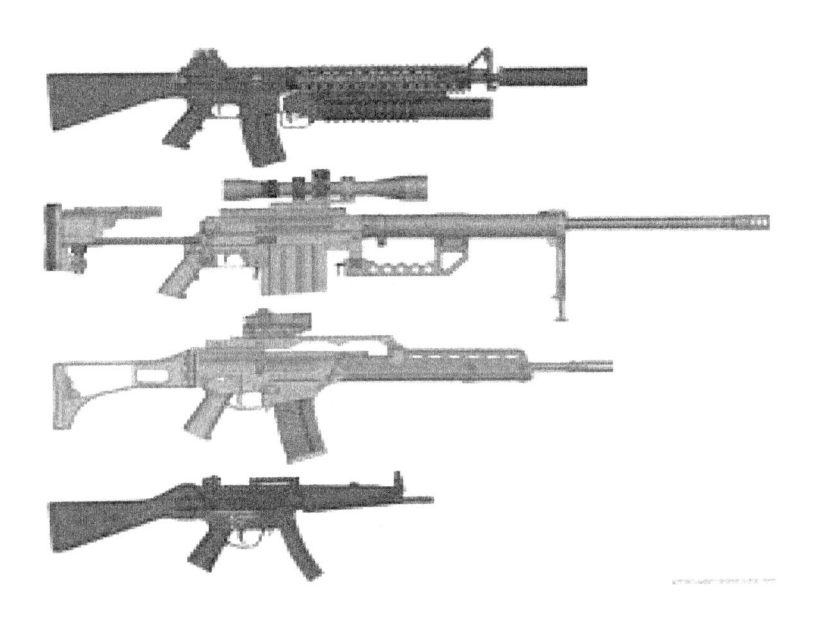

There was a lot more hardware too!
Moose had studied the maps and charts, "what about Hong Kong, always wanted to go back there and see the old strip we all knew, what a posting eh, two and a half years of fun" Moose slurred!
"Where is Hong Kong, I not know this place" Tina asked?
Luke told her all about it, he had to do a topic on Hong Kong whilst he was at college,
"Easy tiger" Dunk grumbled, seeing his Tina looking at Luke and smiling so much, "ye, fuck it, let's go to Hong Kong, wow had too many girls there, what a time, do you remember the time" Dunc was cut off sharply as Tina jumped on his lap and started to kiss him, "you no leave me Duncan" Tina cried,
"Leave you missy, never" Dunc replied.

I was just listening to all the Banta with only one thought on my mind!

"Taffy boyo pass us another bottle of that fire water" Moose slurred!
I passed him another bottle of whiskey, "Ok, me and you, come on, let's have a fag on deck, fresh sea air and that" Moose said,
We went on deck, Moose passed me the bottle, I took a big swig and leaned against the hand rail, the boat was rocking gently,
"Talk to me mate, I can see you hurting too much and it's killing me too, I miss her to bit's bro" Moose said,
I hugged Moose and cried!
"Let it out my friend, let it out" Moose whispered!
Moose hugged me hard,
"Don't you too lads go gay on me now, or I might have to join in, what will Tina say to that, and toy boy down stairs will love that" Duncan announced!
We all laughed!
"Duncan I love you too bits, all of you's, I'll get through this" I slurred,
I took another swig from the bottle, "ok Hong Kong it is then, brings back some memories, Moose tip top in the morning son, get your sailing head on, I think we

need to hit the sack soon, need a watch through the night, I'll do the first one for an hour then Luke can do the next one, I need something to eat" I announced!
"eye eye captain" Moose put in,

We went below, Tina had a spread of food on the table, garlic bread, lamb chops and something she cooked in her tribe, black beans with garlic and all sorts, we all tucked in, it was delicious!
Whilst we were eating moose piped up, "oh by the way, Old Dan has made a few moderations to this boat, I forgot to tell you, ok, the engines have been changed, this thing will out run a fucking dragster, excuse my language, young lady, we have torpedo tubes up front behind hidden port holes, we have radar, we have sonar, we have things on board up there that I still don't know what the fuck they mean, there's a tracking system that means nowt to me, Dan's been a busy man in here, or his friends, this boat may look like an average cruiser but actually is a bionic destroyer, ok I've talked enough, drink please" Moose waffled on!

"Ok Moose, can you get us to Hong Kong or what" I asked
"Excuse me Mr, I can get you to Tim buck two and back, you know I can" Moose announced and burped!
"Hey" Tina called out, "you make bad noise, insult in my tribe" she added!
"Whoops have I offended our little princess" Moose slurred!
I saw Dunc looking annoyed and Luke was waffling rubbish,
Ok that's it, we have a long day tomorrow, time for beddie buy's, drink up comrades and see you all in the morning with headaches" I exclaimed!
I went up to the bridge and had a smoke, Everyone else settled down for the night,
I must have dozed off, the boat was rocking around a bit too strong, something smashed down below,
"Ok ok who shit in my mouth" Moose called out as he made his way to the bridge,
"You been up here all night mate" Moose asked,
I nodded, "suppose so, things to think about" I replied

Moose nodded and patted me on the shoulder,
"Ok let's get this baby started and get out of this shit weather" he bellowed,
Moose turned the key, there was a click but nothing more, Moose turned the key again, another click,
"That's not good, we have mega low power here on the dials, too low, we must have four batteries down below at least to power this thing, ok I need to think" Moose mumbled,
The boat was rocking a lot, things were falling on the floor in the galley,
"Everything ok up there, I just fell out of bed, scared the shit out of Tina" Dunc called?
Moose moved quickly past me and down below,
I heard him lifting up the floor boards to look at the engine,
Me and Dunc were having a cigarette each when Moose came back up,
The way he looked at us was not the stare I liked,

"batteries drained, last night we had full power, I can't think at the moment, drunk too much, brain cells not working" Moose waffled on and started to check around the bridge,

Tina came up, "there's no power, I cannot make any coffee" she said,

"Moose is looking into it my dear" Duncan said to her, the boat was rocking hard,

"Need to lift the anchor and ride the waves for a while folks" Moose announced and continued to check things, he disappeared down below!

Luke came up, "I'll do it" he put in and disappeared quickly,

The rain was hitting the boat heavily, Moose came back up, "I don't understand how the batteries are so dead" Moose exclaimed!

"So what are you telling us mate" I asked?

"Well we have no power, the boat is dead and that's it, were not going anywhere, maybe the batteries will re-charge after a while, I don't know, I can't see it though, were fucked lads" Moose told us,

"My mobile is fully charged now, can I call someone for help" Tina asked?

"Ok a question here, have you had your mobile on charge through the night Tina" Moose asked her,

"I put it on charge when we went to bed" she replied,

"My phones on charge too mate" Dunc announced,

"Mine as well" I told Moose,

"Luke come here" Moose called out!

Luke came up, anchor up as you asked" he said, "mate is your mobile on charge by any chance" Moose asked?

"Yes, down in my cabin, he answered!

"shit, the tv was left on all night too, I should of warned everyone, you only charge things when the engines running, we've drained the batteries beyond repair I think, too many things on charge at one time and the tv left on all night, were in a mess people" Moose announced!

The boat was swaying around and the rain was hitting us hard,

"What can we do Moose" I asked,

"not a lot, send out distress flares, the radio is dead, maybe we can use our mobiles, call 999 and ask for help, I know our rough position, try your mobiles, I'll see what escape craft we have,
I know there's one beneath the back of the boat" Moose grumbled!
I checked my mobile, mine was on charge too, there was no signal, "anyone got a signal" I shouted!
"No, no, nothing here" came the replies!
Moose came up, "ok troops, we are about 200 miles off the coast of Ireland,
the currents here will only drag us further out to sea, we have a collapsible speed boat at the back underneath, a bit too small for all of us, all we can do is wait until its light and hope a passing boat see's up and offers us some help" Moose exclaimed!
It was slowly getting light, no body as talking, just holding on, and the boat was riding the waves and the rain was hitting us hard!
"Reminds me of that Jaws film" Moose commented!

"Show me the way to go home, I'm tired and I want to go to bed, I had a little drink about an hour ago and it's gone straight to my head" Dunc sang,
I joined in too!
Luke came up from below holding a bottle of booze, "anyone" he asked?
"Pass it here young man" I called out!
I took a big swig and passed the bottle to Dunc,
"Well who would of thought we would end up like this then" Dunc put in,
"This is a shipping channel, someone will pass by" Moose announced!
Tina began to cry,
Moose comforted her and took her down below,
We just stood in the bridge and waited and drank.
A good two hours went past, nobody had a signal on their mobile, Moose tried everything, and he went through the boats manual a few times,
 It was light now, the weather had calmed down, and Tina had made some cold sandwiches that went down well.

"Hey look over there, a ship" Luke shouted out,
We all saw her,
"It's a container ship" Moose announced!
"Get the flares out" I ordered!
Moose opened a cupboard and brought out a few flares,
"Get them into the air pronto" Moose growled!
Me and Dunc went outside and fired them off.
We watched the container ship for a good ten minutes, it must have been a good thousand metres away from us probably a lot further,
Moose tried the radio, "dead" He said,
We fired some more flares into the sky!
We waited a few minutes,
"Look, there flashing at us" Moose announced!
I fired another flare, the last one into the sky,
We heard a horn blast, and the ship flashed a light at us,
"Morse code mate" Duncan shouted!

Moose went outside and started to flash a torch at the passing ship, they flashed back, "ok they are coming, Morse code a bit wonky, it's a Polish ship on route to Cambodia with human relief cargo, we need to get a good story together and think about what we've got here, don't know who to expect" Moose announced!.

"Ok here's the story! In fact there is no story, basically we are all friends heading to blab blab blab, and we lost power, maybe they can tow us somewhere, get the weapons hidden in the holdall's, let's see what happens" I ordered!

We watched the container ship turn towards us and waited.

As it got closer it got bigger,

"That's a big bugger" Moose commented!

"Remember the story plan folks, we were just out for the day sailing around the island when the boat died on us,

If we can pinch a tow to the nearest port away from Ireland or they can power up our batteries would be great" I said to everyone!

The container ship was about three hundred metres away,
"Ahoy there! It will get a bit rough when we get to you, hold on"
A voice came over a loud speaker!
The large ship came as close as she could, sailors were on deck with ropes in their hands,
"Secure the ropes and we will pull you in" a voice shouted!
"Polish I think, hm, never trust the polish! Moose mumbled,
The ropes were thrown to us and secured,
We were pulled tight to the ship,
A rope ladder was dropped down to us,
"Come up and talk to me captain,
What has happened to your boat" the Polish captain shouted!
"We have hot coffee or something stronger if you want" the Polish man added!
We were all on deck,
"Coming up mate, a hot coffee will be great" I shouted!
We secured the boat and climbed up the rope ladder.

"So who is captain" a large man asked?
"I am" I said,
"I am too" the big guy replied!
The Polish man put his hand out to shake,
I shook his hand and introduced everyone,
"I take you to kitchen, we have a drink and some food and you tell me what has happened and how we can help,
Good job the sea is calm or we wouldn't have got to you,
I remember once we tried to help a small craft in bad sea, we ended up smashing it to pieces" the captain waffled on,
One of the crewmen picked up one of our bags and went to undo the, Moose moved in and took the bag off him, !easy mate that's full of my dirty underwear and stuff fella" Moose growled, the crewman looked startled as it happen so quickly,
The captain spoke to the crewman in polish of Russian of something, we all looked at each other,
"My friends, my friends, sorry my crew are nosy sometimes, just want to help you" the captain added and laughed.
"ok let's talk about your boat then".

CHAPTER 3:
LUCK OR UNLUCKY ENCOUNTER:

We all followed the captain along a steel walkway, his ship was big,
There was a hell of a lot of steel containers all stacked up everywhere.
"Wow a lot of containers here" I mentioned,

"yes my friend, aid for country we head for, united nations pay well to transport this to needy people, I like to do this, feel like I do my part in this mad world I think" the captain said,
"Here we go" the captain put in,
He opened a thick door and walked inside, we all followed,
"Ok we have plenty of coffee, the chef her can make you anything you want" the captain announced!
"I'd love a bacon and egg butty mate" Duncan asked?
"Of course mate" the captain spoke in a foreign language to the cook!
The cook looked at us suspiciously, he spoke to the captain in their own language!
The cook went to work on Dunc's sandwich and some more for the rest of us,
"So my friends, time is limited here, we stay and help how we then we have to go, schedule to keep, what is wrong with your boat then"
"Basically we have no power in batteries" Moose commented,

"Maybe you can bump start us so we can repower them or something" I added!

The captain laughed!

"my friends when batteries are dead like you say, you cannot as you say bump start and regenerate power, you should have spare batteries no" the captain asked?

"I send my engineer to your boat, he is very good, see what he has to say yes" the Polish captain announced,

"Ok, thanks" I replied, I knew we had well-hidden all weapons and cash away so it was highly unlikely the engineer would find it!

The captain pulled out a small radio from his pocket and spoke in Polish!

A reply came back in the same language!

"Ok, he will do his best, now we eat yes" the captain put in,

The cook brought over a large bacon and fried egg sandwich and the same for all of us with a big pot of coffee and a bottle of rum,

"Now this is what I call a breakfast" Dunc announced as he poured whisky into his coffee,

The captain asked where we were heading and stuff and we continued with small talk for a good hour,

The captain's radio beeped and someone spoke in Polish, the captain replied in Polish,

"Have some bad news for you, engineer reports your batteries are completely dead, he has had a good look around your boat, you have no spare batteries, your engine has had a lot of work done to her, by you call cowboys, I think we call the coast guard and give your position" the captain exclaimed,

"Can you not tow us to the nearest port you come across or something" Duncan asked,

"impossible my friends and very illegal, only way is to call for help, coast from Ireland will be here soon and bring spare batteries and help you on your way or take you back to Ireland" the Polish captain added!

We all looked at each other and carried on eating,

The captain's radio made a beeping noise and someone spoke in Polish, the captain spoke back in his own dialect,

"Excuse me please I have to attend to something, I won't be long, I show you around the ship if you want while we wait for coast guard" he spoke as he stood up,
"Captain, I need a to talk to you about something, we don't want the coast guard to be called, it's complicated" I said quietly,
The captain gave me a stern look,
"ok my friend, we talk when I come back ok, sort things out, but now I have to go ok" the captain replied, the captain as he left spoke to the chef in Polish and he chef looked at us then carried on with his work,
The door to the galley was closed shut with a bang!
"We have a problem here" I whispered,
"How about we pay him off, sink our boat and go with him to where ever" Moose whispered back,
Dunc nodded and so did Tina,
"If we go back to Ireland, it's all over for us, so it is" Luke announced,
I noticed the chef keeping an eye on us,
I stood up and walked towards the door which we came through.

Immediately the chef spoke out and came over to me with a large chopping knife,: "Captain say you stay here" the chef said in broken English and he spoke on his radio!
"Ok mate, calm down, easy with that knife" I said to him!
The chef spoke again to his radio in Polish, The captain walked through the opened door with another two crewmen behind him, "yes my friends we do need to have big talk" the captain announced,
"You captain come with me, the rest of you will have to wait in a secured room for the time being" he continued!
"Hey, what's this all about" Moose growled!
"my engineer found some interesting things on your boat indeed, also your boat has too many technical alterations for just a normal cruising boat, automatic weapons and a lot of cash, I think you are terrorists, with the IRA trying to hijack me or other vessels, but you had some bad luck, am I right" the captain threw to us!

"What a load of rubbish, we are just" before Dunc could say anymore, the Captain spoke in Polish loudly!
The two crewmen who were behind him stepped forward pointing rifles at us, the chef too pointed a pistol,
"Steady on, there is no need for this, we are not terrorists and I will explain" I announced!
"Yes captain you will explain, you come with me now, the rest of your friends will wait in here, toilet is through there and there's plenty of coffee and food if you want it" the captain exclaimed! He spoke again on his radio in Polish!
The captain motioned to me to walk out the door we came through, he followed me out, the two armed crewmen stayed with the others and the chef went back to work,
"Keep going my friend" the Polish captain said to me as we walked along a walkway and went up some steps,
"Open the next door on your left please, I saw the sign: Capitan on the door, another crewman came down the corridor with a slung rifle over his shoulder,

The captain closed the door behind him, "sit down my friend" he said to me, I saw the black holdalls on the bench against the wall and the weapons too, The captain went to a cupboard and took out a bottle of brandy and poured me a glass,
"Cheers" he said and took a big swig from his glass, I did the same, and the captain spoke on his radio again,
"so know we talk, I want to know everything, I have to make sail in less than an hour now, I can just leave you on your disabled ship waiting for the coast guard and I will be gone, with your money and weapons and I am sure the coast guard will be very interested in you from what I could say about you" the captain said, I stood up quickly,
The captain stood up too and pulled a pistol from his pocket,
"I would not leave you out here for the coast guard, I am not like that, I just want to hear your story then we make plan kapeesh" he added!

I told the captain everything, I had nothing to lose, all about us being British missing soldiers on the run from MI5 / MI6 agents, the emeralds and other irrelevant stuff.
The captain's mobile phone rang and he answered it, he talked for a few minutes and hung up.
He stared at me and smiled.
The captain passed me another drink, "It sounds like a crazy movie my friend, but I believe you, I too am ex-soldier from Estonia special forces, most of my crew on board are like you say missing from army as am I, this boat we took over a long time ago, the crew were paid off and warned off and we took their places, false passports etc, no one seems to ask any questions as long as we transport what is asked from one country to another without any fuss, so you and me are the same I think" the Polish captain explained,
I banged the table with my hand, "well what can I say, I am pleased to meet you sir" I announced and held out my hand, the captain shook my hand,

"Have to be careful my friend, I checked on you, your story holds out, but you missed out a lot of other stuff,
Tell me later, we too have friends in high places, you and your friends have left a trail of disaster behind you for a long time, where is your girlfriend" the captain asked?
I explained what happened!
"sorry to hear that, so now down to business, we can take you and your friends far away from here, for a price, I think you have plenty more to talk about and offer me to take you with us yes" the captain added!
"For sure a lot more, there's more in the boat still" I said to him,
My brain was working overtime thinking of a plan.
"I play with you again Englishman, I no want any more, I see plenty here" he said pointing to the holdalls,
"I am not English by the way, I'm a Welshman" I exclaimed!

"I like Wales, I think you and me will be good friends, we are all soldiers here, you and your friends are my guests on my ship till we get you far away from here as you want, I am not going to Cambodia we are going up the gulf of Mexico, I am carrying , Should take a few weeks with stops and stuff" the captain added,

"So we sink the boat then" I asked?

"Of course, like you say, pull the plug and leave her to the depths of the ocean" the captain said,

"So how much is in the bags then my friend" the captain asked me?

"About three quarters of a million, there's more on the boat I think, left in such a hurry, some more weapons and stuff" I answered,

"how about I have one bag for me and my crew and you keep the others, I am not rude man with fellow soldier, I have respect, I keep the weapons for my ships defences if needed, you pay me for bed and breakfast and fee for escape from this area, it is fair yes" the Polish captain asked?

I nodded and put my thumbs up,

"We need weapons on board in case of hijackers, you're supposed to have special licence for small arms on board and maybe hire a team of maritime security Marshalls but in our line of work,
I would rather use my own guys, we have all the high powered hoses around the ship which are just for show, and we have heavy machine guns available when needed!
Three times we have tried to be high jacked by Somalian soldiers or whatever, they had a bloody shock I tell you,
we have much to talk about later I think my friend, come on let's go and see your friends and sort your boat out, we have a long journey ahead of us" the captain exclaimed!
"Looking forward to it mate, another adventure with plenty of money to spend at the other end" I put in!
We both laughed as we walked down the corridor, we passed the armed crewman, the captain spoke to him in Polish, the crewman clung his rifle over his soldier and walked off waving at me,

"I am sorry for speak too much my language, my crew not too good with English, they speak basic and enough to get by when needed but the react and understand me better when I speak in Polish, we have three weeks together my friend, I teach you and we play plenty of poker for money yes, I am happy you are here" the captain said to me,

We got to the kitchen galley and opened the door, the captain went in first and spoke in Polish, immediately the armed crewmen put their rifles over their shoulders and smiled,

"What's going down boss, we stuffed or what" Moose asked,

"far from it troops, in fact we've come up trumps, captain Lotovich here is one of us, long storey, I'll explain later, we are now guests for a few weeks then onto another adventure" I announced!

"yes my friends I apologise, I have to make sure, I never want to deal with the IRA terrorists, I am no terrorist, they are cowards, you are my friends and will be treated as friends, my ship is your ship, make friends with my crew" captain said.

"they are all soldiers like you on the run, I know everything, I checked from your embassy and yes someone compared you like Friday the thirteenth" the captain explained and laughed, "drink drink my friends" he added, the two crewmen came over to make friends, Moose shook hands and asked to have a look at one of the crewmen's rifles, the polish crewman unloaded the rifle and showed Moose the empty chamber and handed it to him, Moose smiled and played around with it, "7.62 nice one, hit someone with this and you know there not getting up, not like the Nancy 5.56 rounds we normally use, designed to maim the enemy and take out more soldiers from battle to look after the maimed soldier, the two crewmen had some drinks and chatted,
"So now we put your vessel to rest Captain Rhys" the Polish captain announced!
"Yes yes, well unload the rest of our gear and let's get going boss" I said to the captain,
"Call me: Lotovich please everyone" the captain announced!

The two crewmen laughed, and one of them made a motion with his hands of drinking,
The captain saw this, he spoke loudly at them in his own language! "Yes captain" one of them replied
We all laughed!
The two crewmen stayed in the galley with the chef whilst the rest of us followed Lotovich to where our boat was secured,
I noticed more crewmen around he place working and just doing their jobs,
The crewmen gave us curious stares as we passed them,
The captain spoke in his language to them and they carried on with what they were doing,
It was raining now as we walked along steel walkways,
It was getting a bit rough,

Captain Lotovich gave us life jackets, not the big bulky orange ones, but the ones like the marines wear, small and comfortable, professional with pouches for your equipment to be stored,

Me and Moose made our way down the rope ladder, we had safety ropes attached to us, Lotovich was concerned for our safety that me and Moose noted and appreciated, "Here we go again bro" Moose commented as we climbed down the rope,

"Don't know what you and Captain Birdseye been up to in his bunk but well done pall, I thought you were walking a bit funny too" Moose continued,
I gave him a dig in the ribs and he shut up,
We got on board and one of the container engineers came with us too,
"You unload I take care of boat" he said and talked on his radio!
Me and Moose brought out more bags and Dunc and Luke pulled them up, we had packed everything away when we knew the ship was coming for us, just in case.
We had other special weapons stashed away on board from Dan's hidden armoury under the barn,

Also another two large bags of cash, dirty IRA money,
We sent them up too, we went onto the deck,
"that's it" I shouted to Lotovich who then spoke on his radio, me and Moose started to climb back up the rope ladder, the engineer appeared and followed us up after he had untied the ropes that was securing our boat to the ship, we all got up and watched the boat start to sick, the ship bounced into our little boat with a large bang, it was getting rough now, our boat went beneath the surf in a seconds and out of site,
Moose stood there and put his hands to his mouth as if he was blowing a bugle and hummed the tune of the last post,
"hmhmmm, hmhmmmm, hmm, hmm hm hm hum" and carried on, "what is this" Lotovich asked?
I explained the last post to him and what it meant.
Lotovich saluted and walked off,
"Come in when you are ready my friends, my crew will show you some bunks"

"There is plenty of room, I have to go to my control bridge now, duties to do, we have to make way now, be careful" Lotovich shouted as he climbed up a steel ladder and disappeared through a door.

"I keep having to pinch myself in case I am still dreaming" Luke commented!

"Yes it's all just too good to be true, however I'm fucking glad it has" Duncan said picking up some bags.

"Right let's get back into the galley before we get soaked" I growled!

It was raining hard now and we got inside with the rest of the kit.

There was a nice smell of cooking in the large galley, the TV was on in the corner, and football was on,

"You like football, I put on for you, I cook dinner for boat, may people to feed" the chef announced!

"So how many people are on the ship" I asked?

"maybe twenty I think, two shifts, 12 on 12 hours off, me I work all day and all night, other chef sick, you sit down and relax, I get you drinks and snacks" he added in bad English!
"so we got a few weeks on this monster boat, let's play the game and be friendly at all times, I think I've gained the captains trust unless he's a false as me, anyway lets chill and take on the captains hospitality until I can think of something, that money is ours and I'm not giving half it up without a fight" I whispered!
"Bang on bro" Moose put in,
"I wonder if they do double beds on these things" Dunc asked.
"Shut up Dunc" we all growled,
Tina gave him a dig!
"want everyone to befriend as many crew as they can, get to know them, joke with them, play along with them, take in as much information as you can, numbers of the shifts, times of change over, crew movements on a daily basis, what jobs need to be done on a daily basis.

I want to know how to run this ship if we need to, is that clear" I whispered as an order,

"Crystal captain" Luke slurred!

"Don't give any more booze to boy wonder tonight please" I asked,

Luke was a little bit tipsy,

"I'm ok, so I am" he announced.

"Ok so how many fingers am I holding up then" Moose asked him?

"Two, three, bollocks Moose you keep changing, I'm going for a piss" Luke growled! 'We watched him walk on a bit of a wonk to the toilet,

"Moose keep an eye on him, don't need any loose tongues trying to show off" I added!

"Roger that mate" Moose agreed,

"Chef" Duncan called out!

The polish chef showed himself, "hello" he said,

"So what's on the menu tonight mate" Duncan asked,

"Ok yes, um, we have: spicy pork schnitzels, we have meatballs, I have sauerkraut with beef inside, and you call big Yorkshire pudding, sausages in curry sauce, rice, pasta, vegetable and potatoes and a lot more, I cook on my own and kill myself, not fair" the chef announced!

"I can help you" Tina exclaimed,

The chef looked at her, "you can cook" he asked?

I can cook, my English not too good, I speak Portuguese better, and you teach me I learn quickly" she said to the chef,

"I know little Portuguese, Linda mavarillioso, encreheevil, vou te ensinar, he spoke in Portuguese! I teach you, brilliant" the Polish chef was well happy, Luke had heard all this, "can I help too" he asked wiping his mouth,

"Of course, come I show you everything, you make me happy, yes wonderful thank you my friends" the chef continued!

"Faggot I think boyo" Moose commented quietly!
"Shut it Moose just play our game with them and let me work a plan ok" I whispered to him,
Moose smiled at me and winked,
Me Moose and Dunc chatted for a while and watched Tina and Luke in the kitchen when the door opened and the captain walked in,
"sorry for the rocking of the ship, got some bad weather out there, the crew can manage it, we've been through a lot worse I tell you, so now I show you to your rooms, or bunks I should say, come with me please" Lotovich announced!
Me, Moose and Dunc picked up the bags and weapons ad followed,
"I want you show me these different weapon's my friend" the captain asked?
"Of course my friend, this one can hit a target over a thousand metres away accurately" I said,

"I buy off you right now Rhys, or we play poker later them I think, make big game tonight when weather is better yes" he asked?

"Yes my friend I look forward to it" I replied!

"Follow me friends" Lotovich called out and opened the door, watch your step, it's wet out here, heavy rain,

We followed him out.

The captain opened a steel door and walked in, we followed him down a corridor,

"ok friends I have five bunks here, nothing special, this ship as meant to hols a lot more crew than I require so these are yours for your stay, i will get you a radio each for communication and bon voyage shall I say, I give you time to sort your selves out and we meet again for dinner in a few hours, we eat, drink and lay poker, I win your money monies and special weapons yes my friends" he said and laughed!

"We will see, maybe you lose your boat to me my friend" I added and wished I never said that,

"Never, will not happen, I know you British people are like" he said sternly and walked away, I saw his eyes,
We waited until he was gone, "I think he's a little bit mental, two can's short of a six pack my friend" Moose commented,
"I agree, just keep him happy, let's get our stuff sorted eh, and pick your bunks, bunkers" I growled!
"Play the game, lardy dee dardy dar" Dunc sang!
"Ok wise guy, you know it makes sense" I told him,
"Can I play gay with the cook too boss" Moose called out!
"If it turns you on" I answered!
We all laughed,
Everyone picked their bunks, Dunc had the bigger one for him and Tina.
The tanoy system crackled!
"My friends, this captain Lotovich, would you like to see where we control this ship from,
I send one of the crew down to show you how to get here" the captain announced!

Within five minutes a crewman appeared in the corridor, "I take you to captain in bridge" he said,
We followed him out up numerous flights of steel steps,
"Is there not an elevator in this place" Moose asked out loud!
The crewman laughed, "no elevator my friend, just too many steps and ladders" the crewman answered!
We got to the bridge.

"Good evening my friends, welcome to the heart of my ship, from up here we can see the whole ship" Lotovich announced!
"Pretty high up, so it is" Luke exclaimed,

"yes young man, we are fifty metres up, so when we have a big load of containers, I can see over them to see where we are going basically, never stack my containers over three high like other ships do, in bad storms when the wind and waves hit the high loaded ships, something might give then disaster, lost load, lost money" the captain added!

"Yes, we have radar that will pick any vessel and size out here as far as fifty miles, we also have sonar, that I got installed, I like to know what is below us too!

We can look all main doors from here, we have CCTV cameras in vital areas, covert cameras too, don't worry there is no cameras in your bunks, we can monitor most radio bands including Military, air force and Naval, police and some others, lake I said to earlier sometimes we transport items that the authorities would agree with so to speak, all my crew respect me and I trust them all, we have armour plating and some surprises for whoever I want to surprise!

"There are secure areas I can hide things and they will not be found, even if an x-ray system is used, this boat has had a lot of moderations, cost me a lot of money, when she needs speed she can put out, we once had a naval patrol boat try and catch up to us but couldn't, we didn't have a load then, we slowed in the end, we had nothing to hide at that time, the Naval captain who came aboard to inspect was so shocked that this ship could match the speed of his cruiser and outrun it, everything was ok in the end though!

Yes, we have cranes and other technical equipment, and lots more" Lotovich announced!

"Pretty impressive mate" I said, "call me Loto My friend" the captain said, "ok and you can call me Rhys,

"Yes yes of course, we go down now, Yakov here will show you around the rest of the ship and explain certain procedures and drills to you if needed, I see you later at dinner, and we talk more and drink and play poker" Loto announced,

"Sure, see you later Loto" I replied,

We went back down the steep steps, following Yakov around the rest of the ship, told us what was required from us if certain scenarios occurred,
A few times Moose asked so what's through there, pointing secured doors, Yakov would reply: "out of bounds, captain's orders" and he carried on showing us around the ship,
By the time we got back to our bunks it was time for dinner, as a message came over the tanoy system!
We all made our way to the main galley,
"Something smells good" I commented,
"Ye I'm hank Marvin mate" Dunc answered,
"Duncan you are always starving" Moose put in,
"I'm a growing lad" Dunc replied!
We laughed and went into the galley,
There was quite a few people in there all over the place in their little groups talking and laughing, we had quite a few stairs too,
We found a table and sat down, Tina and Luke came over, they were wearing chefs white's and looked quite professional,
"Look at you two" I announced!

"I learnt so much, I like this job Duncan" Tina said,
"It's been interesting, so it has" Luke announced!
"Ye this ship is interesting too" Moose commented quietly!
I gave Moose and Dunc one of my stares! They understood!
We got up and joined the queue for dinner, there must have been a good twenty people in the galley,
"Lot of people here tonight, food must be good" I said out loud!
"You must be joking, the crap he cooks up in here, same shit every other day, and yes it's the shift change over, night crew take over now, day shift relax for the night, we drink play games watch dirty movies and occasionally we fight each other my friend" the crewman explained to me, "what is your name" he asked?
I told him and explained to him what happened,
"What do think of Loto then" the crewman asked, I thought he was testing me!

"From what I have seen so far I see a good captain, firm but fair" I answered,
The crewman laughed out loud!
"Did you hear that, Englishman thinks our captain is firm and fair" he announced!
There was a lot of laughter from everyone!
"He is a two faced drunk and not too be trusted, he would sell his own mother to the devil if there was a profit to be made" another crewman said,
"we all know what happen and what your circumstances are here, welcome aboard, Captain Loto will make you play poker later, watch out he is a cheat" another crew member whispered, I smiled, "so am I" I commented! The crew member laughed!
We sat down once we got our meals, there was a smash of a plate and the noise of arguing, we heard punches being thrown and a thud on the floor, Moose went to stand up, I grabbed his arm, "easy tiger, not our problem" I whispered,
"This happens every evening meal time, it is normal to see, one shift always have issues with the other shift, at the end of the day if it came to it, we all stick together",

"We are all ex-soldiers of some sort here, you lot are too I understand" a guy sitting behind us said!
"Just like being in our old cook house, the same there" I said to him, "what is cook house" he asked?
I explained!
"Not too bad" Dunc said eating a double portion of sausages in curry sauce,
The food was ok, we all cleared our plates and put them in the wash area and sat back down, there was a bar area in the corner where some people were smoking,
"I'm going to see if I can cag a fag from over there" I announced and stood up, Moose got up with me, "I'll join you mate, we walked to the bar, "anyone have a spare fag" I asked, the crewman smoking turned around, "no fags here my friend, you want to smoke, these are called papieros like you call: cigarette" the crew man passed me a cigarette and Gave Moose one too,
"You want drink" he asked?
"That would be good" Moose answered

The crewman spoke to the man behind the bar in Polish, the barman looked serious and made two drinks up,
Moose started to cough! "Jesus theses are strong things" Moose said and coughed again, "yes twice as stronger than your capstan full strength cigarette's "more like a Baltchevic fire cracker" I put in and coughed too!
The barman passed me and Moose two glasses,
"this will warm you up my friends" he said and walked away to serve someone else,
""down the hatch mate" Moose said and knocked his glass back, "good god, that's my stomach lining stripped out" he growled, I drank mine, "I am sure you could light that stuff, "it's called slivoritch, plum brandy, very strong, you want more" the crewman asked?
"Later my friend" I said and walked back to our table, Moose followed, we sat down,
"We got a funny crew here, this trip is going to be very interesting indeed" I announced!

We chatted for a while and a young female dressed like the rest of the crew came over and sat next to Tina, Moose was paying a lot of attention to her,
The door to the galley opened and a strong draft came in, the captain appeared,
"He spoke in his own language and a lot of the crew started to leave the galley,
"what's going on now then" Duncan asked, the young lady who had sat next to Tina said: "they go to their duties now, night shift, a rowdy lot, most crew on the night shift have messed up on the day shift so as a punishment the captain puts them to night shift, same as on the night shift, if you show you are good, you will go back to the day shift" she said, "what's your name miss" Moose asked, the young girl smiled,
"Alaina" she replied, "what a lovely name, my name is Moose, pleased to meet you Alaina" Moose spoke softly,
"Moose is name for winter animal I think" she said,
"Well it's not my real name, but all my friends call me it, some say I have a head like a moose" Moose added!

"There's a moose loose around the hoose" Moose announced!

Alaina laughed, so did Tina,

The captain came over to our table, "hello again friends, sorry I should say: Rhys, Moose, Tina, Duncan and Luke, and our nurse: Alaina, I have not seen you for quite a while" the captain said looking at Alaina, "I stay in med station, look after the sick sir, busy busy" Alaina replied, "of course" Captain agreed!

"so you enjoy the evening meal, I believe there was little fight before, it's a usual thing here, like two different regiments mixing together, there is always a bit of trouble, they all know when to draw the line though" the captain told us,

"So we play some poker yes" Loto asked?

"Yes why not" I answered back, the galley didn't have too many crew left in it now, Tina asked Alaina if she would stay and keep her company" Alaina smiled and accepted after a stare from the captain that I noticed, Moose looked happy too!

A few bottles of whiskey were brought to our table with some glasses.

Three packs of well used cards were placed on the table by the crewman who was minding the bar,
The barman put a green table cloth on the table and placed a pile of coloured counters on the table,
"So what poker we play then" Loto asked?
"Stud poker" Moose put in,
"Fine gentlemen and ladies too if you want to play" Loto added,
The two girls shook their heads and carried on talking, Alaina took Tina over to the pool table.
There was eight of us round the table, the captain and three crewmen, me, Moose, Duncan and Luke,
The coloured disks were shared out, "ten thousand each" Loto said and explained how much each coloured counter was worth.
We played a few hands, Moose won most of them, "wish these counters was real money" Moose put in, "it can be my friend if you want to" Loto exclaimed!
"I'm game Dunc announced, I nodded my head, "I'm skint so I am" Luke said,

"We have cash, let's have some more counters out and talk limits" I suggested,
The captain laughed!
More counters were brought to the table by the barman,
"ok so how about we go for five thousand live cash each and see what happens" Loto put to us,
"Game on" Moose growled!
Two of the three crewmen thanked us for the game and left, the other one stayed after talking to his captain in their own language,
"I give him private loan" Loto said and smiled.
The drinks were flowing freely, Luke was slurring his words a bit and making a few daft bets,
"Fold" I said, "me to" Moose put in, Dunc threw his hand in too,
There was a pile of counters in the middle of the table now, probably about twenty thousand pounds worth, we were playing for euros though,
The crewman folded and that Left Luke and the captain holding their cards,

"I see your bet and raise you ten thousand young man" Loto said sternly,
"That's a bit steep" Luke said, "you play big boys game you must to expect big boys bets yes" Loto announced and laughed!
I pushed a large amount of discs across to Luke, your wages for your help young man, good luck Luke" I said,
Luke looked at the captain and took a swig from his glass, "I see you and call you captain" Luke announced!
The captain nodded his head, "ok" Loto said,
The captain showed his cards, three Kings and laughed, "I think I take your money now" he said and went to pull some of the counters from the pile in the middle of the table, "hang on there mate" Luke put in and flopped his cards onto the table,
"Three fucking Aces" Moose exclaimed!
"You're a bit of a dark horse" I exclaimed and laughed!
The captain stood up sharply and spoke to the crewman who was still at the table in Polish,

The crewman left the table shaking his head, he said nothing,

"yes Mr Luke I think you know this game very well, your eyes tell me nothing, three Ace's I was not expecting that hand young man, tonight you win my money, tomorrow I win it back, I send one of my crew down with your winnings, I now retire, I wake early in morning to sort the crew out, it has been an enjoyable evening my friends, make yourself at home here, the chef is on call, the bar is free, there is a jar you can contribute to, enjoy the rest of the evening, I will see you all tomorrow, I bid you good night" the captain announced" he walked out through the door swiftly, you could see on the look of his face he wasn't too happy,

"How much is there Luke" Moose asked,

"I don't know, there's a mountain of chips here" Luke slurred!

"Three bloody Aces son, you bluffing bastard" Duncan exclaimed!

"Dan taught me well I think, we would play poker most nights, he taught me a lot of tricks too" Luke added, "you cheat well young man" I announced,

Luke winked at me, we all laughed!
The crewman minding the bar came over to see if we wanted anything before he finished for the evening,
"my advice to you is be very careful, the captain does not like to beaten and lose a lot of money like that, he was cheating and you still beat him, I think next game you should let him win, he is bad man sometimes my friends, everyone knows of the money you have brought with you and the special weapons, watch your backs I think" the crewman said and left the galley,
"Well what do you think of that then" Moose asked?
Tina and Alaina came over from the pool table, they had played pool with some crewmen, Dunc was watching all the time, the girls were giggling and happy, "we beat them" Tina announced, "we played for money, look" she added showing us a wad of notes in her hand, Alaina saw the pile of chips on the table and Luke counting them, She looked around, "captain Lotovich in toilet" she asked,

"Gone to bed with a sore head" Luke slurred!
Alaina looked worried, "you win him to much I think" Alaina announced, "not good for crew tomorrow" she added and sat down, she poured herself a large drink, "I think tomorrow I have many sick in med station" she continued, she drank her drink and went to pour another,
"Slow down a bit, let me join you, you are too pretty to drink on your own" Moose announced!
"Fancy a game of pool with me" Moose added,
Alaina smiled and agreed, they both walked over to the pool table,
"Be gentle Moose" Duncan called to him!
"Oh my god, I might of made a mistake but I believe I have around fifty thousand euros worth here, he did say the blue ones were thousands didn't he lads" Luke asked?
"He certainly did, after he had had a few though" I put in,
The door to the galley opened and a crewman came in with a briefcase.

He came over to where we were sitting and put the briefcase on the table,
"Comrades, Mr Luke this is your winnings tonight, the Capitan wishes you well and a big well done, the next game he say he will be watching you very carefully" he said,
The crewman opened the case, "sixty thousand euros, and good night" he said, the young man saluted and walked away, with a limp, "you ok my friend" Duncan called out!
"Capitan not happy at the moment, see you tomorrow" the young crewman said and left the galley,
"Wow, unbelievable will I wake up tomorrow lads, I feel a bit uneasy so I do" Luke announced!
"easy boy, you come under my wing now, nothing, and I mean nothing is going to happen to you, all this shit everyone keeps telling us about the captain, just trying to spook us for some reason, but I tell you something, us being on this ship is not good",

"I need to get a plan together soon, tomorrow let's all be nice and play the game, if he wants another game tomorrow night we do it, if we win again, so what, there's one thing I hate, and that's a bully, I sense he is one with his crew, ok that is all, now drink and be happy folks, we don't need to get up early, we are guests as the Capitan said, cheers" I growled! Holding up my glass,

Moose and Alaina were laughing at the pool table,

I sat next to Tina, "listen mate, you and Alaina seem to have made friends, get as much information out of her as you can" I whispered,

"She has asked me if I can help her tomorrow" Tina said to me, "brilliant girl, you help her" I put in,

Luke put all the chips, counters in a large bowl he found behind the bar and put them under the counter with a note: great game captain, here are all the chips, look forward to another game.

"So who wants a game of darts then" Luke asked out loud!

Dunc and Tina agreed, "You coming mate" Dunc asked me? "No mate have some thinking to do now" I answered to him and winked,

I poured myself another drink and went to the one of the port holes, I looked out to sea and thought about Carmem,

I decided to go outside and have a smoke, there was a packet of Polish cigarettes left on the bar, I grabbed the packet and some matches and went outside, the rest of my gang were enjoying themselves,

It was blowing hard outside and I found it hard to light my cigarette, I walked down the steel walkway and found a corner to hide from the wind, I lit my cigarette and coughed!

I finished my drink and threw the glass into the sea, "I miss you Carmem" I said softly and stared at the horizon.

I pulled out my mobile phone and dialled Carmem's number, it went to voice mail, I left a message:

"my love, I miss you so much and will forever mate, I love you Carmem" I put the mobile back in my pocket, I felt a tear roll down my face, I wiped it away and smoked my cigarette and thought of her.

I heard a coughing from somewhere, I turned around and heard someone stumble, "You ok" I asked!

I heard a cough again and a groan, I moved quickly up the walkway and saw in the dark and saw one of the crew slumped in a dark corner,

"You ok mate" I called!

Someone replied in Polish, I moved closer, it was the crewman who was playing poker with us, I pulled him up,

"What happened to you" I asked?

"I fall over my friend, drink too much, I am ok" he replied, I saw his face, his nose was bleeding and he was holding his ribs,

I got him into the galley and sat him down, Alaina came straight over, "Jakob what happened to you" she asked!

They spoke in their own language, and argued!

"Get me drink please" Jakob asked, I did straight away,
He drank it down in one go,
Jakob lit a cigarette,
"so you beat the captain, he is happy with you, but not happy with me, he tell me to help him cheat, I pass to him cards, you still win" Jakob laughed, "now I pay the price yes, Captain Lotovich bad man, be careful comrades" Jakob continued!
"What the fuck is going on here" I announced!
"our captain not as nice as he shows himself to you, he is very dangerous, most of the crew here have run away from the Polish army, Lotovich promises them he can hide them for ever as long as they work for him, he has promised them plenty of wealth transporting things around the world, he pays good when he is paid, so they stay and work for him, crew have disappeared in the past whilst we have been at sea, we took a lot of refugees across the sea once, they were in a container, nobody knew, the container started to smell badly after a week, one of the crew opened the container.

There was thirty black people rotting in there, the captain was very annoyed, the refugees were thrown over the side of the ship and nothing was said, he has a hold on most of the crew from one reason or another, but he does pay well after a good job, people like money and will risk things for it too, I think I have said to much, now I take care of Jakob, Alaina took Jakob to the med bay, Moose went with her,
"Any problems call me pronto" I said to Moose as he left with Alaina,
"I think we finish our drinks and call it a night, maybe we need to be fresh for tomorrow" I announced!
"Yes mate" Duncan replied!
Jake nodded his head and grabbed his case full of euros,
Tina pulled Dunc up, "come on big man, I want to hear you snore" she said and giggled!
We all went to where our bunks were, it wasn't too far, and we had keys to our doors,

"Ok troops, get your heads down and see you in the morning" I announced as I opened my door,
I went to the cupboard and myself a drink, I was thinking about Moose, I was sure he would be ok, I lit a cigarette and thought about Carmem again.
I could see Carmem on our boat drinking champagne, our lesbian made joking with her,
We had so much fun,
I loved her beyond belief, she had save our lives and much more, my best friend lost in the sea,
I blamed myself and hated me for it!
I heard my door banged! My head was ponding!
"What" I shouted!
Duncan came in,
"Hey boyo, Moose is not in his bunk and I feel like shit, how are you by the way" Dunc growled,
I was on the floor wrapped in my blankets,
"Dunc give me a hand here" I groaned!
Dunc pulled me up and I slumped in the chair,

"What a night ah partner" I said to him, "Rhys, I think we need to talk, I've got a bad feeling being abroad this ship, too many people talking bad about Captain Birdseye" Dunc announced!
"Ok mate, give me five and well go to the galley for breakfast and see what's going on ye" I told him, Dunc nodded and left.
I sat on the edge of my bed and got my head together,
What was going on here, I asked myself!
I got dressed as Dunc came in, Tina and Luke were there too,
"You look like I feel mate" Luke put in!
"So nobody seen Moose then" I asked?
"Nope" Dunc answered!
"ok, let's go and get some breakfast, too much going on for my brain, need a greasy fried egg on toast and I will be fine" I announced and lead the way,
We walked into the galley, we were actually late, the night shift had had their breakfast and the day shift too and gone to their duties, a few of the night shift hung around, playing pool and darts, a few were drinking and smoking at the bar,

Alaina and Moose was sat at a table talking and smiling at each other,

We went over, "so, here you then looking cosy, how's the patient then" I asked with high eyebrows!

Moose got my stare and smiled, I winked at him,

"Jakob is ok, he has took a good beating but will be fine" Alaina said,

"Did he say who did it" Duncan asked?

"He doesn't know, too dark he said" Alaina put in,

"Ye captain Loto for sure is behind this, so he is" Luke said quietly!

"You must not say things like that on this ship, people have just disappeared in the past for being too nosey" Alaina announced!

"Ok so I'm off for breakfast" I said and walked to the hot plate, Dunc, Tina and Luke followed.

We got our food and went to where Moose and Alaina were sitting,

"Bon appetite" I said as we sat down,

We ate in silence and finished our meals.

"I needed that" I put in and drank my coffee,
"I'm off for seconds, anyone else" Duncan exclaimed!
Tina slapped his bottom as Dunc stood up and made his way to the hot plate again,
"So, I am very unhappy with what's going on here my friends, too many of the crew are talking badly of the captain here, we need a plan to get off this Mickey mouse boat as soon as possible I think" I put to everyone!
"I totally agree mate" Moose said.
"so let's play his game as I said before and sus out this ship, I want to know as much info as possible, we still got weapons and ammo, if and when we need it, we help out as much as we can, make friends with the crew, play the captains games and not beat him too much Luke, ok" I said quietly,
"Received and understood boss" Luke replied!
"I'm going to help Alaina in the med centre" Moose announced,
"I will help the chef with Luke, if he wants to" Tina said, Luke nodded,

"That's fine, me and Dunc will scout around the ship" I put to everyone,
The galled door opened and the captain came in,
"good morning to you all, I hope you had a good rest after an adventurous day you had yesterday, so, last night was fun, I look forward to playing again, today I show you your duties around the ship, if that is ok, I thought that you did not want to be bored as its going to be a few weeks before we see land, I will send some crew to show you your duties soon if this is ok with you" the captain announced,
"Captain I was wondering if I can help Alaina in the med centre, she is busy and I am a team medic" the Captain gave Alaina a hard look, "of course of course" the captain replied,
"Can me and Luke help the chef as he is on his own" Tina asked?
"You pick you own jobs, I like this, yes of course" he said,
"Loto, me and Dunc are yours mate" I mentioned!

"ok Mr Rhys and Mr Duncan I will show you some duties to attend to when required, it seems I have too many crew going sick lately and I need their jobs covered" the captain announced!

"Alaina I understand that Jakob has hurt himself again, drinking too much on a ship, no good, I wish to speak to you when I go up to the bridge" Loto told Alaina,

"yes Capitan" and she stood up, "Moose, you know the way to the med bay, look after things in there for a while till I return please"

Alaina asked Moose,

"Yes boss" Moose answered and saluted. Me and Moose left with the captain, he made us both go back to our bunks and get our life jackets, I put some of my own equipment into the pouches of the jacket and so did Moose!

The captain took us to the front of the boat where all the containers were,

"Ok soldiers I need you to check all the containers, make sure they are all secure" Loto announced, he showed us what to do and showed us some more jobs too.

The captain left us to get on with things, "you have radios, so if you need help just call, I will see you later tonight after diner for another game" the captain put to us and went off.

"So let's do our jobs and have a good look around this bucket boat" I told Moose,

I saw a few of the crew going about with their checks, they waved to us and carried on with their jobs,

We both did what the captain asked of us then we walked around taking a lot in, we went down below and saw some secured doors that had a notice saying: Out of bounds in Polish,

"Wonder what's in there then" Moose asked?

I saw a camera on the ceiling and coughed, moose saw my eyes and clocked the camera, we moved on, we went down some more steel steps, we must have been at the bottom of the ship, we came across another secured door with a key pad, I looked around, there was another camera on the ceiling,

Moose saw my eyes and we walked on, there was some more doors that were not secured, Moose opened one of them and looked in, "hey take a look at this mate" Moose exclaimed!

We both walked into the room and saw a body on the floor, "check it out" I told Moose, Moose looked for a light switch, then turned on his torch he took out from a pouch on his life jacket,

"I think we have a stiff here" Moose put in, the room was smelling badly!

"We got a dead woman here mate" Moose announced!

The dead woman was dressed in the same uniform as the rest of the crew, but was slightly different, looked like the same overalls as Alaina wore, "bad karma" I mentioned, we left the room and closed the door, we made our way back up the steps to where we were meant to be doing our checks on the containers,

"What now mate" Moose asked, "I don't know yet, let's carry on with our jobs and wait till we see the rest, need a good chat" I told him.

Me and Moose carried on working and being nosy for a good few hours, we found another area deep at the back of the ship that was out of bounds also, the door had a key code pad on the door, Moose said he could hear splashing water through an air vent next to the secured door, there was a camera on the ceiling so we got out of there, We made our way back to the galley and found the captain there eating a meal, "Hello my friends, how was your day, I'm glad to see you wear your life jackets, too many accidents happen on my ship that do not need to happen" he said sternly!
"Good day Captain, all our jobs done and we had a look around your ship" I told him, I know, just to let you know that there are some areas that are sensitive and out of bounds, only certain crew can access, it's a captains thing, we all have restricted areas for the ships security that is all" Loto put in, "Of course captain, excuse us for being nosy, big ship here, just like to explore unknown areas, it's a soldier thing, I am sure you understand" I announced!

Captain Loto looked a bit confused, "yes my friends, of course, you are my guests, you can explore anywhere, we are friends here, I look forward to play poker again tonight with you, I hope young Luke will not be so tough tonight" he said and laughed,

I looked at him, I had him confused and a bit stuck for words, plan successful I thought!

"I look forward to a good game too my friend" I replied,

"So back to work" the captain announced and stood up, he said a few things to the chef in Polish and left,

Me and Dunc sat down and talked, I noticed the chef trying to listen,

Dunc went over to the bar and made us two drinks, "here you go bud, for a good days work" Dunc said,

The chef came over with some sandwiches, "I make cheese and tomato for you after your day my friends, so what do you think of the ship then" he asked, I felt he was digging for info, "yes interesting boat, so big, so many places out of bounds too, had a good day, need a god shower soon and look forward to your evening meal mate" I replied,

The chef smiled, "yes some places out of bounds, key personnel allowed only, captains orders, ship's security and weapons in case we get hijacked" the chef put in and laughed!

The chef went back to his kitchen,

Duncan gave me the eyes, "what the fuck was all that about" he asked quietly,

"too much going on here pal, we all got secure pagers, if we feel we need to talk to each other in confidence or whatever, find a bog and text the message,

I have some spare pager's for Luke and Tina, so hard to get these things, thanks to our ex drunk Sargent Nash, Dan got me some more" I said quietly,

"so what we going to do, there's a smelly stiff down below, I am sure captain Birdseye has seen us going down there, so no dought it will be gone by now somehow",

"We need to find the key code for those doors and somehow knock out the CCTV cameras" Moose whispered!

"Good god Moose, you surprise me with all this stuff, I like it mate, when you're ready give me some more" I told him,

"Jerk" Moose said!

We sat there for a good hour when Moose and Alaina walked in laughing and touching each other,

"You two look happy, how is Yakob" I asked?

"he will be ok, needs rest, he gets drunk and falls over too much" Alaina said, "you believe that" Dunc exclaimed!

"no I do not, I know too much, Captain watches and listens too, I cannot say too much here, I tell Moose later, he can tell you everything" she added,

"So the walls have eyes and ears do they, I'll be back" I said and stood up,

I went to the toilet and wrote a few things down on a piece of paper for Alaina that I hoped she could look into, I went back into the galley and sat down,

I buttered another piece of toast and took a bite, I was looking at Alaina, she saw my stare, my other hand was under the table with the piece of paper in it, and I touched her leg, Alaina's eyes widened! I touched her leg again, she frowned at me and looked at Moose, I looked down with my eyes, she took the bait, her hand touched mine and she took the paper from me and hid it, "Alaina got up, "so back to work, are you coming with me Moose" she asked? "Not now, Moose said, I gave Moose a hard stare, he got what I meant, "actually I will my dear, rather be in the sick bay than swabbing the decks with these two scallywags" Moose replied and winked to me,

They both walked away to the med centre, "Make a good couple, I think" Dunc put in, "so you two helping the chef today" I asked Tina and Luke, yes, I think we are stuck there, the other chef just disappeared apparently, the captain told the chef he must of jumped ship or something" Luke announced,

This boat ride feels more like the highway to hell to me" Duncan commented!

"Don't talk too much in front of the chef ok, I whispered!

"Befriend him and see what he spills" I added,

"Ok Dunc let's go up top and see what the captain wants us to do then" I growled!

"arrr, Jim lad" Moose replied!,

We left the galley and may our way up to the bridge,

We got up to the bridge, "ahoy there" Dunc announced as we walked in!

I saw three crewmen busy at the controls, "captain around" I asked?

"not today, he is not feeling to good" one of the crewmen said, another crewman made the gesture with his raised hand as if drinking a drink, "he was fine at breakfast" I said,

The crewmen shrugged their shoulders and carried on with navigating the ship,

Me and Dunc left the bridge and made our way down the steel steps away from the bridge,

"We need to get off this ship mate, I have a bad feeling" I whispered, "me too mate" Moose replied!

"I say we find the captain and have it out with him, we got weapons downstairs, let get them and kick some butts" Moose put in!

I nodded and we made our way to our bunks,

I opened my door and looked around, I sensed something, and the weapons were not here,

I went to Dunc's bunk, he came out, my gat's gone mate, even the pistol I hid Under my mattress, sneaky fucker" he growled!

"We find captain fish finger and have some words I think ye" Dunc exclaimed!

"Let's do it, we need to warn the others first" I ordered!

We went straight to the galley and spoke to Luke and Tina as the chef wasn't around for some reason, we made our way to the med centre and told Moose and Aliana,

"I see note you gave to me Rhys, we need to talk" she said softly,

What is this about a dead girl down below with nurse's uniform" Alaina asked?
"yes we found her dumped in a room deep below, bottom of the ship, out of bounds area I think, or close to it" I replied!
My nurse, went missing two weeks ago with the other chef, not good" Alaina added,
"Ok captain Lotovich is bad man, he has something on all the crew he takes on, he picks the crew carefully from our messed up country, mostly soldiers who have run from Polish army or are on the run from the police for some reason, he pays them well when he can, but has a hold on them.
He works for some rich British man, who has covered up so many problems with this ship, most of the crew have false passports, this ship used to have a different crew that disappeared after being paid off well, he smuggles all sorts around the world" Alaina continued,
"How do you know so much about this bum bag" Moose asked?
"Because I used to sleep with him" she said softly,

"Kick me know" Moose exclaimed!
"Polish army bad and hard, small pay, long story,
Lotovich needs to be stopped" Aliana complained,
"Well we can't call the authorities can we" Dunc announced,
"So he has our weapons, can't put up much of a fight with no weapons, need a plan, knives from the kitchen could be handy" I put in,
"wait I know numbers for keypad looks, I know there are rooms down below with weapons inside, Loto told me he had an escape boat that can be launched from the back, there is hidden doors that can be opened or something, I don't know, maybe alcohol talk, Loto talks too much when he is drunk, he also slept with my nurse, who is missing, I want to see this dead lady, then I take you too locked rooms" Alaina growled,
"We need to disable the CCTV cameras somehow, I f he is watching from somewhere, or take over the bridge" Luke exclaimed!

"Well look at you, I like it, keep it up young man" I said to him,
"I want to help" came a voice!
We looked around and saw the chef standing there, "I want to help please, he got rid of my chef and I have been working like a dog, he got me drunk one night playing poker, I lost big time, I cannot repay dept it was too much, he take me to his room and rape me, I cannot say anything or he will tell to everyone I am gay" the chef announced!
We all stared at him in silence for a moment,
"Unbelievable, he's a nonce too, I so want to have a chat with him again" Moose growled!
"Ok troops, this is what's going to happen" Chef here, what's your name mate, I asked?
"Dimitri" I am ex recce platoon like you guys, I listen to your stories, I had to, captain order me to, I am very good with knives" he said, in an instant Dimitri threw three sharp knives strait into the dart board with accuracy within a second!

"I'll buy that for aa dollar" Duncan put in and laughed!

"ok, so, have some walkie talkies thanks to the captain, we change the frequency, keep checking the other frequency though to see if the Capitan is chatting, Dunc and Luke, with the chef go up to the bridge, once Alaina has shown us where the weapons are, me and Moose will go and find Lotovich, Tina and Alaina, I don't know girls, what do you want to do" I asked?

"We fight with you Rhys, we have nothing to lose" Tina answered,

"ok, Tina you come with me and Moose, Alaina you go with Duncan and Luke, ok let's go down and see what we can find, grab some knives you lot, that's all the defence we have for the time being" I announced!

The galley door opened with a bang! There was two crewmen standing there with raised rifles, "so captain would like you to stay here until he arrives please! One of the crewman announced, the other one shouted in Polish to the chef!

Within a second the chef had thrown a knife into the two crewmen, they fell and didn't move.

"Get some" Moose announced and quickly went and took their rifles,

"We need to move fast Duncan and Luke take the rifles and get up to the bridge and hold it" I ordered!

"We have hand guns here" Luke announced as he searched the dead crewmen, "another radio and a bunch of keys" he added!

"Ok the girls get the hand guns and off we go" I growled!

We left the galley, Dunc, Luke, Tina and the chef went off to the bridge, me, Moose followed Alaina quickly down flights of steel steps, over the radio I could her Loto talking in Polish, sounds like he was calling the two crewmen who had come to the galley,

We kept going down and came to an area that said: Out of bounds, the place I saw before,

"down there" I called to Alaina and pointed to a door, Alaina opened the steel door and looked in, she started to cry, "son of a bitch"

she sobbed, Moose went to her and hugged her,
"It's her, my nurse" she announced!
Alaina came out of the room, "this way" she said, we all followed, she led us down the hallway, "here we go" she announced!
Alaina tapped in a few numbers into the keypad, we heard a beep, Alaina pushed the door open, "here we go gentlemen" she said and turned on a light, me and Moose walked in.
"Well look at this" Moose announced quickly grabbing a shotgun and ammunition,
The room was had shelves with loads of weapons and ammo scattered ever were,
I grabbed a rifle and some ammo, Alaina did too,
"Ok let's rock" Moose announced!
"Wait I need to show you something" Alaina announced!
She led us down the corridor and down another flight of stairs,
"This is where Moose heard water behind the door" I exclaimed!

Alaina tapped in a number into the keypad, the door clicked, Alaina puled the door open,
"Shit, he wasn't talking rubbish" she said
I looked in,
There was a boat moored in the water, what the hell is this, like a James bond movie" I exclaimed!
"I mini harbour, I love it! Moose announced!
"Moose check that boat out" I ordered!
Moose was straight onto the boat!
Me and Alaina sneaked around, the was a cctv camera in the corner I noticed, we looked around, it wasn't too big in there, enough room to berth an averaged sized cruiser boat and some small rooms that we checked out, I found a control panel for the rear doors, I switched the power button on, the panel lit up, "good sign" I whispered,
We left the loading bay where the boat was moored and made our way back up the steel stairs,
I lead the way, the radio crackled!
"Rhys you receiving over" I heard Dunc call!

I stopped and replied: "roger, send your message over"

"Hello my friends, if you would please come up to the bridge now or I will shoot the young lad" Captain Lotovich announced!

"yes I have been watching you Mr Rhys, I see you have found my Ace in the pack, I will have a good talk to Alaina when I see her, I see you have also found my spare weapons, I would like to tell you there are no firing pins in your weapons, so this time I think I win the poker game yes" Lotovich added,

There was an announcement over the tanoy system: "can I have your attention please, there is a lock down in place, only essential personnel are allowed on deck all other personnel are confided to their cabins until further notice" captain Lotovich announced! Aliana told us what he said as he announced it in Polish!

"Roger that, on route" I replied.

"let's go troops" I growled and moved forward rapidly down the corridor.

I pushed open the first door I could and entered, I looked around for any cameras, Moose and Alaina followed me in, "check for any listening devices" I announced!, "will you tell me what is going on mate", Captain Birdseye wants us up top for a chat and we have no firing pins in these weapons apparently" I told him.

Moose quickly striped his weapon down, "son of a bitch, I need some tools, any bits of metal, a file, I can fix this, remember I worked with the company armourer for two weeks mate for punishment, he showed me a few tricks" Moose announced!

I told Alaina, she nodded and lead the way, "hang on, we need to stay out of view from the cameras" I told her, she nodded again and lead the way.

We took a quick left and went up a ladder, Alaina opened a door, "I think you will find what you need in there" she said and went in,

She turned on the light, "maintenance office, we used to have five men working here, now have only one man, he should be off shift now" Alaina announced!

Moose quickly went to work!
My radio crackled!
"Yes I am waiting and I am not a patient man, if I sense you try some tricks I shoot Mr Luke, you have five minutes" Lotovich announced!
"Whatever you doing Moose hurry up mate" I exclaimed!
"Getting there, pass me your weapons" Moose answered!
I could hear Moose filing down metal and banging hard at metal,
We waited more than five minutes,
The radio crackled!
"There was a loud bang over the radio, "you bastard" I heard Dunc shout!
"One down three to go my friend" Lotovich spoke,
"I am so going to fuck this wanker" I growled!
"Moose hurry up man" I announced!
"I'm done" Moose put in!
Moose handed back our weapons, "they will work now" he announced!
"Alaina show us a way to the crane possibly avoiding the cameras" I asked her!

"Will do my best" she said and went off.
We heard another shot from somewhere!
Aliana led us down a ladder and along some wonky walk ways,
We heard another shot!
"Ok Moose I want that crane to smash that bridge up fast" I ordered!
I sent Dunc a message on his codded pager and hoped for the best,
I got no reply,
I told Moose to wait for my signal before taking out the bridge,
I and Aliana headed to the bridge, I spoke on the radio: "Rhys to Captain Lotovich over"
"Yes I am here and waiting to see you, one last game of poker I think, you are out of time I think and I am tired of this game" Lotovich announced!
I made my way up the steps to the bridge, there was three armed crewmen standing close to the door way, I saw captain Lotovich standing next to the controls with a pistol in his hand, there was another two armed crewmen in the bridge too,

"So we meet again, I missed you sir" I announced!
"Yes, you still carry useless weapons, I know you British are sarcastic, Aliana come here now" Lotovich ordered!
Aliana went past me and walked towards the captain, in an instant Lotovich slapped her hard across the face and she fell to the floor,
I moved forward and but was stopped by rifles pointing at me,
I saw Luke lying on the floor and blood coming from him, Dunc was lead over and he had blood on his shirt too, Tina was sat on the floor looking at me hard!
I saw the chef lying face down in a pool of blood,
"Someone had some fun here, turn you on does it, yes I know about you Captain, like young men do we" I announced, the crewman looked at each other,
"Shut up you are already dead, where is your other friend" the captain growled!,
"He twisted his ankle down below" I replied!

I waffled on talking crap to him, whilst looking at Dunc, Dunc opened one eye and winked,
"Yes my friend what I will do to you I am thinking, we are so different", the captain said to me and talked on his radio in Polish.
"So now I think it is time to get rid of my headache yes" the captain exclaimed!
I looked at him and smiled, he smiled back, I saw Dunc grab a fire extinguisher off the wall next to him and set it off!
I swung my rifle up and fired a volley of bullets, I saw Dunc swing the fire extinguisher around and he took out two of the armed crewmen that were close to him, Lotovich fired his pistol blindly as the foam from the extinguisher was everywhere in the air,
Tina threw herself at one of the crewmen and flew backwards as he shot her!
I felt a sudden pain in my arm, I heard rifle fire next to me, Moose was there firing his rifle into the mist of foam! More shots rang out!
I heard a groan!

I moved forward and took out one of the crewmen who moved, I saw Moose take care of another one,

"Everyone out of here now" I shouted!

I saw Dunk drag Aliana out, Moose pulled Luke out too, we just got down the stairs when there was a big crashing noise and the whole area shook!

I fell down the stairs and landed hard at the bottom, Duncan landed next to me with a thud with Aliana on top of him, I looked up and saw Tina stager down the steep steps, Another loud crash came from the bridge!

We all made our way further down the ship away from the bridge that was taking a pounding from the crane that Moose was operating.

I loud bang was heard from the bridge and a load of stuff came down the stairs on top of us,

"We need to get out of here folks" I announced!

"Luke's gone" I heard Dunc moan out!

"I got Aliana, she's ok" Moose called out!

I saw Tina climb next to me, "we need to get off boat" she said,

I got myself up with a struggle,
I staggered down the steel staircase, the rest followed, the fire alarms went off!
Another loud crash was heard from the bridge, I shouted on the radio! "Moose that's enough, you nearly killed us you fool, I said give the bridge a slight nudge to shake things up a bit, not flatten it"! I growled!
"Roger that got a bit carried away, got excited" Moose replied,
"I'll give you excited when I see you, get down to the galley Moose, we need help, some of us are a bit shot up, and Lotovich is about somewhere" I told him!
We all made it to the galley and started to attend to our wounds and stuff, Moose came in,
"Jesus H Christ, you lot" Moose bellowed!
"Moose I need you to be outside in the shadows, Lotovich is out there somewhere, when we get patched up we make our way to the boat downstairs" I demanded!
The door to the galley opened and a lot of shocked crew personnel came in talking in their Polish language!

I stood up, "ok you lot, as I am sure you are aware that the ship is in a state, you can blame that on your Captain, the bridge has been destroyed so I don't know how to advise you other than abandon ship" I announced,

A shot rang out! I felt a hard punch to my shoulder and fell backwards,

I landed hard against the wall, I saw captain Lotovich leaning over the chef's hot plate, where the food is served, he was smiling at me, he raised his weapon and aimed at me, I pulled out my knife and threw it as hard as I could towards him,

Two more shots rang out!

I tried to talk but only coughed, my mouth felt wet, I wiped it and saw a lot of dark red stuff, my blood,

Alaina was leaning over me, "you'll be ok Rhys don't worry" I heard her say,

Duncan run past me with his rifle looking very mean, "its payback time troops" he shouted out and disappeared through the door, I heard a lot of shooting and cries of pain!

I looked at Alaina, I couldn't find the words
I wanted to say, things were going blurry
and I felt numb, I heard more shooting,
Things went dark.
I heard the noise of an engine, I felt myself
rocking about, and my body hurt all over,
I was lying in a small bed and I was
strapped in, there was a small round
window next to me,
I saw water splashing against the window,
was I dreaming I thought to myself?
I lead there and thought about my Carmem
and closed my eyes.
"Hey boyo you with us or what" I heard
someone say!
I opened my eyes and saw Duncan standing
there,
He was smiling, "you all right mate, Aliana
sorted you out, you will be fine dood, you
got him good with your knife, what a
throw" Dunc said to me and patted my arm,
"What are you talking about mate" I asked
him?
"Captain Nob head shot you in the galley
and you got him with your knife, before he
passed away and you passed out, he said:

"look forward to a game of poker with you later my friend" Dunc said.
I had been laid up for a good few days in my cabin, Alaina looked after me,
Moose told me what happened:
We had lost Luke and the chef who helped us,
The ship was on fire when we escaped on the boat we found below,
The rest of the crew escaped on the emergency life vessels,
We watched the ship on fire, and some of the crew were fighting the fire as we pulled away,
We got all the bags of money and a lot more from captain Lotovich, we have a lot of weapons too,
There was a silver hip flask next to me with a big dent in it,
I took a closer look at it,
It was a present from Carmem from long time ago, and I took the cap off and took a big swig from it and laid there looking out of the window.

The door opened,

"look at you bro" Moose said,
I smiled, "so where we heading mate" I asked?
"not too sure mate, this boat is a bit crap, I see us going towards Thailand ish, soon I hope, we are getting low on fuel and we have basic food on board, you just rest here my old mate" Moose put in,
"So what happened to the hip flask here" I asked him,
"Saved your life dood, you took a bullet to your shoulder and this old flask of yours, that was in your inside pocket took the other bullet, there is a God" Moose exclaimed!
I looked at the hip flask, "thank you Carmem" I said and closed my eyes.

CHAPTER 4:
VOYAGE TO ASIA:

I awoke to find the boat rocking quite violently,
I pulled myself out of bed and got dressed, I had to hold on to things as I was still a bit unsteady, I went out into the small corridor and made my way towards the galley where I could smell bacon cooking,
"Make a place for me darling" I announced!
"Rhys, you should be resting" Tina exclaimed!
"I'm ok, need to stretch my legs, bum too numb" I said," what is bum too numb" she asked?
I laughed, "too much in the bed my dear" I put in and slapped my bottom, she laughed!
I made my way up a small ladder to the bridge, the boat was jumping around,
"Moose you never told me how you passed your driving test" I shouted!
"Hey look at you, get your arse up here mate" Moose bellowed!

The bridge was small and basic, Moose was fighting with the wheel, Dunc and Alaina stood there looking at me,
"Where we going then" I asked?
"Not too sure yet boss, How about somewhere around Thailand" Moose announced!
"Why not" I answered to him and sat down on a wall bench,
"You ok Mr Rhys" Aliana asked?
"I think so mate, feel like I've been scrapping with an elephant though" I said to him,
"you were busted up mate, shot up, concussion after you fell down the stairs bla bla bla" Aliana and Tina patched you up though, got a good team her mate" Moose threw in!
I looked out to sea,
"Ok according to this sat nav I will take about twenty two days, we need to stop soon and refuel and get supplies, and I have a place in mind" Moose put in,
"Where Captain" I asked,

"Coast of France, a small island called: Ile D' Yeu, I know someone there, been AWOL from the Army for years, I think you know him, Billy Mack, Irish lad, from C company, always kicking off in the bar, runs a run-down bar and stuff there now, haven't heard from in a good while, he owes me from the past, but we need to stop somewhere and I know this is a quiet place" Moose exclaimed,

"Get us there pronto mate" I replied, "oh one thing mate , you and Dunc get the weapons checked and ready to use, you never know, we've got enough fuel to get us there, so let's chill out for a day or two" Moose put in, "did you say check out the weapons" I asked?

Dunc just shook his head and went down below, "here we fucking go again, Moose I'm getting a bit old for this and you are too may I add" Dunc growled making his way down the steps,

Moose looked at me with a smirk on his face, I laughed and it hurt.

Aliana pushed Moose and went below smiling,

"Here mate have a swig of this, numb the pain" Moose said and passed me a silver flask, I took a swig and coughed!

The radio was playing music, Moose started to sing I joined in.

Tina came up with some bacon sandwiches that went down nicely!

"Should get there tomorrow mate" Moose announced!

"need to keep going through the night though, I'll get my head down soon for a few hours, then take over tonight, Aliana can handle the boat till then" he added!

I left Moose to it and went down below,

I went back to my Dunc and laid on my bed thinking of Carmem, I must have drifted off to sleep, I felt the boat jumping around, I got up in pain and went to the galley,

Dunc was sat by the table cleaning weapon parts,

He saw me, "all weapons cleaned and ready for use boss, you ok" Dunc asked?

It was dark outside,

"whose driving" I asked

"Aliana and Tina, Moose is still out for the count as usual, snoring like a baby, wake him in a few hours, the girls are following the sat nav indicator" Duncan announced, "Want a snifter, looks like you need it mate" Dunc added!

I excepted, Duncan passed me over a bottle of whisky, i poured some into a plastic cup and took a big swig, "so we heading for France, some little island, to meet Billy Nash, he was a fine one, went nuts after Bosnia, lost his whole team, they found him in a ditch talking to his zippo lighter, sent him to ward 13, padded room, the nut house, he did a runner bla bla bla" Duncan told me,

I do remember the name, of course, what is Moose getting us into now" I put in!

"Another adventure mate" Dunc growled and drank from the bottle,

"We got a shit load of cash from Captain Nobhead as well as ours, he was a bad boy, if you hadn't of done him, I was looking forward to it mate, damn good shot with the knife by the way" Duncan announced,

"I don't even remember it, that's the worst part of it" I told him and took a swig from my cup, I coughed!
Me and Dunc chatted for a while, when Tina came down, we have problem with sat nav, signal lost" she said, I went straight to where Moose was kipping and woke him up,
"What, what, what man" he growled,
"We got no sat nav mate" I told him,
"Bollocks, need to navigate by maps and the moon then" Moose burbled!
"You ok mate" I asked!
"Will have to be wont I, how are you by the way" Moose inquired,
"So Moose you trust this Billy Nash nut job" I asked as he stormed past me,
"no, never, would sell his mother for a bottle of booze, however we need to refuel soon and that island is the closest, we have little choice, we got weapons, he will have a big shock when he sees us, if he's still there, need to find a gap in the coast's rocks, he has or had a small place there, he runs the islands bar, gets hooky booze shipped in for the locals and other stuff".

Hookers, drugs whatever" Moose grumbled and went up to the bridge,
"Ok girls, let uncle Moose take over, well done you two by the way, have a break, yo done well" Moose told them,
The girls came down to the galley,
"someone has a grump head on" Aliana announced!
"Mr Grump" Tina put in!
I took the rest of the bottle of whiskey with me up to Moose, he was looking over nautical charts and writing figures down,
"Bollocks mate, the girls done well until the sat nav packed up, will have to navigate the hard way,
I recon we should come across the island in the morning, if not we are in the shit, get the paddles out boss" Moose put to me,
I passed Moose the bottle, "I'll be here with you mate" I replied!
Moose navigated the boat through the night with precision, he kept checking the charts and looking at the stars,
We drank the rest of the bottle and talked about the good times,

It started to get light and get a bit rough, "I told you I'd get you here, look" Moose shouted!

I was dozing off in the chair, Moose pointed out the window, I looked and saw the coast of a small island in the distance, "well done mate" I told him,

The boat made a strange noise and stuttered,

"We are on fumes here, needle well in the red" Moose exclaimed!

"Come on baby" Moose growled!

The engine of the boat made some strange noises and started to jerk,

"Come on you piece of shit! Moose bellowed!

Duncan came up, "what's going down boss, boat doesn't sound too good"

"No shit Sherlock, better find some paddles people! Moose put in!

"Good morning to you to squire" Duncan announced!

I saw Moose give Dunc a hard stare, "ok boyo I get the message, can I do anything" Dunc asked!

The boat shuddered and made some strange noises, "let's hope the tide is with us eh" Moose commented!

The engine came to a stop and we rode the waves, we were about a good thousand metres from the coast,

Moose shot past us and went below, "When I say so, turn the key ok" Moose bellowed!

We heard a lot of banging from the back of the boat and swearing, Tina and Alaina came up to see what was going on,

Moose shouted to turn the key, I did and the boat started, "don't touch nothing" Moose shouted and he dived into the bridge and pushed the throttle forward gently, the boat spluttered and moved forward, "hold on folks" Moose told us,

he pushed the throttle forward and the front of the boat rose and we lurched forward, "had a brain wave, these models have a reserve fuel section that you have to switch over by hand, not recommended really but we should get closer and float in" Moose added!

The boat bounced around and we did get closer to the island.
Moose had the boat going at full speed, we all had to hold on hard as the boat bounced around, we got closer,
I saw a cove that we were heading for,
"Come on you bitch" Moose growled,
Alaina slapped him on the back!
"Easy tiger" she told him,
The boat jerked and slowed down, "that's it folks, we drift in now" Moose announced, we rode the waves,
We were still going quite fast and approached the island,
"It's going to be a rough landing everyone, best get below and secure things" Moose shouted!
The boat rode the surf and Moose steered her expertly through the opening to the cove, which was next to impossible with no engine power.
We cruised through the gap and into the cove the boat slid into the sand and stopped.

The girls screamed and a there was sounds of breaking glass,
The boat tilted to the left, "ok we need to secure the boat, pull out the ropes and secure those lines lads, Moose put to us! Me and Dunc went to work, we pushed the boat out and pulled her round the corner away from the opening to the cove and secured her.

We all got off the boat, there was a canoe in the water and some old buildings close to the sand,
We both walked towards the old building,
"Stand your ground, stand your ground or you'll get two barrels I tell you"! Someone shouted from the broken down building!
A double barrelled shot gun poked out of the window,
I stopped but Moose didn't, a shot rang out! Me and Moose hit the deck,
"Next one goes in your bellies you varmints"
Someone shouted!
"Billy, its taffy you drunken oaf, recce platoon, I saved your arse too many times by the way" I shouted, I heard him reload the shotgun,
"What you talking about, I see you but don't know you" he shouted!
"Remember Bosnia, the ambush, you dragged me out of a pool of mud, I nearly drown, I saved your as in that mine field we stumbled into mate" I shouted back!
"That you Taff" he shouted!
"Of course it is you nutter" I replied!

"Less of the nutter, you still shagging sheep Welshman" he growled back!
We saw a man come out of the building holding a shotgun, he had long grey hair and a grey beard, the cloths looked dirty, "well stone the crows, what the fuck are you doing here, no one comes in here, the surfs too bad and the tide makes it almost impossible to get out",
"well done to the driver by the way, you in trouble boy, heard too much about you already, MI6 after your arse, done a runner with stolen silver bullion from the Serb's or something and messing with the IRA, you should be six foot under already" Billy announced!
"Billy boy" Moose shouted!
"Jesus Christ, he had to be with you, brothers in arms, who the hell have you brought here" Billy asked?
"We have Duncan and a few girls, booze, weapons and money" I shouted!
Billy started to laugh!
"Duncan show your ugly face to me! Billy announced!

Duncan and the girls had been lying in the sand after taking cover,
"Billy boy you owe me a beer by the way" Dunc exclaimed,
Billy laughed again,
"Well look at you, never would have believed it, get your asses up here lads, excuse my language ladies" Billy rabbled on,
"Look at you Billy boy, how you doing" I asked?
"What the hell you doing here, how did you find this place and me, why, what have I done now lads" Billy asked?
"Calm down mate, we need some help that's all" I put in!
"Hope you aint dragging some nasties behind you boys and girls" Billy inquired!
"So you boys been on the run too long, I heard too many wonky stories about you lot of mercenaries,
Fighting your way out of Bosnia with nicked silver bullion from the Serbs, Sarge Nash stitching you up, on the run from the regiment, IRA and MI6 involved, a trail of bodies behind you",

"then disappeared in Brazil where you took out a protected Indian tribe and stole a large haul of emeralds too, shall I go on, Billy laughed! "I'm bloody jealous boys, sounds like great fun" "had Smudger Smith here a while ago in a mess and on the run, I got him on a boat to Thailand and that, so why dig me out mate, been a long time, bringing back some bad good and bad memories I tell you, I heard you had a Brazilian wife, god knows how you ugly Welshman, where is the lady" Billy asked?

"Long story mate, lost at sea, don't go there pall, let's sit down and have a drink and talk things through, we need fuel and provisions to get us to Portugal, we can pay you plenty my old friend" I announced! Billy gave me a hard stare,

"I can help you boyo but I hope you can see me right, seeing as you have all these emeralds and stuff" Billy put in,

"No emeralds, no silver bullion mate, just cold hard cash and some interesting weapons if you're interested" I told him,

"of course, we go in to town to my bar, good food and some home brewed ale, I'll get your boat fuelled up and give you a load of jerry cans for reserve, got plenty of supply's from the local shop that I control, this is my island now, maybe two hundred people on here now, the authorities don't pay too much attention to us unless we call for help, it's so hard to land here with the tides and the high rocks all-round the island, hele drops come and go every so often, we are left alone and that's how I like it lads" Billy informed us!

We had a quick drink in Billy's broken down house and jumped in his old land rover, Moose and Aliana stayed with the boat, I made an excuse that Aliana was unwell with the bug and Moose wanted to look after her,

Billy gave the eyes but was fine with it, we went to town in his land rover, the road was not too good, "easy mate, you want to give us whiplash here" Duncan growled" "shut up man, Dunc you're going to get a steak you will die for my friend" Billy announced and laughed, "we got some catching up to do boys, shame Moose can't join us though" Billy added!

"He will have a good drink with you before we leave you nutter" I put in,
"Less of the nutter boyo" he replied!
We drove through some thick vegetation and saw a small village, about ten stone buildings and some shacks, there was a few old jeeps around, we stopped,
"Ok troops, debus! Billy announced!
We all got out and followed Billy towards one of the larger of the buildings,
"Here we go, my pub, the last Post" Billy announced,
"Why the last post mate" I asked?
"Well this is my last post mate and that's it" Billy exclaimed!
We followed Billy into the building, it wasn't posh, there was a large bar and a load of chairs and tables scattered around, there was a pool table and a pinball machine, there was some local people sitting quietly drinking, the bar went quiet when we walked in,
"Say a big hello to my friends everyone" Billy called out!
A few people turned round and raised their glasses to us,

"Ok folks take a seat",
"I'll get the grub on, need a doggie bag later for moose and his girl" Billy exclaimed and went behind the bar, I watched him fix up some drinks and give orders to the kitchen behind!
"Things too good for my eyes mate" Dunc whispered and kicked my ankle,
"You carrying mate" I asked him?
"Of course, I hope you are too amigo" Dunc replied!
I nodded, Tina nodded as well, I smiled,
"Let's just play his game and get the stuff we need, he will get his money for this" I put in,
"I just hope he is not expecting more" Dunc exclaimed!
I nodded.
We talked and waited for billy to bring us some drinks,
"stay soba Dunc ok"
I put to him, "no probs, got a young lady to look after now" he replied,
Billy came over with a tray of drinks and put it down on our table,

"Cheers to you all" he said and raised his glass,
We all raised our glasses and drank,
"Wow, what is this mate" I asked and coughed!
"My own brew, a bit strong with a hit that's all, enjoy" Billy said to us,
"It's the hit that worries me Billy"
Billy laughed,
Aliana gave me the big eye stare,
I winked at her, she winked back,
Billy went back to the bar, "come on woman, hurry up with the food" Billy shouted,
"You just can't get the staff these days I tell you,
Billy joined us and we talked about the old times,
We had a few more beers just to be sociable,
"so let's talk about what you are going to give me in return for my outstanding hospitality and help to get you all off safely to wherever and I do not want to know where by the way, just in case, you know what I mean" Billy announced!

"so billy boy you know what we've been up to, what about you, how you end up here, and by the way here is not too bad I might say, your own pub and more, a nice place in a secluded cove out of the way, nice set up mate" Duncan waffled"
"Well big man, another long story, will tell all after we've tasted one of my famous dishes, a few more locals came into the bar talking their own language,
Billy stood up,
"Tonight in my bar we will have only English if you please, make my guests feel welcome, I thank you, drinks on the house you scum" Billy shouted!
"thank you misère" some shouted back, people went to the bar and it started to get loud, some guys were playing pool with their women, the gambling machine was being played and a few men were playing darts,
"tonight we have a good time, no closing time, we talk, we eat, we drink and play some games of pool, tomorrow we sort the boat out after your hangovers have gone" Billy growled!

There was a call from the bar from a young lady! "There she is, Chantelle, my girl, the best cook on the island I tell you" Billy announced!
Billy stood up and banged the table, a few drinks fell over and billy shouted for some more, he went to the bar and came back with some more drinks, Chantelle followed him carrying some plates, she put them down and went back to get the rest,
"Bon appetite, I am Chantelle, pleased to meet you all, please if you want anything else let me know" she said,
Billy grabbed her, "lassie you're the best" he growled! He slapped her bottom, "you too, shame about your breath though my love" she replied and went back to the bar,
"This looks nice mate" Duncan announced!
"Yes what we have here is, prime beef with a fried egg on top, spaghetti and black beans in a fantastic sauce" Billy informed us,
"Never had a steak with a fried egg on top" Alaina said,
"Enjoy" Billy replied,
We all started to eat,

"Billy boy, this is great, Chantelle is a good cook, and this is great mate" Duncan announced!

"Yes mate, the taste with the fried egg on the beef is so different, lovely" I told him, We all enjoyed the meal and kept on talking about it,

"I will send Moose and his girl some food down with a little pick u up" Billy announced and got up and went to the bar, Me and Dunc talked quietly, "feeling a bit uneasy here, don't know why but I do mate" Duncan whispered,

"That was lovely" Tina announced and giggled!

"Steady on the fire water young lady, this is strong stuff" I told her, "well I can tell you sir that after the venom I had to drink at my village, this is puppy food" she announced! She laughed and took a swig from her glass, Me and Dunc laughed too, "you got a good one there Dunc, I'm jealous, look after her mate" I told him, "roger that" Dunc replied!

Billy came over, "so who wants a game of pool then, get your cash out taff, I remember you were a bit of a hustler back in the regiment" Billy growled!
"Ye you done me too for a few bucks as well" I called back!
Chantelle called from the bar!
"Ok we have food for Moose, I'll get it taken down to him no worries" Billy announced!
I watched Billy talk to a man at the bar, the man looked at us and gave me the thumbs up sign, I nodded in agreement,
"Need a pee" I said and made my way to the toilet, I gave Dunc a look and made a quick sign on my hand, he knew what I was going to do,
I went into a cubicle and sat down, I took out my coded pager and sent a message to Moose, warning him of what was coming and be ready,
"Hey boyo, my food upset you already" I head Billy shout as the toilet door went bang!
"Food was brill mate, I'm still bust up don't forget" I replied!

I heard Billy have a pee,
"Don't be too long, going to kick your ass at pool Welshman" Billy put in
"We will see" I replied!
I quickly sent a message to Moose on the boat: be aware food on its way to you from Billy stand too mate, I sent,
My pager vibrated, I read the message: roger that will signal if I need help, the message read,
These coded hi frequency pagers we all had, were issued by our ex platoon Sargent, Sargent Nash, what a man, could get all the kit, but sometimes full of shit, he passed on to me where I could pick up these pagers, which I have done over the years, very handy to silently communicate with whoever has another linked pager to you.
I left the toilet and entered the bar, Billy had set the table up,
"Come on then boyo, what's the wager" Billy growled!
I smiled at him, "ok Billy boy, let's say five hundred, big boys game eh" I replied,
"Bring it on" Billy put in,

"More drinks over here, big game on folks"
Billy shouted!
A few of the locals came over to watch,
Dunc and Tina came over too.
Billy broke and potted a red ball and
continued to put down five more reds,
"On you mate" he said and smiled, "easiest
five hundred squid ever" he announced and
laughed out loud!
Billy had only one more red to put down
and the black to beat me, I had six yellow
balls all over the table in bad positions, I
took my shot and put the white ball behind
one of my balls so Billy could not hit his red
ball on his next shot,
"Good shot, a bit dirty though" he said,
Billy fouled and hit one of my balls,
"Two shots to you boyo" he growled! He
finished of his beer and shouted for another
one,
His friends were jeering him on, I looked at
Dunc and he shook his head, I knew what
he meant,
I winked at him and finished my bottle,
I lit a cigarette and looked at the table,
"Game on" I announced!

I had a free ball and made good use of it, I knocked Billies last red ball tight against the cushion and continued to pot all my yellow balls with precision, the drunker I get the better I play, all my mates knew this, Billy did too,

"You're a crook Welshman" Billy exclaimed!

I laughed and took my shot, my last yellow went down but I did not have a shot to put the black ball down, I hit the black which nudged Billies last red over the pocket,

"you lose boyo" Billy announced and put his last red ball down, he took the shot on the black ball, he hit the white ball to hard showing off, the white ball shot into the black and the black ball bounced out of the pocket and luckily for him stopped tight on the middle cushion,

"Pockets need sorting out, will buy a new table soon, unbelievable, so do you worst, another boring safety shot no dought" Billy slurred,

I looked at him and took the shot quickly, I hit the white onto the black, and the black bounced off the cushion and went straight into the middle pocket.
"bollocks" Billy shouted and went to the bar, his friends and the other locals who were watching the game thinned out quietly and went back to their tables, a few left looking a bit worried,
I sat next to Duncan and Tina,
"You playing with fire mate" Duncan whispered!
"were not here on a pick nick pall, I want to put that across to this plonker, he's a drunk and do you remember that night in Colchester, we lost a good friend that night, stabbed for nothing, Billy caused that, messing with a civi's wife, he dropped us in the shit with the military police, he did a runner and we all spent the next two weeks in jail, I will not forget it" I growled!
"Ok bro, I think things could get ugly here" Dunc whispered,

Billy came over with some more drinks, "Ok you lot, game over, the best man won for now, let's talk, whilst I am still able to" Billy slurred,
We talked about tomorrow and how much we would pay him for helping us out,
I offered Billy twenty thousand for knowing nothing about us being there and another ten thousand for the fuel and supplies and stuff,
Billies eyes went really wide, "I think you are very generous indeed, I could do so much with that amount, the island is in need of a few new things, me too, lovely jublee" Billy exclaimed,
"right you lot I need to go have some words and get your fuel sorted out, I won't be long, this place is your place tonight, Chantelle will show you were you can kip for the night and freshen up if you want to" Billy said to us and finished his drink, he looked back at us and winked then walked to the bar, he had a quick word with a guy at the bar and they both left,

It was getting dark outside now, I was a bit concerned that Moose didn't reply to my message,
"let's have a game of pool mate, you and Tina against me, lets waste some time and then ask Chantelle if she can show us where we are staying for the night" I told them,
Chantelle was flirting with some guys at the bar,
I didn't want to ring Moose and cause eyes on us, we played pool.
My pager buzzed in my pocket, i gave Dunc a signal and went to the toilet and checked it, and a man followed me in,
I went into the cubicle and read the message: nice food – two men in Billies place now – all quiet here – hope you are having fun – eyes wide open mate, the message read, "you all right in there mate" a voice called out,
"Fine mate, spicy food always plays hell with my arse" I replied,
The man laughed!
I came out of the toilet and joined Dunc and Tina at the pool table, I winked at Dunc and I joined in the game of pool.

More drinks were brought over to us by Chantelle who was a bit drunk,
I asked her if she could show us where we would be staying tonight, "I show you now" she replied,
Me Dunc and Tina followed her through the bar and went into the kitchen, she lead us to a cupboard and opened it, "it looks like a cleaners place but we have a secret door here" she announced, she pulled a panel out and revealed a passage way, "here we go, it's nice in here, no windows but nice, Billy hides who he needs to hide in here" she added!
We followed her in, she turned on the lights, there was a few doors, she opened one, "here is a single and next door is a double bunk bed, sorry not quite the Ritz but I'm sure you will sleep ok and in the morning I make you my fine breakfast, there is a shower just next door and toilet, Billy has put in a phone so you can be contacted or if you want to contact him, I'll bring your bag through for you" she said and left.

I waited until she left, "got a bad feeling about this place, Dunc, too many people pally with Billy, they all look like crooks, too many eyes on us, Billy now knows we have money too, need to keep our wits about us, as soon as I see Billy I will try and get us out of here first thing, maybe tonight if I can, the sooner the better" I announced! Dunc nodded, "I not like here Rhys" Tina announced,

"Leave things to me mate" I told her, Dunc stared at me, "ok mate I see you" I said to him,

We sorted our stuff out, Tina took a shower and we went back to the bar, there was some shouting noises that we heard from the bar, we went into the kitchen, there was some food burning in a frying pan on the cooker, "ok, ok" we heard Chantelle shout as she came through to the kitchen and saw us, Tina was trying to rescue the burning food, "hey bitch what you doing there" Chantelle slurred!

"I just try and help" Tina replied,

Chantelle pushed past us and threw the frying pan into a sink, she spoke in French angrily!

I pulled Tina away and we went into the bar,

Billy was there with his hands around a man's throat, "yes I give you a bone and you want the whole thing" he shouted!

Billy pulled a knife and stabbed th man in the ribs, two other men at the bar grabbed Billy and threw him to the floor.

A shot from a gun rang out!

"Ok, ok, that's enough" Chantelle shouted!

She was stood in the door way with a revolver in her hand,

I picked Billy up and plonked him down in a chair, "what's going on mate" I asked?

"ok mate, happens every night, welcome to the island, all the scum come here from the main land, authorities don't come here much, too hard to awkward to land, I am the law here if you can believe that" Billy slurred!

"Not sure what to believe mate" I put in!

"Ok, your fuel is here, your stores are in the local shop,

I don't blame you is you want to leave here, take me with you if you want" Billy exclaimed!

"Love to mate but the boat is not that big and I'm sure you don't mean that" I put in, Billy stood up, two guys from the bar dragged the dead man out of the bar, most of the bar cleared too, after swearing at Billy on their way out, Chantelle gave the gun to Billy, "ok I think we let you go tonight, the tide is good to go now, I will get the fuel down to your boat and the supplies, you finish up here and Tobias will take you to your boat, I will see you in my place in half hour" Billy slurred,

Ok mate, not here to tread on your toes, looks like you've got enough troubles here to deal with on your own" I put on!

Billy called at a man at the bar, "Tobias take my friends to my place and come back for their supplies" Billy ordered!

Tobias nodded and showed us to the door, We jumped in the jeep that was outside and Tobias got into the driver's side, "ok, I take you to boat and get your supplies ok" Tobias announced!

"Yes great mate" I answered,
We all left the bar, Billy started to shout at people when we left!
Tobias took us to Billies place in the cove where our boat was moored, I quickly texted Moose that we were coming!
We got to the cove and jumped out of the jeep,
"Ok I go back to Billy and get your supplies ok" Tobias said, I nodded and he drove off,
"Ok troops, lets sort things out" I shouted!
Moose was stood on board the boat next to Aliana.
"All ok mate" I shouted!
"So, so, got baddies in there" Moose announced looking towards Billies place,
"ok mate, we got a load of supplies on its way and fuel, Billy kicked off in his bar, someone got stabbed, basically were off tonight as soon as we can, Billy is up to something, I'm sure of it, his misses is a can short of a six pack too" I told him,
"Thirty grand I offered him and some high calibre weapons thrown in too" I told Moose,

"And he's ok with it" Moose asked? "we know Billy don't we, would sell his mother if there was a profit in it, no dought he will be after more before we leave so let's keep our eyes peeled" I put in,

Moose was in the wheel house, bridge looking over some charts and checking a few things, Alaina was with him, I went below with Dunc and got some weapons ready just in case, we all knew what Billy was like from old days,

Tina was in the galley making sandwiches for later,

It was starting to get dark now, Dunc was keeping an eye on Billies place, and there was two thugs walking around torches,

I heard some vehicles approaching, their headlights lit up the boat, which I wasn't too happy about,

They stopped at the end of the track about a good hundred feet from the boat, the two men that were hanging around Billies place walked over to the front vehicle and started to talk to the driver, "hey boyo, got room for a small one" Billy shouted out!

"Come on down Billy, let's get you paid and have a good bye drink eh" I shouted back! "for sure" he agreed and spoke in French to the help he had brought with him, ii counted a good eight lads and the two that had been skulking around Billies place, keeping an eye on us,
The fuel tank was dragged down onto the beach and the fuel hose was stretched out by two young men, the other men were bringing down boxes and fuel cans, "ok boyo give me a hand up then" Billy exclaimed and held his arm out to me, I pulled him up, Billy got very close to me, looks like he stumbled, I was ready for him, "steady on mate, too much ambernecta" I said to him, "I need a tad more mate, I know you got a shit load more you can offer me for my troubles" Billy whispered, he laughed out loud, "I thought you were going to give me a good bye kiss then mate" Billy bellowed, he stared hard at me, "let's go below and have a chat" I said, "billy before he came down shouted in French at his helpers and followed me down to the galley.

The boxes were being passed onto the back of the boat, Aliana and Dunc were helping, "Hey Moose you old dog, come down here and have a drink with me" Billy called out! Moose came down, Tina stayed in the bridge watching what was happening, "Billy boy, been a while, what you doing in a place like this then" Moose exclaimed, "you know me, not too many places for me to disappear into now, won big in a dodgy poker game and landed myself governor of this island, don't see any authorities coming here, the tides and the surf make it almost impossible to land here, and well done for coming in through the arch in the cove by the way, I only know a handful of captains that can guide a boat through there, when the surf is coming in, tides going to turn again soon by the way, so let's have a drink then lads" Billy announced, Billy went to put his hand out to Moose, Moose shook his head and opened a bottle of whiskey, "so boys, this is how I see it" Billy exclaimed, he took a big swig from the whiskey bottle and passed it to me, "I know what you lot have been up to.

the silver bullion from the Serbs, Sargent Nash stitching you up, IRA after your arses, MI6 agents disappearing, Brazil, emeralds, some protected tribe wiped out and the chiefs daughter kidnapped, I know you held up in Ireland too on some Provo's farm, you left a trail of bodies behind you all over the place, took over a Russian container ship and wasted half of the crew" Billy announced!
"So who's been whistling to you then mate" I asked and passed the bottle back to Billy, "your all over the news lads, the underworld news that is, your government is trying to sweep up your mess and cover up your mess, before it turns embarrassing for good old UK, on the run, ex- British army mercenaries kidnapping and murdering anyone steps in their path, they are saying some bad stuff about you lot" Billy added,
"what's this kidnapping shit, she wanted to come with us" Moose growled, he sat down, "I say we get the hell out of here and fast, don't know where we are heading yet, just pay this fool" Moose exclaimed,

"come on now Moose me old mate, remember the good old times we had" Billy was cut off by Moose stepping in, "you were no mate of mine, you're a coward, I remember the night club, we all took a beating and you hid in the shitter, then dropped us in the shit, I went down for six months for that mess you caused by the way, good job you transferred elsewhere, a few lads after your hide then" Moose put in,

"Long time ago eh lads, lets brush old dust back under the carpet out of the way" Billy said,

Billy sat down, "so Rhys your offer was ok but I recon you can do a bit better than that eh" Billy added,

I stared at Moose and looked back to Billy, "ok you old dog" I said and stood up, Billy stood up with me, "steady there Billy boy, a bit jumpy there, just going to get you some cash and some extra, you and Moose carry on with your mud pies" I spoke, I walked out of the galley and to the forward bunk, I pulled up the pillows and the boards.

there was quite a few bags stored in the hidden storage place, I pulled one of the bags up and another one, I checked the bags, I was sure there was a good fifty thousand in each bag, I had some emeralds too, that I put in my pocket, I put the boards back in place and the cushions and made my way to the galley ,I heard a scuffle from outside, I walked into the galley to see Billy standing up with a handgun pointing at me, there was a man stood next to Billy with a rifle in his hand, "what is this bollocks" I head Duncan announce, he came down the steps with Tina quickly, followed by another man holding a pistol, someone spoke in French from outside, Billy spoke back in French, "you doing pretty well with the old French Lingo old mate" I put in, "had no choice, this is a French island, right as you can see, things have become a little bit messy, what I would like to happen now is, you three into the front cabin, Taff you sit there, now!" Billy ordered!
The two armed men motioned Dunc, Moose and Tina forward with their weapons!

"secure the door and watch them" Billy told one of the armed men, they went out of the galley, I heard the front cabin door shut, another man came down the ladder and threw a set of keys to Billy who passed them to the armed guy watching the front cabin, I heard the door being locked, "you want to hope I never see you again Billy boy" Moose shouted from behind the locked door, "shut up Moose or I will have to pay some attention to your sweet lass hiding up top" Billy shouted back!
I gave Billy a hard stare, "I don't know what you have planned here Billy but I tell you something you mess with Moose's lass and you had better put me down before I get my hands on you" I growled, the armed man close to me prodded the barrel of his riffle into my ribs and told me to shut up!
"Open the bags Rhys, let's see what we have here" Billy ordered!
I opened the bags and Billy looked in, "how much" he asked? "Hundred grand plus" I told him, "you have more, I know it" Billy exclaimed,

One of the armed men started to drink from the whiskey bottle and passed it to his mate, they were both smiling after seeing all the cash, "there is two more bags under here" I told him and tapped the wooden bench I was sat on, "get them out then boyo, don't be shy" Billy said!

I removed the pillows and the wooden board, I pulled out the two holdalls and put them on the table, I replaced the wood and the pillows, Billy opened the two bags, he spoke in French and showed the two armed men in the galley with us, they smiled and spoke in French, and they continued to drink the whisky.

"how much" Billy asked me, "another hundred, probably more, Billy there is no need for this, you're going to have to kill us all if you want to get away with this, you know that, I have one more thing to give you and to stop this crap, emeralds I have, you get them and we leave, you can do whatever you want with them" I growled!

"You have them here" Billy asked?

I pulled out three big sized emeralds and placed them on the table, "good god, are they for real" Billy asked?

"Raw uncut emeralds from the Brazilian rain forest, must be worth a good few hundred thousand bucks, if more" I put in, "you make me want to say just fuck off now mate, take whatever else you have, disappear off my island, however, I am a cunt and you know it so I will strip this boat and find whatever else you are hiding, I've got another boat to disappear on, leave you lot here to rot until MI6 arrive and believe me they are on their way, so don't think I'm fucking you, your fucked anyway pal" Billy exclaimed!

"Oh and I won't be doing the hurting here, I couldn't do that to you, however I have made some hard friends on this island" he said looking at the two armed men opposite me,

They both smiled at me, there was a scream from on top of the boat, Alaina came down the ladder hard, followed by another armed man, "you ok" I asked, "I will be fine" she replied and sat next to me on the bench.

Billy zipped up all the bags and put them at the bottom of the steps, "so what am I going to do with you all then eh, I was thinking of taking your boat but and leaving you all here to fend for yourselves, however getting this boat back through that arch and out to sea not a good move, or I just send you off on your way on ya boat, you'll have enough fuel to get you Portugal or somewhere, I'll see you right, but no, I know you lot, you'd find your way back here to old Billy out, so I am thinking a bad accident on the boat, whilst refuelling, so bad, so sorry, no one got off the boat" Billy informed us, "you'll go to hell for that one" I announced, "ye, well I know all about hell and soon you will to, chow" Billy said and threw one of the bags up the ladder to another waiting Frenchman, he passed the other bags up, Billy spoke to the two armed guys, "watch these fuckers whilst I sort things out"
The two stood opposite me and Aliana, they carried on drinking the whiskey, Billy jumped off the boat with the other armed guy, and it sounded like there was someone else walking around up top.

One of the armed men in the galley called out in French to the other armed man who was watching the forward bunk where Moose, Duncan and Tina was locked inside, he came to the galley and excepted the bottle of whiskey, "you have more" one of the men asked? Aliana opened a cupboard behind us and took out a bottle of rum, she passed it over, the three of them talked and drank from the bottle, there was a slim window behind the armed lads and I saw Moose show me some hand signals then moved slowly out of site, Aliana saw this too, she tapped my leg under the table and passed me a pistol, I put it slowly in my jacket pocket, I asked if we could have a drink too, "the bottle was passed to me, Aliana got two glasses from behind us and poured our drinks, the bottle was snatched back, one of the armed men went back down to the door that was being guarded, I started to talk to Aliana, "no talking, just sit there and drink your last drinks" one of the armed men growled, I knew there was some hidden rifles in the front cabin where Moose and Dunc were.

One of the armed men slumped next to Aliana and put his hand on her shoulder, talking in French, the other armed man started to laugh, I laughed too, there was arguing coming from the front cabin, a scream rang out, the man outside the door shouted in French! Another scream came from inside the locked cabin, followed by a lot of arguing, I heard the armed man unlock the door and shout in French as he pushed the door open, I heard a muffled noise and at the same time, Aliana slapped the Frenchman hard in the face who was next to her and screamed! The boats lights went out, thanks to Moose and the fuse box, Two bodies came flying down the stairs landing on top of one of the armed men, I fired quickly where I last saw them, one of them fired back, I fired again and there was silence, Duncan came into the Galley with a torch looking mean, he gave me a hand signal, to say bad guy down, Moose came down the ladder in a shot, "two monkeys down here, I recon there's another four about" Moose exclaimed and went back outside, the lights came back on, "ok make sure they are all dead, don't want any more surprises, Dunc you check out Billies place, I'll be up top, the girls stay here, get the rest of the rifles from the front and if anyone comes in once we are out, you know what to do" I ordered!

Me and Dunc left the galley, shots rang out and one of the boats windows smashed, one of the girls inside screamed! I had one of the dead man's rifles, with a full mag on it, Dunc jumped to the sand from the front of the boat, the whole area was lit up from the headlights of the jeeps, I heard a weapon being fired! Thee lights on the front jeep shattered, more fire went off and the rest of the jeeps lights were ousted! I saw a few figures running around where the fuel container was, it had been dragged back to the track after the refuel, "here take this" I hear Tina say as she passed me up the 50 calibre sniper rifle, "thanks mate "I replied, I laid down quickly and turned on the scope to infa red, more rifle fire went off, the side of the boat was hit again, I scanned the area where the vehicles were parked,

I saw a man loading the back of jeep with the bags Billy had took from the boat, I fired my rifle, there was a silencer on the end of the barrel, I reloaded and fired again at the front jeep, there was a large bang and the jeep exploded, I hit its fuel tank, the fuel container went up too, there was two men running around on fire screaming, someone fired and the burning men fell to the floor, Dunc ran past the boat, "man down in the house, you watch what you're doing with that elephant gun" Dunc growled as he stormed off.

I picked up the rifle and jumped to the sand, I scanned the area when I felt a huge blow to my back, I fell to the ground and saw Billy standing over me, he had hit me with the butt of his rifle, "you and me big boy" Billy announced and dropped his rifle to the sand, he pulled out a bowie knife and took up a fighting stance, billy threw me a smaller dagger, more gun fire was heard and the sand was kicked up close to us, I saw a man climb onto the boat and go below, two shots rang out!

"Show us what you got then Welshman" Billy growled!
Another armed man came close to us, he fired his rifle at me, I dived for cover, and billy picked his own rifle up and shot him dead.
"You all right" Billy called out!
"Never better Billy boy" I answered, I got up and held the knife in front of me, "do you know what I can't be bothered with this" Billy announced!
He raised his rifle towards me, there was a shot from the boat behind us, Billy slumped forward onto the sand, I looked at the boat, Tina was on the back of the boat holding a pistol, and Billy coughed!
"Ooh you sneaky fucker, he also shouted out in French, there was no answer.
Billy looked at me, he tried to reach for his rifle, a large boot trod down on his hand, the crack of breaking bones was heard, Billy cried out in pain!
Moose kicked Billy in the ribs and he went over, the other jeep started up and screeched off in our direction, Billy started to laugh out loud!

Dunc came over limping, "one ugly left I think" he groaned!

The jeep must have been fifty metres away from us, I dived behind the 50 cal rifle and loaded a large bullet into the chamber, "shit, make it count boyo" Moose called out as he pulled the trigger on his weapon and nothing happened,

"I'm out too" Dunc announced, he shouted to Tina to get off the boat, the jeep bounced onto the and heading straight for the boat, I fired and fired again, I reloaded and took aim for the front of the jeep, I fired, the jeep turned sharply and bounced past us and straight into Billies place, with a bang, no one got out of it, I told Dunc to check it out, he limped off with Tina,

Billy was lying on the sand laughing, "who's got a drink for Billy then" he asked, blood came out of his mouth, I pulled out my hip flask and threw it to him, "so what now, you got room on this boat for a small one, I promise to be a good boy" Billy said and coughed, Moose went to give him another kick, "that's enough mate, he's finished" I sounded off, "that's right, old Billies finished" he groaned, Moose spat on the sand and started to walk away "I'll let you rid of him Boyo" Moose called out as he walked away!

I stood up and looked at Billy, "I'm going to leave you as you are mate, were going, you live you live, you die you die, you were right, this is your last post" I announced! I picked Billies weapon up and mine and went to walk away, "see you Billy" I called, I heard the noise of something I didn't really want to hear, and Billy laughed! Billy had pulled out the pin of a grenade with his teeth, Billy was sitting there on the sand with a grenade in his good hand, "always wanted to go out with a bang ay Taffie, didn't know I would be taking you with me too old boy, so sad, so sorry" Billy coughed out!

I kicked sand up into Billie's eyes quickly, I dived at Billy and snatched the grenade from his hand, as I rolled over him I stuffed the grenade down the back of his trousers after I had pulled the pin out,

I heard Billy laugh again! I dived for cover, "grenade" I shouted, "Boom" the grenade went off and so did Billy, "bye bye Billy boy" I whispered!

"You bad boy" I heard Moose call out! "I saw that you naughty boy" Dunc called as he came back from Billy's place carrying the bags of cash with Tina,

"I take it Billy won't be coming with us then" Aliana announced,

"No just his fuel and supplies, Moose get this boat running, it's looking rough out there" I growled!

"I know ugly" Moose shouted back!

Moose was on board, and the rest of us pushed as hard as we could to get the boat off the sand and back into the water, it took all our strength but we did it, Moose started the engines, I went up the beach to where a load of jerry cans had been dumped, I kicked them. They were full!

"Let's get these on board too" I yelled!

Moose put on the spot lights and the cove lit up, the waves were coming in strong and the boat was rocking around,

"Need to move now or we'll never get out of here folks" Moose announced, we all got on board, the jerry cans full of fuel were dumped on the back of the boat, "need to secure them lads in case we take a bashing getting out of here" Moose ordered!
Me and Dunc tied the cans down the best we could, "ok Moose do it, the girls went below and held on, we moved off, "need to go around the cove once get speed up, when I go through I need to give her full throttle, one chance at this only" Moose yelled!
The boat shot forward and we sailed around the cove, the boat turned towards the archway were we came in, the boat roared and flew forwards, "hang on you lot" Moose shouted!
The boat bounced over the waves, it was dark, the boats spot lights was all that was lighting up the place, "come on you bitch" Moose growled! The boat turned to the left and then to the right, the girls were screaming down below as stuff was falling about the galley and smashing!

I was holding on to the side rail with all my strength and looking forward at the entrance to the cove, the waves were coming in high, we flew off another wave and landed hard as we rode up another one, "Here we go" Moose bellowed!

The boat rose over another high wave and we went down, into another wave, the waves knocked me back into the back seats at the rear, Dunc grabbed me,

We went through the archway, the boat swung to the right as we hit the archway, some windows smashed and the girls screamed! The boat flew forwards, the top of the bridge where Moose was steering hit the top of the archway with a crash, bits of wood fell back onto me and Dunc, "Moose get us out of here will you" I shouted!

We flew off another hard hitting wave and bounced through, "yes baby" Moose shouted!

The engines went a bit quieter as we left the cove behind us and headed out to sea, "Unbelievable" Moose announced!

Me and Dunc were covered in bits of wood and holding on to the jerry cans full of fuel, "bloody maniac" Duncan shouted out!
We slowed right down once we got well clear, "damage report troops" Moose called out!, "roger that" I shouted back, me and Dunc went to the front of the boat, we took a bash but it looked ok, a few licks of paint after some sanding down, you would never notice I told Dunc, we went back to the bridge where Moose was, "need a stiff one dude" Moose asked, I slapped him on the shoulder and went down to the galley, Dunc stayed with Moose, they started to argue straight away!
The girls were doing their best to sort things out,
"You two ok" I asked?
"A few scratches and broken plates, we are fine, well done to Moose" Aliana announced, "ye he did well, you got a good lad there mate" I put in, "I know" she replied and smiled, Tina went up top with a flask of strong stuff.

I sat down in the galley and looked out of the side window, I thought of Carmem. Aliana left me alone and went up top.
I made myself a drink and lit a cigarette.
I must have nodded off.
"Rhys, you ok mate, want some food" I heard a voice call out!
I opened my eyes, "Duncan was standing over me, "waky waky sleepy head" Dunc said softly, he sat next to me and patted me on the shoulder, we've took a battering lately, my body wants to shut down too mate" he added,
I looked at Dunc, "everything ok" I asked, Dunc passed me a glass of water, "you giving me water, that's not a good sign mate" I mentioned!
"you been kipping for nearly a day, you lost some blood as usual, Aliana patched you up mate, you took a bit of the grenade you stuck in Billies arse" Dunc put in, "see I knew it, the bastard got me back after all" I announced, we both laughed,
The boat was rocking about, I tried to get up but my side hurt too much, I laid back down, I was in the front cabin,

"rest my friend, Moose has worked out where we are heading, we are going to stop in Gibraltar then on to Malta, should take a few days or so, Moose has set the route in the sat nav and has coursed it out on the maps as a backup, when you're ready come through mate" Dunc announced, I nodded and Dunc left the cabin, I laid there thinking of Carmem and drifted off to sleep.

I heard a lot of laughter from on board the boat, my eyes were a little bit blurry but I managed to get myself out of bed, I put some decent cloths on rather than the pyjamas I had on that smelt too much of sweat, I opened the door to the cabin and made my way to the galley, I heard more laughter!

The galley was empty, I saw a plate of sandwiches on the table, I helped myself as I was hungry, I climbed the short ladder to the back deck and went up to the bridge, "Room for one more" I asked?

"Boyo you're up, great" Moose put in, everyone turned round and welcomed me in, it was a bit cramped in the bridge,

"So what is all the cheering about, you woke me from my beauty sleep" I announced!
Moose has plotted our journey out, all the way to Thailand" Dunc exclaimed!
"Has he really" I put in!
"Sure, took me a good few hours, here I'll show you" Moose told me,
I went to Moose and he showed me the whole route.
"ok mate, basically I think we get to Asia, Thailand, lay low for some time, too much heat on us pal, ok so from here we head to Portugal, pass and into the Mediterranean on to Malta, stop refuel get supplies, I know somewhere, a small island called: Isola Di Linosa, I know someone who can help us out there, ex-Army padre runs a missionary, owes me a favour, from there we head east to Egypt, Cairo, we need the port Said, we go down the Suez canal and into the red sea and onto the Gulf of Eden, we cross over to the Arabian sea and land somewhere on the Maldives, I know a place called: Fonagardhoo, another lost pal hiding there can sort us out,

from there we cross the Anta man sea and into Thailand, I think Phuket, there's a small island called: Ko He, a diving island, not too many inhabitants, John Jones is there, runs a bar, remember him Moose paused, "Bloody ell Moose, I don't think I am too ready for all this information in one go mate, fuck me, you have dodgy mates all over the world, this John Jones was a right twat if I remember" I put in!
"relax mate, I thought of Mexico but the route there is not to good, need to keep as low a profile as possible, it will be fine, don't worry" Moose added,
"God help us" I exclaimed,
"I don't think God is with us on this voyage boys" Dunc announced!
He was pointing behind us,
There was two boats heading towards us at speed.
"here we go, Moose get us out of here, Duncan get below and get some weapons up here pronto, girls get below and secure things I sense a rough ride coming up" I shouted, the engine made a loud roar and smoke came out of the back,

"Moose, tell me that's just a smoke screen your making yes" I shouted!
"We got problems, man the wheel house bro I need to check something" Moose bellowed! He ran out of the bridge, jumped down the ladder and went to the engine down below, I rushed to the bridge, and there was a lot of smoke coming from the back of the boats exhaust!
Dunc came up with the fifty calibre sniper rifle and some more automatic rifles, "bloody ell mate, give me a hand here" Dunc exclaimed! He dumped the weapons on the cushioned seats at the back of the boat, Tina came up with a few more bits and pieces, "down below if you please" I growled, Tina gave me a stern stare and went back down below,
The boats were a good five hundred metres away, I was observing them through a pair of binoculars, I could see a few men on each boat hanging on as the boats bounced towards us at speed, there was gun fire and the water was kicked up to our stern,

"Moose do something before we say hello to Davy Jone's locker" I shouted!
Dunc took up position behind the fifty calibre sniper rifle and fired off a round, "hit them hard Dunc" I growled!
"Roger that" Duncan announced!
I fired at the boat too, they returned fire and hit our boat, wooden splinters flew up as bullets hit the back of the boat, "Moose were in the shit pal" I shouted, "start her up boyo" Moose bellowed!
I pushed the starter button and the boat rumbled into life and stopped again, gun fire hit the back of the boat again, Dunc was firing back with not too much accuracy, "hit her again mate" Moose bellowed!
Again I pushed the start button, the engine started and some more black smoke came out of the back of the boat, "love the smoke screen chaps, however I can't see what to shoot at" Duncan exclaimed!
"Just keep firing Dunc" I shouted!
There was an explosion!
One of the boats heading for us broke apart in a ball of fire,

The other boat was getting very close, our boat shuddered, Moose jumped into the bridge and took over, "come on you bitch" he growled!

I carried on shooting, Moose cried out! I looked back and he was holding his shoulder, another spray of bullets hit us! The boat roared and jumped forward, more bullets hit the back of the boat, "we are in the shit here lads" Duncan announced!

Tina came up quickly holding a law, Light anti-tank weapon, "I have had enough of this rubbish" she exclaimed! She knew what she was doing, she got the Law weapon ready and fired it off, and there was a whoosh! And we watched the missile fly into the front of the other boat, there was a big explosion, "game over" I shouted!

"You amaze me every day" Moose called out, Alaina went to him as she saw he had been hit.

"Ok troops, I suggest we get the hell out of here, apart from Moose who else is hurt" I shouted!

Everyone called back: ok mate!, Alaina quickly patched up Moose and we shot off towards Portugal and onto Malta, Moose said it would take a good twenty four hours, me and Dunc cleaned up the back of the boat as much as we could, "shot to fuck mate, were going to draw a few eyes with our arse shot to shit like this" Duncan announced, "well we had better disguise it the best we can, I saw some paint somewhere, tape it all up and paint over it" I told him, "oh, improvise, adapt and overcome is it" Dunc put in, "you got it soldier" I answered him, we both laughed! Tina went below to sort out the galley, Alaina patched Moose up and we were on our way.

We sailed through the night taking it in turns to drive the boat, the sat nav was set on autopilot so it was pretty strait forward. My alarm went off on my watch, it was three o clock in the morning, my turn up top for two hours, I got myself up to the bridge after I grabbed a bottle from the galley, Dunc and Tina was on watch, "hello mate, you alright" Dunc asked, "aching like a downed donkey, I'll get by" I answered, I showed him the bottle I grabbed from the galley, "easy tiger, numb the pain yes, don't numb the brain too much bro" Dunc exclaimed, he patted me on the shoulder and gave me a quick brief on what was going on, "sat nav started to give me shit, I had to wake Moose up, Moose said we still go with the sat nav, however if we head off North East on the compass, turn the wheel till we are back on it, the sat nav will sort its self out again, double Dutch to me, Tina understood though, women eh" Dunc growled, Tina gave him a dig, "shut up big man and take me to bed" she put in, Dunc didn't say a word, I saw his eyes and smiled, they both left me,

I sat down and checked the compass, we were heading in the right direction, it was getting a bit choppy but not too bad, I took a big swig from the bottle and looked out to sea.

I remember thinking of my lost Carmem when I banged my head on the front window, the boat was rocking around quite a bit, I checked the compass,
I remember Moose saying head North East, the needle was pointing north,
I looked at the sat nav, it read, readjusting,
I turned the boat to head North East again with a strain, the wheel was hard to turn, and rain was hitting the boat pretty hard now.
"I fell out of bed mate, what's with the sharp turn mate" Moose asked looking stressed,
"Get your arse in here and sort things out Moose" I announced!
Moose took control and sorted things out, I went below to the galley,
Tina came in, "ok I will make us all some food" she said,
"Sounds good to me" I replied, the boat was bouncing around,
"Going to be a bit choppy for a while folks" Moose bellowed! "Passing Portugal soon rough sea" Moose added,

Moose sorted things out and took control for most of the day, I slept for a good eight hours or so in Dunc's bunk.

"Malta coming up lads and lasses" I heard Moose shout! I pulled myself onto the floor and felt like shit as usual! I made my way to the galley to hear the girls scream out!

"Rhys put some clothes on please" they shouted and laughed! I realised I was in my underpants and that was it,

"Sorry girls" I replied and went back to find my clothes,

I got changed quickly and went back to the galley, "sorry girls" I announced! They both smiled, Tina passed me a bacon sandwich, and "eat up man and less of the booze" she said!

I got up to the bridge,

"you knocking it back too much my friend, so I know a quiet bay where we can stay for a while and get refuelled and get stock and stuff dude" Moose told me,

Dunc came in,

"Hey boy what's going on Rhys, you starting to worry me boyo, not the Rhys I am used to" Dunc announced!

"Sorry guys, I can't stop thinking about Carmem" I told them!
"We all know mate" Moose put in,
"So what now" I asked?
"We moor up, sort the boat out and head off again" Moose exclaimed,
We cruised around the island and found the place where Moose wanted to stop the boat,

I was out on top with Dunc, we saw a few other boats moored in the area, and Moose brought us in nice and slow and found a spot,

We had to get into the dingy to get a rope to the rocks, everyone was in a good mood, acting like we were all on holiday and stuff, rather than being on the run,
"nice place here, so you know where to get stuff from then mate" I asked Moose, "of course, lot more people here than used to be as I remember it, if he's still here" Moose replied, "if who's here mate" I asked?
"ok boyo, you remember bogger Baz from support company, worked in the bedding stores, he pissed 10 mattresses one night, pissed up and passed out in his stores, well he did a bunk years ago and married a chick from Malta and as I remember a while back as I came here on leave, he runs a bar café and a diving school with his misses" Moose every day you surprise me, Bogger Baz, he was a minger,
I was in care bare platoon when I got to the regiment in Northern Ireland, we weren't eighteen yet so we weren't allowed to go out on the streets, did guard duties and shit, oh yes I remember him, we had to give him a regimental bath the minger"

"I thought you were bringing us somewhere quiet, there's quite a few boats here mate" I announced,

"Divers on hol hoping to find a bit of lost treasure down below, Baz used to dive down and leave fool's gold and car boot sale crap don there" Moose exclaimed,

"I sense this is going to be interesting, let's go and find him then" I Putin,

We secured the boat and went for walk, trying to look the best like holiday makers, We walked for a good ten minutes, Moose lead the way, a beach buggy went past us with holiday people shouting out,

"Moose were the hell are you taking us mate" Dunc grumbled!

"Relax just a bit further if I remember" Moose growled,

We walked around a corner and saw a few buildings, "not too impressive" I announced!

There was a sign on one of the buildings saying: Baz and Cloe's diving school, there was another building with a sign outside saying: Bazz's Bar.

There was a walkway into the sea where the bar was, on wooden stilts,
We heard some laughter from inside the building, Moose pointed to the bar,
"Let me go in first lads, see what the score is, hang fire out here ok" Moose exclaimed!
He walked down the gang way towards the bar,
We all waited by the trees and watched Moose go into the bar,

There was some shouting from inside the bar!

I made my way down the walkway,
The rest followed me,
We went inside to see Moose at the bar shaking hands with a bearded man,
"Come and meet Bazza you lot" Moose exclaimed!
The bearded man came over,
He smiled, "hello Taff, Dunc and pretty ladies, what the devil are you doing here" he asked,
He came closer and offered his hand out to me,
I shook his hand and so did Dunc, "hello Baz you still smelling then old boy" Dunc announced,
"Still got your sour banter I see, come to the bar and have a drink, and introduce me to your pretty ladies and talk" Baz exclaimed,
I smiled and we went to the bar,
"Drinks are on pals, snacks coming,
Baz spoke to a girl at the bar and she went into the back,
Another girl made us some drinks,
"Hope cocktails are good for you, all we do here, got some strong stuff if you want it" Baz announced!

"Cocktails will do mate" I put in,
The drinks came,
"So chin chin and lets have a chat" Baz said
I told Baz what we needed and he told us he could get us fuel and whatever else we needed,
We drank for a good hour and ate snacks,
I told Baz I could pay well,
He laughed at me,
"I know what you lot have been up to, you're the talk of the town" Baz exclaimed,
"Ok pal you refuel us and get us supplies, I'll pay you well and we just disappear and you never saw us ok" I put in,
"Fine with me mate, don't relay need too much attention here as to speak, diving school ticking over nicely so to speak" Baz exclaimed.
Baz left the bar and left us, it took a good two hours to refuel the boat and get the supplies on board the boat.
I paid Baz with some extra on top,

"So it's true then" Baz said as I passed him an emerald stone, "maybe, been to hell and back mate" I put in,

We shook hands and left the bar, we made our way to the boat,

"Was expecting some funny stuff here, but never happened" I said out loud!

Everyone agreed and nodded their heads,

"You say you can trust this Guy Moose, you sure" I asked?

Moose gave me a hard look,

"If I say I can trust him hen I can ok boyo" Moose growled back,

"Alright, easy tiger, who took your donut" I replied a bit shocked at Moose being like that,

Me and Moose starred at each other in a way that we had never done before, I dismissed it and lit a cigarette,

Something didn't feel right I knew that.

We left the island safe and sound, I was still very suspicious but never let on, everyone was in a good mood as we sailed off.

"Next stop Cyprus, then down the Suez Canal and onto Thailand" Moose shouted out!

CHAPTER 5:
CYPRUS SCANDLE:

Moose got a roster set up for us all to take it in turns driving the boat, music was playing and the girls were dancing around the back of the boat, I went below and sat down in the galley, I thought of Carmem.
Tina came into the galley, "want something to eat Rhys" she said, I shook my head and took a swig from my glass, "I think that will not mend your loss" she said to me, I looked at Tina and nearly started to cry, I felt a tear roll down my face, Tina came over and sat next to me, she wiped the tear away, "very hard missing someone you have lost, I have been there, I understand, will hurt forever my friend and some more" Tina exclaimed,
She poured me another drink, "I think you eat something and get some rest, your body is beaten up" Tina put in,
I nodded and watched her make some food. Tina nudged me, "rhys mate, eat some food and rest please" "yes boyo, get your head down" Duncan put in,

I ate some bacon sandwiches and went to Dunc's bunk, as soon as I got on the bed I must have passed out.

The boat was rocking, someone was holding my arm, I felt pain there, "hey" I called out, I saw Ariana standing next to me, there was a drip plugged into my arm, "you need this mate, you'll be fine, your body has taken too much and it is not too happy with you, you lie here and get better, I bring you some more water and some light food, take these tablets Mr" she commented, I smiled and remembered who used to call me Mr, Carmem, I t was her favourite word when she was a bit annoyed with me or something was on her mind,

Aliana came in with some sandwiches, she tapped me on the leg and left, I ate one and lead back on the bed.

I woke up, it was dark, I was sweating big time, I raised my arm to look at my watch, there was no watch, my hand was shaking, there was a tube connected to my wrist, I pulled the needle out, I felt annoyed for some reason, things did not make any sense to me!

I was rocking about on the bed and felt sick, I didn't recognise anything, I thought I must be dreaming, my arm was wet, I looked at it, there was blood where I had pulled the intravenous drip out of my wrist, "Guys what's going on" I called out!
No one answered.
I sat up my head was all fuzzy, the bed was all wet underneath me, there was two small round windows that I tried to look through, I strained my eyes to see, the room rocked again, I remembered where I was,
"Lads I need some help here" I shouted!
No one came, I got of the bed and went to the door, I fell over as the boat swayed, I sat on the floor, I needed a drink big time, I got to my feet and tried to open the door, it was locked, "not funny guys, I need out now, need to take a dump for Christ sake" I growled!
I waited and thumped on the door, I didn't have enough strength to force the door open, and I sat on the floor and thought about things,

"Coming sir" I heard someone call out!
I didn't recognise the voice, I quickly looked around to defend myself, there was nothing, and I waited staring at the door, The door was unlocked and man stood in the doorway, "you ok mate" I heard him say,
"Do I look ok, what the fuck is going on here" I announced!
"Taff, we had to sedate you, sorry pal, trying to detox you and let your body mend mate"
I strained my eyes to see the person talking to me, "Duncan you git, help me up here" I asked him!
Dunc smiled and gave me a hand, I felt samba and didn't like it much! "you been banging on the door crying like a baby, don't hate us mate, you got yourself into a bad way dude, you been down here for a good five days" Dunc announced, "if I had the strength id give you one you know that" I growled!
"Ok, let's get you out of this sess pit and let you have some fresh air" Dunc said,

He helped me get dressed and helped me shave and sort myself out, let me walk to the galley, "hey look at you, that's the Rhys I remember" Tina exclaimed, "yo bro, welcome back from highway to hell" Moose commented as he came in,

I sat down and ate a sandwich Tina had made for me, I wanted a drink but kept quiet, "so where are we then" I asked?
"Just off the coast of Cyprus mate, there's a small island on the west side of the island called Mazaki island, you should remember it from when we were posted here, did some adventure training there, Sargent major Gill, is apparently still there semi-retired now running a shot gun range for the toff officers when thieve had a few and feel the urge for some daft officer fun, he's been in the army since doomsday, he can sort us out if he's still around, another old friend told me a while ago" Moose put in, "bloody el, I remember him, six foot tall Indian, a hand full in the army, does things by the book and not by the book, his favourite phrases were:

"jowley jowley I can't see no fucking trees, take a fucking baring my son" I announced, we laughed, "come up top mate and get some fresh air, drive the boat for a while, we are nearly there" Moose put in,
I finished my sandwiches and went up top, the fresh air made me feel a bit giddy, "hello stranger, you look better" Alaina exclaimed,
"Thanks for looking after me mate, I owe you big time" I announced, "I still owe you mate for getting me out of the jungle and giving me Dunc" she said,
I smiled and took control of the boat, "Cyprus here we come, the island was in view, we got posted there back in the nineties for two years, I went through a bad marriage there, another story,
Moose told me where to sail, a few boats sailed past us, some big rich ones, military aircraft flew over and that was expected, there was a big RAF base on the island, we sailed round the island and headed to the Mazaki island, not too far,
The island was coming up and we slowed down to cruise in to the mooring area,

wooden walkways came out into the sea from the beach, there was one boat moored up, looked like a fishing boat, we slowed up and stopped, Dunc and Tina jumped off the boat and tied us off,
Moose looked at me, "you suffering aren't you pal" Moose said to me quietly,
I nodded,
Moose opened a draw under the steering column, he passed me a silver hip flask, it was mine,
"Been looking after it for you bro, I am not too happy giving you this, however I can't see you suffer like, just don't go to banana land again ok" Moose exclaimed!
"yes boss" I replied and took a swig and closed my eyes as I felt the strong stuff go down my throat, "that hit the spot I tell you" said, "hey what is this" Aliana came up and looked very annoyed, "we nurse him for nearly a week and now you give him that, you crazy both of you" she growled!
"It's ok love, I know what I'm doing, been looking after this bum for a long time haven't I brother" Moose put in,

I nodded and went outside.
I could hear Aliana telling Moose off, I smiled and took a big swig, I didn't have too much interest any more, all I wanted was my Carmem back and I blamed myself for her loss, I thought about something else and jumped of the boat, the hip flask was put into my pocket till I needed it again, I walked up to Dunc and Tina, "so here we are then back in sunny old Cyprus, I always said I would never return to this place, too many bad memories, broken marriage bla bla bla" I announced, Dunc gave me one of his stairs, "how you feeling mate" he said, "just fine now, let's try and find Mr Gill and keep going" I put in, Dunc grabbed my arm, "easy lad, Dunc's here for you" he said, I looked at him in the eyes, he looked back into mine, "come on bro, let's go and shoot some shot guns eh" Dunc growled!
I knew he knew that I knew he knew that I had had a drink, I told myself to buck up for my mates,
Moose joined us with Aliana who gave me a stern look,

"Ok people, you can't change a leopards stripes, I will drink, but in moderation, I hurt too much inside and you know why, now let's have a look see of this place ye" I growled!

I walked off and started to whistle an old tune from our regiment that the corps of drums always played,

"Hey what's that rucas, I know that tune" an Indian accent sounded!

A large man appeared from out of the bushes with a shotgun in his hands,

"so, sound off, I have had no news of anyone coming here, and what's with the whistling tune that I remember from long ago, come on speak up don't be shy" he growled!

"Sargent major Gill, bloody good to see you sir" Moose called out!

The major looked at us, "Jesus H Christ, you lot still alive, you bad boys, heard a few stories of your adventures, if they are true I wish I could have been there with, jowly jowly! The major announced!

"Come come, let's get inside and talk, who fancies a curry" the major put in,
He patted me on the back, corporal Evans, I take it your in charge here, Moose and Dunc were always behind you, and you have some pretty ladies with you to, lots to talk about my boys, take a fucking baring son" he growled!
We all laughed!
"You guys are in a world of shit, I hear you turned mercenary and wasted a few MI5 agents and a lot more, you're the top talk of the mess by the way" the major grumbled,
"never mercenaries, just got stitched up and all things went messy sir" I told him," I know son, I heard about sergeant Nash and what happened, come on let's get you inside and talk" the major exclaimed,
He stopped sharp, "oh by the way my unofficial rank is now major not Sargent major, they are being soft with me promoted too much, trying to get me to retire, once a soldier always a soldier" he put in, he swung round and gave me a punch in the ribs, "getting a bit slow there taff my lad" he growled!

I got my breath back, "missed you sir" I grumbled!

"Who drives that thing then" Major Gill asked? "me sir" Moose replied, "right let's get you out of site then, you make yourself at home up there, he pointed to the shacks, and I'll show Moose head where to park that beaten up raft of yours,

The Major and Moose got on the boat and sailed round the corner, the rest of us walked to the three out buildings, the set up was still as I remembered it from when we used to come here for adventure training for a week,

We tried the door to one of the buildings, it was locked, and we found a door that was unlocked so we entered.

There was a bar at the end of the room, it looked like a function room, soft backed chairs scattered about the place,

There was a lot of pictures on the wall of officers in uniform,

We went to the bar and Dunc got some drinks sorted out, "chin chin" he said and raised his glass,

We all took a sip, and chatted,

I was just about to say something when a side door was pushed open with force, same time as the door we had come through was opened,
Army Uniformed men burst into the room wearing army style clothing brandishing some high calibre weapons, there was silencers on the end of the barrels,
They wore balaclavas to hide their faces,
"On the floor now, get down ya bastards" one of the men ordered!

We did as they ordered,

We had no choice as two men in black pushed me down and frisked me, my hand gun and grenade were taken so was my knife and various other bits and pieces I always carry on me whilst working, they put a hood over my head, I could hear a scuffle from Dunc and Tina and Aliana screamed!

"Tango two one alpha, four targets down and secured fifth target being dealt with now over" someone spoke,

"What the hell is going on" I growled and got a thump in my ribs, "shut your mouth if you know what's good for you" someone yelled at me!

I heard a door open and there was a thud on the floor, "stitch up folks, any chance of a quick drink before the party starts" I heard Moose comment, he groaned and I heard him being punched around, "funny man eh shut your fucking mouths all of you's" another voice called out, he had an Irish accent!

"I want them separated, take the girls into the other building bind and gag them, split these fuckers up".

"Take the big man out the back and put the funny guy over there, tape them up" another order was shouted!

I was pulled by my feet and slumped into a chair, "who's Rhys" someone shouted! We all remained silent, I heard the door open just as I received a punch in my stomach, I could hear Moose and Dunc moaning too, "that one there is Rhys" I recognised the voice, Major Gill,

My hood was taken off, "you bastard" I growled!

He came over fast and punched me in the jaw, "you call me a bastard after what you bunch have been up to, "search the boat thoroughly then well start having some fun with the girls" another man said in an Irish accent,

"You did a bad thing back in Ireland boys so you did, took out one of the big men, naughty naughty" a tall man in front of me whispered!

"we would like the money and other stuff you took from Sam's farm so we would" another man said.

there was six armed men in the room with us I wasn't sure who many were outside, I guessed a good twelve here all together, "major, why, and to the fucking IRA of all people, you've killed us sir" I announced, I received another blow to the side of the head,

"Long story my boy, they been tracking you for a while, so I understand, one of you lot has a tracking device on them or maybe you have a bad boy amongst you" the major put in "impossible" I growled! "Anyways, I was offered too much to turn down at my age, army trying to kick me out anyway, fuck em, and you crazy bastards fleeing around causing havoc, I remember the day on the ranges when you had a cook off in your weapon, a young whippersnapper then you was, fresh out of training, knew shit, got cocky with me laying behind your weapon, "wasn't my fault colour Sargent you said, I gave you a good dig as we did in those days and you reported me, cost me a long time to get promoted and I could not train on the ranges for years after that", he paused,

"so when I heard of the chance to get my own back on you I jumped at it" major announced, I laughed, "waste the English scum" one the others said,
"later, he goes back with us, someone wants to have a private word with this one so he does" another armed man said in a heavy Irish accent, "you dirty Irish scum, you touch those girls and ill rip you apart" I heard Dunc shout after we heard one of the girls scream! Two thugs were on top of him straight away, "you fuckers" Dunc shouted, "silence him will you someone" one of the armed men growled, two thuds went off quickly, "Duncan" I shouted! I was hit in the ribs again and slumped to the floor, I didn't hear anything from Dunc,
I laid there on the floor trying to sort things out, I looked over to Moose, he just sat there quiet, I thought he was playing things out till he could make a move, I would be ready,
One of the Irish men was talking on a radio, "roger that" he replied,

"Where's the fucking money English, tell me know or we start to play with your whores" he demanded!

"Come on man, tell them where it is and lets end this" the Major put in,

"Fuck you sir, you served our queen and country for a long time to end up with these wankers" I exclaimed!

I was hit again, I saw Moose shake his head, I saw him stand up and take his hood off, He stood there staring at me, I was wondering why no one was throwing him to the ground.

"Sorry old pal this is how it is" Moose commented!

One of the armed men gave him the thumbs up and threw him a pistol,

Moose took the radio off the guy who had spoken on it earlier, "Tango two one sunray two control, sunray compromised, Charlie target is down three targets left, will bring one back with us, Charlie one secured and in order over" Moose spoke over the radio,

"Unbelievable, am I drunk or what, I am not seeing this Moose, what the hell" I announced,

Moose came over and punched me in the face, "been wanting to do that for a long time old pal" he exclaimed!
"You bastard, I never would of believed it, I trusted you like my brother" I coughed out!
"Why" I asked him before I took another blow from one of the armed men, "that's enough for now, need to take him back in one piece" Moose ordered!
Moose pulled me back into the chair, "bring me some whisky Mick" he shouted! He pulled up another chair and sat down, "if my hands went taped they'd be around your neck pal" I whispered, "I know" he whispered back, "why Moose" I asked again?
Major Gill brought a bottle of whisky over, "take a drink major you have earned it" Moose announced, "sure" the major took a long drink from the bottle and passed it to Moose,
I saw Moose smile, he then shot the major twice in the chest, still smiling, "last post Major" he put in.

I just stared at Moose and shook my head. "get rid of the women, dump them in the sea with this fat piece of shit, chuck the other one, moose pointed to where Dunc was laid, on the boat and sink it" Moose ordered!

"let's have a drink old pal, Moose said, one of the armed men forced my mouth open, I had no strength to resist, Moose poured a good quarter of the bottle down my throat, I choked and felt the burn in my throat, "Chin chin" he said and took a good swig himself.

I felt drunk instantly and started to laugh, "Any chance of a fag" I asked him,

Moose gave me a cigarette, he put it into my mouth, "take his tape off, he won't be a bother, drunk and stupid, if I think he's getting frisky I'll put a slug in him myself" Moose growled, the tape around my wrists was pulled off fast and I felt the hair being ripped off, I laughed, "give us another swig will ya, let's get pissed together for the last time, been a lot of times though eh Moose" I slurred and took a big swig from the bottle,

I passed it to Moose, a lighter was passed to me, I lit my cigarette and sat back, "well well well so who am I to meet when you get me back to Ireland then, don't tell me, Mr Paisley himself hiding behind the church" I added, "I don't like your drunk Banta so I don't" one of the armed men announced, "ok you lot, help unload the boat and wait for the chopper, get rid of the girls, don't mess with them ok, I'll be fine here with the piss head, Davey you stay here and keep us company" Moose ordered!
I sat back and smoked my cigarette, I saw Dunc pulled out of the door, and there was a lot of blood on the floor from him.
I laughed again, "last post old friend" I said and flicked my cigarette at him,
"taff I have always hated you, you were always above me in command, I dragged you out of so much shit in the past, you came up with the honours after my hard work, did I tell you my father was a bare knuckle fighter and good at it, he pulled me up and thumped me in the stomach twice, I slumped to the floor and laughed!

Moose went to kick me, I grabbed his leg and twisted it around with skill, I heard a snap, knew I had put his knee cap out, he dropped to the floor, I grabbed his pistol and shot the other armed man dead, Moose grabbed my legs and I fell over, I shot him in the shoulder, I saw Moose slide back against the bar, "you sneaky bastard, could never know when you were pissed, you hide it so well amigo, what now pal" Moose asked holding his shoulder,

"You fucking rat, how big are you then with the IRA" I asked?

"Big enough, maybe I'll tell you one day" he coughed out!

I took the weapon off the man I just shot and went to the window and looked outside.

I saw a good eight men taking holdalls and weapons off my boat, and taking them to another boat moored next to mine, two other men were pulling the girls towards the other building, the girls were screaming, one of the men slapped Tina across the face to shut her up, "I thought you told your guys to lay off the girls" I growled!

"We all need some fun trooper" Moose said and coughed!
"You wanker" I growled!
I put another bullet in Moose's leg "ok enough already, I have no dought that you won't kill me or leave me here to slowly die, pass me the radio, I will tell them to leave the girls alone and to bring them back here, I'm interested in how you recon you can overcome eleven armed men, I will enjoy this, no tricks mate" Moose moaned,
I kicked over the radio, Moose picked up the hand mike, "Mick, change plan, bring the girls back here, over" Moose commanded, "roger that" came the reply, Moose reached for the bottle of whisky and took a big swallow, nice here, front row seat" he commented,
I remembered as they dragged Dunc out I noticed his hand was pointing back, I took a look behind the bar, "you bloody beauty" I growled, Dunc had left two grenades under the bar, "thanks mate" I said to myself, I heard a scream from outside,

"Game on "Moose put in and laughed out loud!

"Another word and you will be in a world of pain my friend" I growled!

"I already am" Moose answered and took another swig from the bottle, quickly looked around, there was a shotgun case that I got open pretty sharpish, there were boxes of cartridges in the bottom, I loaded two shot guns up and put a load more shells in my pockets, I looked at Moose, he was watching me, "Taff's last post" he yelled out! And laughed, I put another bullet in him and he slumped over, there was a scream from outside and an automatic weapon was fired, I could hear the radio talking away, I went into the back and rigged up quickly the grenade on the door trick, I went to Moose and slumped him in a chair with the bottle in his hand, I put a hood over his head, he moaned,

I thought about going behind the bar but thought otherwise,

I waited behind the snooker table, the bar would be the first place I would look at or shoot at if I came in here under the circumstances, brain still working I thought to myself,
There was another scream from outside and some more gunfire,
The back door opened, "we got trouble boss, girls tried to do a runner" someone shouted! There was a loud explosion, the grenade taped to the door when off, I heard a few groans, I emptied the shot gun at the back door, I reloaded and waited,
"Rhys what's going on in there" someone shouted in an Irish accent!
I saw someone at the window, I unloaded the shotgun without hesitation, one of the windows smashed and I heard a clunk on the floor, at first I thought it was a grenade, it was a smoke bomb, I grabbed it and launched it out the back door,
There was smoke in the bar now, I saw two men come in, they sprayed the bar with bullets and shouting out for Moose, I already had the pin from the second grenade pulled,

I rolled it to where they were, the grenade went off and there was quiet, "you stupid bastards, kill this sun of a bitch will you" Moose yelled out!, "your last post mate" I growled! I shot him dead,

The side door was shredded by bullets and followed by a figure in the smoke, I fire off the shot gun twice and grabbed the other one, I scrambled my way to the back and into the kitchen, I looked around for some cooking fat and threw it into the microwave with a metal knife, I set the timer for five minutes and crawled out of the back door, three bodies laid on the ground, I took one of their weapons and is spare ammo clips, there was a lot of smoke outside from the smoke bomb, I had a packet of mini flares inside the back of my trousers that was missed when I was searched, I crawled over two dead bodies, and made a dash into nearby bushes, I reloaded the shot gun, there was a lot of gunfire from inside the building and shouting!

I heard a helicopter start it engine, I couldn't see it from all the smoke, I crawled to a better position,

I saw my boat was on fire, I got up and ran to a low wall, I dived over it, and bullets ricocheted off the wall above my head, more shouting I heard!

Through a gap in the wall I saw the chopper, there was three men next to it, I fired off my mini flares at the chopper, I didn't miss, the chopper went up I smoke and exploded!

There was a few screams, I saw two men running up to the chopper carrying holdall bags from my boat, I moved through the bushes, bullets flew around me, "fucking ye" I growled to myself, I returned fire with the shot gun and moved again, I waited.

I heard some more machine gun fire and then there was silence, I stayed where I was, my heart was pounding and I was sweating big time, I thought I was going to get a heart attack.

Another shot rang out!

I stayed where I was, my body had no more energy, I took out my hip flask and had a good sip, I crawled into a small ditch and checked my pockets, no more shells for the shot gun,

I had lost my hand gun too, mini flares gone, I sat there, I checked my pockets and found a packet of fags, I lit one and thought, what the hell I'm finished here.
"Rhys" I heard someone called out, woman's voice!
I heard it again!
I looked up from behind the rocks to see Tina standing there with a rifle in her hand, "sons of bitches tried to have their way with me, Aliana gone, everyone gone" she announced, she fell to the ground, I got up and went to her with a strain,
"You're ok girl, I got you know" I told her. She passed out on me, I checked her over, she had bullet wound in her shoulder and one in her leg, I let her lie there, I knew she would be ok, it was quiet, just the sound of burning metal could be heard, I picked up a rifle from a dead soldier and walked around.
What a mess, bodies everywhere, I found the holdalls taken from my boat that was now burning away where it was moored, I went into the building where I left moose, more bodies laid on the floor,

I went to the bar and got myself a drink and lit a cigarette, I sat on one of the bar stools and just stared at Moose and Major Gill, what the hell has gone on here I was thinking to myself.
"Ok you fuckers, this is your last post" I murmured!
I found a few cans of cooking oil in the back kitchen and threw the oil about the place and stopped I had to think of a plan out of this mess, the smoke from burning helicopter is bound to attract attention, there was a fire extinguisher in the kitchen, I grabbed it and went out to the burning chopper,
I extinguished the fire quickly.
My mind was working overtime, how was I to get off this place, I walked around, I heard someone coughing and took cover instantly, It was Tina, I went to her, she had sat herself up,
"Hello you, where are the rest, I know Aliana has gone, I know I'm in a state" Tina whispered.

"you'll be fine, I've put the fires out, there's another building up there, I am thinking it's where the major lived, can sort ourselves out there and think of what to do next, I announced, Tina pointed down the hill," I saw a boat down there when I got away from those scumbags, two of them wanted some fun with me, they took me down to another small harbour, our boat and another posh boat is there, I lead them to believe I was game, I played with them both, then grabbed a rifle that one of them had put on the floor, I kept firing at them till the bullets ran out and ran, she said, Tina started to cough!

"Good girl, Dunk would be proud of you, I put in,

Tina looked at me, I saw a tear run down her cheek, I leaned forward and wiped it away, she came forward and hugged me, and "tell me what happened please" she whispered in my ear, we just hugged in silence for a few minutes.

She pulled away and coughed,

"I told her exactly what happened, she looked shocked, "Moose, oh my god, I can't believe it" she said,

"Ok I need to have a look at this boat, I stood up, there was a noise from behind me, I turned to Moose standing there with a gun in his hand, and he was in a bad state,

"You can't kill me Rhys" he laughed, he was using a rifle as a crutch,

"You two looking cosy here, I saw you, I wonder what Dunc would say to that, moving in on his girl" Moose announced, he coughed again,

"You fucking pig" Tina shouted out! There was two thuds and Moose fell backwards over a low wall, I looked at Tina, she had one of the soldiers weapons with a silencer, her stare I will not forget, "bye bye you rat" Tina said and slumped back, I checked Moose, this time he was dead!

There was a radio in his pocket talking away, I listened, "tango two one sunray send sitrep over,

I grabbed the hand mike, "roger that, targets all down, one casualty to look after, over" I said in a bad accent, "roger that, Alfa whisky is not responding do you have the biscuits, send sitrep over" someone on the other end of the radio asked in a strong Irish accent, I knew what they were asking, army talk, sitrep was situation report, Alfa whisky was the chopper and I guessed biscuits meant the cash and weapons, I spoke again, "roger, Alfa whisky has coms down, biscuits secured, need some time to patch things up here then will be on our way" I replied,

"who is this over" I heard on the radio, "go fuck yourself you bogie twat" I growled and dropped the hand mike, I spat at Moose and went to Tina, I patched her wounds up as good as I could, I found a med kit in the kitchen, we slowly made our way down to where the boats were, I could see my boat smouldering away, "we need to put that fire out quickly, I am sure we will be expecting company soon, those radio messages I sent to whoever, well I know they know what's happened" I said to her,

There was a small hut next to the harbour where I found another fire extinguisher and set to work to put the fire out,
Tina got on the other boat that the Irish lads had come on,
I got the fire out and said good bye to Dunc, I pulled the holdall bags down to the harbour with a lot of strain, I was knackered!
I heard the boat start up!
Tina came out on deck, "there is a lot of provisions here, a full fuel tank and looks very technical in here" she announced, I gave her the thumbs up!
I got the bags on board and some weapons, Tina helped as good as she could, I opened the door to another small shack to find a small armoury, "shit" I said to myself, there was rifles, shotguns, trip flares, boxes of grenades, claymore mines and lots more,
I was wondering what exactly was the Major running here and dealing with the IRA,

I had an idea, I knew there would be nasties on their way here to find out what was going on!

I grabbed all the stuff I could and went out, "get the boat ready to leave, I need to rig a few surprises up" I shouted, I told Tina to take the boat a bit from the harbour wall and steps so I could leave a surprise on the steel steps, I went off and put booby traps in places I thought anyone coming here looking for trouble would stick their noses into, I had to go back to the small shack a few times, I was running out of energy, but I had to do this, for Duncan and Aliana, I left a nice surprise next the main path up the hill from the harbour, another in the bar, and a few more scattered around, must of took me a good half hour, I brought a rucksack I had found in the Majors shack and filled it with bits and pieces I thought would need and be of use, and limped down to the end of the harbour wall, Tina reversed the boat and I got on, I went through to where Tina was at the steering wheel,

"ok let's get off round to the other side of the island out the way, find some cover, we need to plot a course where to go next and not sail of blind" I told her, Tina nodded and pushed the throttle forwards, the boat moved off and we sailed out of the harbour and made our way around the island, we found a little cove and put the boat under some overhanging trees, I got to work looking at sea charts and maps,
Tina was checking out the sat nav and the other controls and switches that were a lot different from our boat, I'll give Moose one thing, he taught everyone good skills as a captain and how to navigate water craft, we learnt from him!
An explosion went off!
"time to go I think" I said looking at Tina, I told her the coordinates to put in the sat nav, she did with speed, it took a few minutes for the sat nave to accept the settings, another explosion went off and smoke was now rising, we could hear gunfire and shouting, "I think someone's found my surprise welcomes" I exclaimed! Tina smiled and we pulled off!

"Bye my love" Tina said looking back, she looked at me, "just you and me know, if I make it" Tina said looking at me, "oh boy, you will make it and that's an order sailor, and besides I get scared when left on my own" I put in, she laughed and steered the boat out to sea.

We sailed for a good few hours, it was starting to get dark, and the sea was good as we bounced along at a reasonable speed, Conversation was minimal, we just took it in turns to steer the boat,

"According to the sat nav we have 36 hours sailing time till we reach Cairo and get more supplies, hope you can put up with my bad habits mate" I announced, "don't you think I am not used to you by know Rhys" she replied in a soft voice, she smiled and went red,

 "You blushing young lady"
I asked?
"I never blush" she replied'
"You need to rest, it's a good job those bullets were small calibre and went straight through you",

"take it easy, you've lost a lot of blood, ill navigate through the night" I suggested, Tina nodded with a smile and went below.
I steered the boat following the sat nav and the sea charts that really confused me and thought of Carmem.
I could smell cooking from below, made me feel hungry, I felt for my hip flask, it wasn't there in my waist pocket, "bollocks" I growled out loud!
Tina came up top, "what's happened" she asked?
"Lost something I have had for a long time, has a lot of good and bad memories, maybe I was meant to of lost the damn thing" I exclaimed,
"You mean this" she said and handed me my silver flask, "I saw it on the floor and grabbed it, knew it was yours mate" she said and smiled, "me and you are going to get along just fine" I told her,
I opened the flask, Tina held out her hand, I gave the flask back to her, she took a big swig and passed it back to me,
I smiled and took a swig myself.

CHAPTER 6:
A BLIND AFFAIR:

Tina brought up a plate of food, it smelled nice, thin pieces of steak with fried eggs on top, I could smell garlic and herbs, "you made my favourite food mate, wow and may I say you look very pretty Tina, I wish you would rest some" I told her, "I will later, we need to eat and thank you Rhys, makes me feel better when I feel like a lady, not all roughed up and dirty" she replied, I set the boat to auto pilot, steady speed and sat at the small table in the bridge,
I looked at Tina, she looked very pretty, "not happy but a big thanks you, looks lovely" I said, Tina smiled and sat down next to me, there wasn't too much room at the table we were close to each other, I banged her elbow as I cut into my beef, "sorry, sometimes I have no manners, I am Mr dog with a broken tale" I said, I had no idea what I meant but it made Tina laugh, she nudged me in the ribs, "ah" I groaned, "I am so sorry Rhys" she said, and looked really concerned!

"Its ok mate, we are both beaten up, what we need is a good night's rest" I put in, she smiled and had a drink,

Tina had found the music system and soft songs were coming through the speakers, We started to eat the food, "this is great mate" I said and took a swig from my silver flask, thanks for this" I said holding the flask in my hand, "no problem" she replied, The boat bounced and Tina bumped into me, my plate fell into my lap, there wasn't too much left but I was covered in bits of food, "bloody hell, can you imagine if this had happen to Dunc, it would of broken his heart, lost his food like that we would ever hear the end of it" I said, I didn't mean to say that I thought to myself, "sorry came out wrong, will never forget him" I put in, Tina looked at me, "I know" she replied, she put her hand on mine and kissed my cheek, "what do we do know" she asked? I looked at her, "we will get through this I promise you" I told her, she smiled again and kissed me on the mouth quickly and pulled away!

I looked at her a bit shocked, "sorry Rhys, I didn't mean that, I hurt all over and I am not thinking straight" Tina announced, I nodded at her and picked up my plate, "can't waste this" I said and licked the plate, Tina laughed, "you pig", Dunc did that" she said, Tina put her hands on my face and kissed me again on the mouth, this time with passion, I responded.

We broke apart and looked at each other, "ok you, now I'm in shock by the way, ok, we clean up this mess and go down below and sort your wounds out, I'll make sure the sat nav is correct and the auto pilot is ok and let's get some rest" I announced, "I think you talk too much Rhys, don't be too long" she said and went down below with the plates, I saw her eyes and I felt butterflies in my stomach, I took a swig from my flask and checked things out in the bridge, "I'm just going to have a cigarette" I shouted!

"I think I will join you" Tina replied, she came up and we lit a cigarette each, the sea was quite calm and the stars were so bright, Tina blew out her smoke and grabbed my

hand, I held it, we both looked out to sea, "it's hard when you lose someone you really care about, seen this so many times, you never get used to it, hurts too much, god damn you Moose, how in hells name did this happen, we've been together watching each other's back and stuff for a long time, I hurt too much inside to believe it" I announced, I took my flask out of my pocket, Tina took it from me and took a long swig, she passed it to me, I drank some and put the flask back in my pocket,
Tina flicked her cigarette into the sea, "bye my love" she said quietly, Rhys will look after me now" she said, Tina turned around and looked at me hard, "can I have your flask again Rhys" she asked!
I passed my flask to her and she took a big mouthful and coughed! I took the flask off her and had a swig, I put the flask in my pocket, I flicked my cigarette over board, and we stood there in silence for a moment. "Come on, I need to be looked after" she said to me and pulled me down below.

I felt a bit scared as I was thinking of my Carmem, I took a swig from my flask as I went for a pee.

I went into the galley, Tina wasn't there, I heard a noise from the cabin at the front of the boat, and I grabbed the first aid kit and went to her,

I opened the door and saw Tina lying on the double bed, all she had on was a towel, she was wiping her wounds, "hey, hang on let me see that" I asked? I opened the first aid kit and found some antiseptic cream, let me put this on you please" I told her,

I saw Tina's eyes, "just come here before I pass out" she slurred,

I turned the light off and took my clothes off, I got underneath the blanket, Tina turned to me, "I am hurting inside Rhys" she whispered and hugged me, I could feel she had no cloths on, I could feel the heat from her body, we kissed and made love.

I woke up as the boat rocked, I looked at my watch, it was six o clock in the morning, there was a beeping sound coming from somewhere that I heard, my head hurt and so did the rest of my body,

I turned around to see Tina lying there in the bed with me, I remembered what had happened, I took a cigarette out of the packet and lit it, I laid there feeling quite happy, my silver flask was next to the bed, I reached it and took a swig from it, I smoked my cigarette, and thought about what we were going to do next, I felt good, I remembered last night, Tina was very affectionate with me, I knew she was in pain but she made love to me and fell asleep, I finished my cigarette and looked at her, she looked peaceful whilst she slept, I was about to get out of the bed and go and make some breakfast when I felt something sticky on my leg, I brushed my hand there and looked at it, I saw blood, I turned towards Tina, "you awake mate, want some breakfast" I asked, there was no reply, I touched her face, she looked very pale, she was very cold, "Tina" I called out and gave her a nudge, she didn't reply, I pulled back the quilt and saw blood everywhere,

I shook her again, there was no response, I checked her pulse, there was no pulse, I gave her mouth to mouth immediately, and she was stone cold.

"Bollocks" I shouted! I tried my best to revive her but she was long gone, there was too much blood in the bed, I slumped to the floor and cried.

The boat rocked and I opened my eyes, my watch said it was three thirty pm, I took out my flask and had a big sip, I wished I had been dreaming, I looked at the bed, Tina was there looking like she was fast asleep, "Tina" I called out, I touched her arm it was ice cold.

I sat there for what seemed like ages, I finished my flask, and I felt sober and very annoyed!

The boat rocked quite strongly, I needed to up top and see what was going on, "sleep tight Tina mate" I said softly and left her there, I went to the bridge, it was getting rough, I checked the sat nav and corrected the boat, four hours to get to Cairo, I didn't know what to do, I felt completely lost and alone.

I lit a cigarette and thought about things, Navigating a boat and mooring up is not too easy on your own, not impossible but awkward, I didn't want to cause attention to me when I had to moor when I get to Cairo, I didn't even know where I was going anyway, "fuck" I growled out loud!

I stood there in control and navigated the boat with the sat nav.

Two hours went past I could see the coast line of Cairo, Egypt coming up in the distance, I slowed the engine down and went below.

I looked at Tina, I had made a decision, I had to get rid of her, in case someone came on the boat whilst I was moored up and went bananas if they saw a dead body on my boat, I picked her up and went up to, I said a quick prayer and let her go to sea, I saluted and bid my farewell to her, I cleaned up the bed and got back up top.

I pushed ahead to Cairo, and then hopefully go down the Suez Canal into the red sea and onto Eden Sea, from there I cross the Arabian Sea and onto Thailand,

I was scared to death, Cairo was coming up.

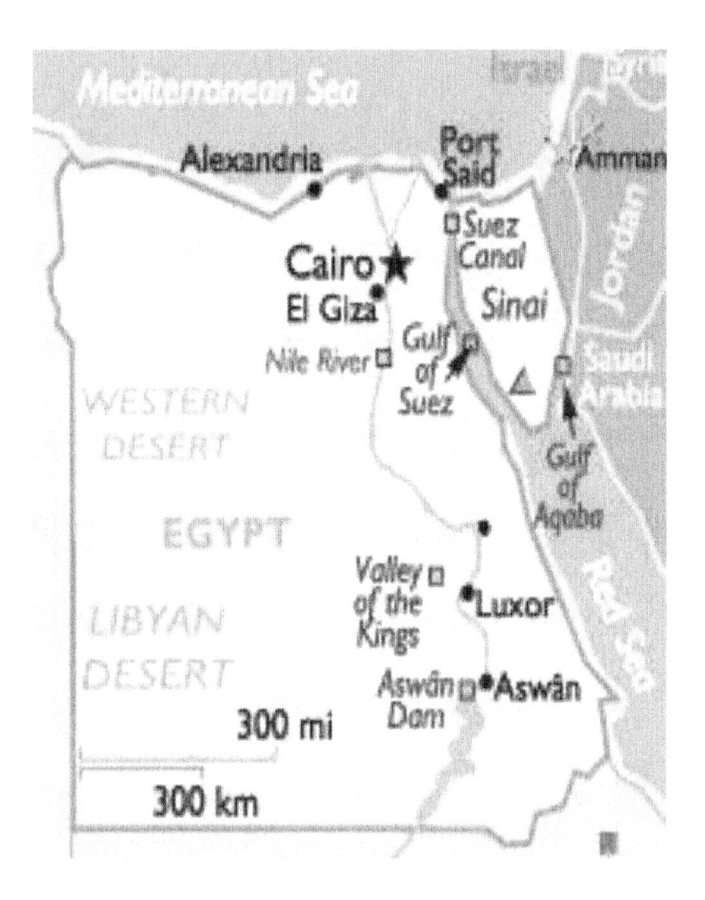

The coast was getting closer,
I sailed past and looked for somewhere a bit quiet, there was too many expensive boats everywhere for my taste.
I carried on around the Coast, the sat nav said I was next to Alexandria, never heard of it, too busy for my liking,

I carried on, I went round a corner and was a secluded cove, and I went in.

I got up as close as I could to the sand and threw the anchor overboard,
I jumped off with the front rope and tied her off round a spike, banged in hard, and some kids were running towards me,

I didn't understand their language they were shouting out!
The kids were jumping around and shouting at me!
"Hey you have problem with boat" one of the kids shouted! I need fuel" I shouted back!
"hey Mr I get fuel for you, you pay me good, I get anything you want, you need lady for night no problem, want massage I get for you sir" the young lad shouted back to me!
"Ok ok, come here young man" I announced!
The young boy climbed aboard and came out to the bridge where I was standing, "hello sir I help you" he said, "yes great, I need fuel and supplies" I asked him, "I do for you no problem, he held out his hand, "wait here" I said and went below to get some cash, I only had British currency, I grabbed a big wad out of the holdall and went back up top, the boy was sat on the chair looking at the sat nav and controls, "he saw me come up, "nice boat sir" he said, I held out my hand.

He was the money and took it, "British, good money, I bring you what you want sir, you want massage or anything" he asked, "massage would be good" I said, he nodded and jumped off the boat, he showed the rest of the kids the money and they all started to shout and scream, they ran off.

I felt a bit worried, I wasn't sure how much I gave the lad, maybe a five hundred pounds or so, I thought he might bring back some nasties so I got prepared and sorted some weapons out and waited.

Time went past, I had something to eat and sat on the front deck, my hip flask was filled and I was enjoying a cigarette, I had a hand gun in my pocket in case, Carmem was on my mind, so was Tina and the rest of the gang I had lost.

I waited maybe a good hour when I heard a boat approaching from behind, I wasn't paying too much attention as it was close to me, and I jumped up and looked at the boat. "Hey Mr I have fuel for you sir" someone shouted!

I saw a man on the front of the approaching boat, "you pay my son too much, he very happy, I help you sir" he shouted!
"Yes come on" I shouted back!
My boat was refuelled and a load of supplies was given to me, it was getting dark now,
"I send you nice lady, give good massage to you, relax you sir for the night yes" the man said, "ok, ok" I replied, I was keeping an eye on the other chaps he had with him, they were all talking in their own language and looking at me.
All was done, they said good bye to me and sailed off.
I wanted to go but it was dark now,
I went below and sorted out the supplies they had brought me,
I had asked for some extra fuel which they gave me in jerry cans,
I gave the guy more money too, he was very happy.
I checked what they had got me and was a bit surprised:

Coffee and sugar, powdered milk, some sort of beef, eggs pasta rice, there was slices of ham and cheese, bread and some sort of fish spread, there was a lot of drinking water, and other stuff,
I was surprised to see two bottles of brandy too, I put it all away and decided to make some food.
"Hello Mr" I heard someone call from outside, I quickly went up top
There was a young lady standing on the rocks, "you need to move your boat further down,
I show you, you get bad waves through the night if you do not move sir" she called out!
"Thank you young lady and what can I do for you" I asked?
"My brother and farther help you today, I hope I can help you relax tonight, I cook for you if you want" she shouted!
"Ok miss, come aboard" I replied!
She untied my lines and got onto the boat, she showed me where to go, we didn't go too far just a few hundred metres round the bend, and she helped me tie the ropes off.

What is your name" I asked her, "Tula" she replied.

She had a nice smile and looked very pretty, not too young for me I thought, she asked my name, I told her.
"Where you come from Rhys" she asked?
I told her a story and she was very interested,
"Ok I make you food and give you good massage" she said,
"Ok, sounds god to me" I replied.

I tripped over something and my hand gun fell to the floor, "you no need that with me sir" she said, and she passed the gun to me, "thanks Tula" I replied, I secured the top deck and we went below, Tula went straight to the galley and started to prep the food, I went for a shower, I still felt a bit uneasy, in a foreign place on my own, on a boat, what the hell was i doing, I thought to myself!
I showered and smelt a nice smell from the galley, I dried off and got dresses, I went through to the galley, the table had a cloth on it and was laid out nicely, plates, glasses the works, "wow something smells nice" I announced!
"I cook nice beef for you sir, we eat and I give you a relax massage, I clean boat and watch out for you, you have good rest tonight, I stay with you tonight, it will be late, I scared to go home in dark, please" she asked, I looked at her, "you are very welcome to stay" I replied.
She smiled and sorted out the food, I went up top and had a cigarette, Tula came up with a glass of beer, "here you are sir" she passed the glass to me,

"thanks and you Tula, call me Rhys, I would like you to drink with me, I hate drinking alone" I said, where the hell did that come from, I thought to myself, Tula smiled and went below to get her drink, she came back up with a glass in her hand, "chin chin sexy" I said, "salud" she replied and she took a drink, she smiled at me, we had a chat about where I came from and stuff, I lit another cigarette as I felt a bit nervous, not being used to this stuff I thought to myself, I told a few jokes, she laughed and I knew she didn't understand them, "I smoke too" she said, I passed her a cigarette and lit it for her, she told me about her life, her English was bad and broken but I got what she was telling me, her mother was dead and she cooked and helped her brother, she did everything for her farther, I felt sorry for her, she told me she gets beaten by her dad if she doesn't do things for him and his friends and more, I was annoyed, "its bloody wrong" I growled!

"Enough talk I think, we eat now" she said, I nodded and we went down below to the galley.

I poured us some drinks, she was drinking whiskey with me and getting a bit giggly, The food was delicious, the company was great, her English was broken but ok, she asked me so many questions about me and what I do, she seemed very interested, I liked it,

We finished the meal, "that was great" I announced!

"ok, you go have cigarette I come to then you lie down I do washing quick and come to you ok" she said, "yes sir" I growled and saluted with a smile, she laughed and followed me to the back of the boat, it was dark now, the sky was full of stars and the boat rocked steadily, we smoked, Tula did all the talking, as women do!

We went below, I went to the front cabin and got comfy, I could hear her washing up, she came through, "now relax, you give too much money to my brother, he very happy, I look after you now" she said, I laid on the bed and enjoyed the massage, "too many injuries, why" she asked me, "long story" I replied, "you tell me one day, I wait" she put in and carried on massaging me, I had my shorts on and that was that, "too many tattoo's make you look like bad man, I think you good man but you look hard outside but soft inside" Tula said, I was nodding off, I grumbled a yes and laid still,

The massage took a good hour, she massaged everywhere except my privates, she clicked all my fingers and toes, snapped my knew which actually scared me, arms, legs, back front, face feet and hands, I felt so relaxed, I think I actually nodded off for a while too.

Tula slapped my leg and walked out, I felt I had said something wrong, I felt a bit confused, too much whisky I thought, I put my clothes on and went to the galley, she wasn't there, I could smell cigarette, I went up top, she was standing there looking out to sea, "penny for your thoughts" I said, "what that mean" she replied, "nothing really, you look serious, I worry" I put in, "I have too many problems here" she added!

I lit a cigarette and smoked with her.
We went back down to the galley, "drink" I asked, "ok then you rest, I stay here and watch out for you, I know you come from trouble, I let you know if I see something wrong ok" she said, I looked at her, she really meant it, "no way, we both sleep tonight, in my bed, I look after you" I replied!
Tula smiled and nodded, we finished our drinks and went to the cabin, she took off her clothes, I could see she was shy, she had a fit body, Tula got under the blanket, I did too,
"Goodnight Rhys" she said, "good night Tula, sweet dreams" I replied and turned off the side light, I turned over and put my arm around her, "thank you I like that" she whispered, I drifted off to sleep.
I awoke to the smell of cooking, I dreamt Tula robbed me through the night, thank god it wasn't true, I saw a nice person in her a person who need help, I decided I would help her, I liked her, and wanted her company for a while and some more,

I got dressed and went through to the galley, "something smells nice" I announced standing in the door way, Tula was startled, "oh you up, I thought I would make you breakfast for being a gentleman last night, I have never been treated like the way you treated me last night without having to give something back, you are a nice man Rhys" she exclaimed!
"Well what if I said get your arse in that bed sexy" I said, she looked shocked, I laughed, she laughed too,
I went up top for some fresh air she joined me, we smoked and drank strong coffee,
I heard kids shouting and saw the same one who helped me yesterday, they spoke in their language to Tula, "I must go Rhys, I have problem to sort out with my father, too bad" she announced!
"can I help" I told her, "no you no help, give you problem, you told me things last night, I think you drank too much and tell me too much, you have fuel and food, if you want to go then go, it was very nice to meet you, I have to go now" she put in looking very distressed!

"hang on" I told her and went below, I had hidden all the money and other stuff, I got to it and grabbed a load of cash, I rushed back up top, Tula was off the boat and into a small boat that the kids had brought, "one minute" I shouted, I rushed below, I put the money into a bag quickly and went back up, I threw the bag to her, she caught it and wiped her eyes, "I wish I could come with you" I shouted!, "no Rhys, bad for you, I go now" she replied and the boat pulled away, she waved until the boat went out of distance.

I sat down and lit a cigarette and did some thinking.

Too many things going through my mind, I went down below and found my flask, I filled it up and had a good drink, went up to the bridge and put in the coordinates for port Said that leads down the Suez canal into the sat nav, one hour and 12 hours down the river Nile into the Suez canal, I checked the boat, plenty of fuel and some spare in cans,

I was about to set sail, I had Carmem on my mind and felt a bit guilty paying too much attention to another woman, I was sure Carmem would want me to get on with my life, it was hard, I loved her so much!
I heard a boat sound and looked, there was an army boat coming into the cove slowly, I thought its game over now,
I had no way of escape, the boat got closer and there was a soldier standing on the front, he waved at me,

I waved back, he shouted something in their language, I made the gesture with my hand to say I don't understand, "hello are you lost" he shouted, "no sir, I came last night, it was getting dark, I found this place" I shouted back!
"We come and check boat sir, regulations" the soldier shouted!
"Ok ok yes fine" I replied!
The boat pulled up next to mine, "you are British sir" another soldier asked, he looked like the captain, "yes, I got lost last night" I told him,
He smiled, "why you come here, all foreigner's go to main marina" he asked me, "I got lost, it was dark, my sat nav went bonkers on me" I replied, "what is bonkers" he asked? I explained, he wasn't too happy and came aboard the boat,
"So what is your name sir, I need your identification and boat details" he told me, I knew I was in the shit!
"In the shit" the officer said,

"yes in the shit, in trouble, did not know where to go, too dark and found this place, some nice boys helped me out" I said, "young boys, all thieves and vagabonds around this area, you luck know one assaulted you here last night and stole your boat" the officer exclaimed!, he spoke in his language and another officer came on board my boat, "we have to search your boat, you are in a restricted area" the captain announced, "ok, just need to make sure my girlfriend is dressed, you might scare her and you look like a gentleman sir" I put in, I went below quickly and made my way to the front, I found two handguns, quickly checked them and stuffed them down the back of my trousers, I grabbed a few knives from the draw and put them under my belt, "darling you ok in there" I shouted!
I put a shotgun behind the cushions on the bench in the galley and went up top, "lady problems, she's been sick, it's a bit smelly down there sorry" I announced, I looked at their boat, I could see one man at the controls of the boat and another at the front of the boat tidying up some ropes,

"is it ok if we check your boat now sir, we have to follow rules" the English speaking officer exclaimed!

"sure" I put in, I was watching the two other men on their boat not paying too much attention, I followed the captain and the other crewmen down below, "I need to see paperwork for your vessel, your captains licence and some sort of proof of where you have come from, your passport for instance sir" he asked me!

I stared at him, "its ok darling it's just the shore police doing their checks, don't worry" I shouted, I started to look through some drawers, "its hear somewhere" I announced, the crew man went forward to the front bunk and the captain looked about, it was now or never.

I took the knives out in an instance, I silenced the captain in an instance and threw my other knife into the man who went forward, no noise, I checked and finished them off, I sat there and took a big swig from my flask, I took a peep through the small window and watched the two other sailors on the patrol boat.

The man at the front was just standing there looking at the shore, the driver was doing something, looked like he was texting, I made my move, I came out of the front hatch and jumped on their boat from the rear, their boat rocked, my mistake, the driver turned round, I shot him straight away the man at the front stumbled over the ropes and dropped his rifle, rookie I thought, I stared at him as he got up in shock, two shots rang out, one scratched my shoulder and I fell backwards, a sailor burst through a small door and took aim at me, I shot him twice in the chest, the man at the front jumped off the boat, I put bullets in him and he sank, I checked their boat for what I had no idea!

Their radio crackled and someone was talking in a language I didn't know!

I got on deck fast, I made the decision to sink their boat, and do a runner before people came looking for them.

My head went into panic mode, I took a swig from my flask, it worked, I jumped onto my boat and went to the front of the boat where the weapons were hidden,

I found some grenades but thought to much noise and smoke I took out the fifty calibre sniper rifle, make a lot of holes and let their boat sink, it was deep here, I dragged out the two bodies from my boat and slumped them below on their boat, I went below and fire off three magazines of bullets into the bottom of their boat, water sprung up everywhere, I thought about the investigation afterwards when they were discovered, didn't really matter I hopefully would be a long way away.
I got onto my boat and watched the police patrol boat slowly sink, I felt numb, four people gone because of me again, I felt a pain in my heart and worried about it, "shit not a good time for a stroke" I said to myself,
I got the shot gun and fired a few shots into the side of their boat, their boat went down a bit faster, sat in the bridge and checked the sea charts and set coordinates for an island in the Arabian sea as Moose had suggested, down the river Nile and into the Suez canal and onto Thailand, three days,

I made some quick calculations and worked out the fuel would hold till then as I had some spare in jerry cans, I looked out to sea and thought about Tula and Carmem, I smoked a cigarette, something was holding me back, I drank some more and watched the patrol boat sink, it took a good twenty minutes and I watched It go under, there was some debris that I pulled in, there was no trace of the patrol boat, the radio was on and the international news was talking about lost soldiers, I heard the Last Post being called out, I stood up saluted, I stood there for a good time until my arm ached, I went below to fill my flask then I was going.

I heard some shouting from outside and went up top, the kids from yesterday were on their small boat, I saw Tula sitting at the back of the boat, she waved, I suddenly was happy again, the kids were pointing to the water as if they could see something, Tula stood up, her face was bruised and scratched, "I came to say goodbye, I thought I would not see you Rhys" she said, their boat bumped against mine,

I pulled her on board, and looked at her, "bloody hell, who did this" I asked?
"My father and brother are bad, If I do not go out and massage people they get very angry,
I sat her down and went below for the first aid kit, I also put a load of cash into a small bag and went back up top, I wiped her face with an antiseptic wipe, she was crying, I will miss you Rhys, you are good friend to me, I don't have friends anymore because they think I bad girl do massages, I was pushed into it by my father, my real job is teacher" she replied and tears rolled down her cheek, "take care Rhys we see you again" she added, I just stood there looking at her, I felt pain inside, I sat down next to her and passed her my silver flask to her, she took a swig and coughed, "it pains my mouth" she said,
I passed her a cigarette, the kids were talking in their language, Tula looked over board at the water, "something happen here today" she asked, I looked at her, "that's a another story I tell you" I answered,

"so I have a plan, will you come with me and be my guest on my boat, I go to Thailand, I will look after you, I give money to your young brothers, what do you say, she smoked her cigarette and spoke to her younger brothers, they all smiled and laughed with joy,

She took the silver flask off me and had another sip, I watched cigarette fly into the sea, she smiled, "you no regret this I promise Rhys, friends for life" she said and put her arms around me, I threw the bag of money to one of her brothers, "what is that" she asked, "about thirty thousand British pounds" I said, she pushed away, "you crazy man" she growled, she spoke harshly to her brothers, they had looked inside the bag and were shocked,

They spoke back in their language, "Rhys I as a favour, can you take us round the island, I give my brothers to my other sister and Aunty, they will look after them and with amount of money they can buy some business and be good for life, why you have so much money to give away" she asked, "another long story Tula, I will tell you don't worry, we have a long journey ahead of us" I replied, she patted my shoulder, "I dream to meet someone like you" she said and then spoke harshly to her brothers, they hooked up their boat to the back of mine and got on board, "ok Skipper where are we going" I asked, "what is Skipper" she replied,

"you're the boss, show me where to take you and we need to have a storey if we get stopped or something" I put in, Tula looked at me strangely, "its ok, we go to tourist place, plenty of boats no problem there, where we are now is problem area of city, I glad to get out, you save my life and my brothers, thank you Rhys" she exclaimed. "Ok we go that way" she said and pointed, we sailed out of the cove and set off round the coast, I thought to myself and listened to her directions.

We sailed for a good two hours, right round the other side of the island, Tula had been talking on her mobile phone, and "she will meet us in the port" Tula said,

"Who" I enquired?

"my sister she ran away long time ago from the beating, my father killed my mother, bad mad with my older brother, he takes drugs with the money I earn from massage" she told me, I nodded, the boys were looking around the boat, one of them came up with the shotgun in his hand, "wow, carful there young man, it's loaded" I exclaimed, he passed me the shotgun,
"I think you have many things to tell me Rhys soon, I like to know everything about you, I tell you my life too, It very important for friends to communicate I think" she said, with here broken English I had to guess what she meant sometimes but it didn't bother me, I had to do that all the time with Carmem.
We carried on round the coast, "I make some food for my brother's ok" Tula said and went below,
I let the boys have their fun around the boat and sailed ahead, I was thinking of Carmem and feeling a bit guilty, and what was my intentions with Tula, I wasn't too sure myself.

We were closing to a busy port, Tula was on her mobile, I slowed the boat down, Tula pointed where to go, I found a space and stopped the boat, the boys were on the ropes and secured the boat with skill, they shook my hand, "take care of sister please, one of the lads whispered, I nodded, I got off myself, there was a lot of other boats here so I felt at ease, I was introduced to Tula's sister, she was a lot older, they both cried and talked a lot in the language, her sister kept smiling at me and nodding her head, I nodded back, I thought of a line for a dirty joke and stopped there, I was in a good mood, the kids were running around, I noticed two men in white uniforms walking towards us, and started to feel a bit uneasy, I started to play with the boys and jump about, the officers got closer, I saw that Tula noticed my change in manner and quickened things up, we all said our goodbyes and we got on board the boat and sorted things out, the officers were nearly at our boat when we pulled off, one of them shouted and waved to us, he raised his radio and talked into it, "what did he say" I asked Tula? "he wanted to know why we have no name or number on our boat" she said, I never even realised, "shit" I replied, every boat has to have a name or serial number, we had to get one quickly and maybe change the colour of the boat from black to a softer colour, I asked her if she knew where this could be done, "I can call my sister" she replied, she did and told me where to go, it wasn't too far, ten minutes and we pulled up along a wooden mooring point, there was other boats there, Tula got off the boat and talked to someone, a man came back to the boat with Tula, "you English man" he asked, "actually I am Welshman" I replied, "what is Welshman" he asked? Tula explained as I had told her, "ok Mr, I take boat inside, what colour you want and name, most important" he asked, I remember Carmem's favourite colour, green, I told him green, I went forward and whispered into his ear, the man laughed, "yes yes, good name sir, well done" he replied, he spoke to Tula in his language, "he say how you pay" "British pounds" I replied,

He got a calculator out and tapped away, "ok, I think five hundred British pounds" "you have a deal, how long it will take" I asked, "twenty four hours, paint to dry, three coats, under coat, over coat, the name, I think" he said straining his eyes,
I looked at Tula, "it will be fine, he is good friend of my sister's husband, I have told him how good you are and what you did for me" she said,
"ok so show me around the place, I tell you what, let me get some money and lets buy you some cloths mate" I announced, Tula pulled me to her and kissed me on the cheek, "you call me mate, like two wild deer's together, mate's for life" she said and laughed, "one minute" I said and claimed on the boat, I wanted to hide a few things and secure the money and weapons away from sneaky eyes, I filled my flask up and lit a cigarette, I jumped off the boat, I gave the thumbs up to the man who was going to sort the boat out and we walked off, Tula asked me for cigarette, I gave her one, we walked into town.

"Are you hungry" she asked, I nodded, she pointed to a café, "sit, I get us some drinks and food" she said.

I sat down outside this café, I lit a cigarette and looked around, the street was busy with people, and there was a lot of tourists about asking for information, Tula came out and gave me a glass of something, "salute" she said, I guessed she said cheers to me, "Yakidar" I replied and smiled,

"What is Yakidar" she asked? "My Welsh language, for cheers, same as Salute, or chin chin" I told her, Carmem used to say: "chin chin" when we drank together,

Tula smiled, a waitress came out and put a plate in front of me, I wasn't too sure what was on the plate, I looked at Tula, she smiled, "its baby hearts from rabbits with garlic and their own sauce, try, if you do not like I as for fish and chips" she said and laughed!

Tula passed me a cocktail stick, I watched her spike one of the hearts and eat it, I did it and chewed, the taste was quite amazing, the hearts were so small, the size of my thumb nail, they tasted really nice,

"Well, what can I say, wonderful" Tula smiled and ate,
I drank my drink, I didn't ask what is was, I tasted aniseed with something a bit stronger in it,
We finished the meal and I paid for it and left, Tula took me to where the main shops was, I saw a MacDonald's restaurant, "dog food" I commented!
She laughed, we found a cloths shop and went in, there was a café bar there, "ok I wait hear and you go and get what you ok" I said, she smiled and went off.
I sat there and had a local beer and thought about things,
I must of waited a for a good half hour, I went to the bar and asked if I could exchange some British money for some coins, I saw a gambling machine there, I pointed to it, I was given a load of coins and another beer that I had asked for, I noticed other people smoking here so I had a cigarettes myself and played the machine, I didn't know what I was doing, just put in the coins and pressed the buttons, my mind was a bit numb after what had happened,

The machine started to flash and a siren noise came out of it, I stepped back, I saw a line of four gold bars on the screen, coins kept coming out, it was quite loud, "chunck chunck chunck, for a good two minutes,
I noticed people looking at me, "Jackpot" I growled! I wish I never, two large lads came over to me, they spoke in their language, I put my hands out to say I don't understand, "must be a bit of the Welsh luck" I said, another mistake!

One of the lads spoke in an aggressive manner!

"Sorry lads, must be a bit of Welsh luck" I said,

"What is welsh luck, you are British yes" one of the lads asked?

"Yes I am British, is there a problem" I asked?

"British man on his own, where are your friends, you win big on machine, we play all day, have no jobs, you take our money" one of the lads said, "ok my friends, you have the money, I had fun, I wait for my friend she has gone shopping here, take it" I said and stepped back, "mother fucker" the other lad said and pulled out a knife, "you laugh at us I think with your money, I give you nice scar to remember us yes" he growled, the other lad picked up my empty bottle and held it up to swing at me.

I blocked his arm and grabbed his wrist, I twisted it round in a second, there was a snapping noise, at the same time I stuck my fingers in the eyes of the other lad before he could do anything, I kicked out and the lad with the knife flew backwards into some tables, I pushed the other lad away and he fell against the bar, I stood by the machine and finished my other bottle of beer,

People in the bar started to clap, some bar staff appeared and got rid of the two lads, police were outside talking in their language to the staff, and they approached me.

"You think you are James Bond sir" one of them said! He took out his hand gun,

"WO, hang on, I was playing the machine, I won the jackpot, these two men came over and started on me" I announced!

The two officers talked together and spoke two the bar maid,

"Ok sir, I need to see your passport please" one of the officers asked?

Tula appeared, she spoke in their language to the two officers,

They both looked at me, "enjoy your vacation sir and be careful" one of them said, they walked away,

I looked at Tula, "I don't know what you said but well done" I announced!

"What happened" she asked?

I told her and she pulled me out of the bar, there was still some people clapping their hands to me and talking in their language,

"Why you cause problem Rhys" she asked me?

I looked at her, "I don't know, It happens all the time, I am sorry, you hate me now" I said, "no, I just worry for you" she replied.

I paid the bill for her clothes and walked out, Tula followed me,

"Sorry" I said to her, I seem to attract trouble all the time, like a magnet" I growled!
Tula patted my shoulder, "I don't think so Rhys, there is trouble everywhere, you sort it out your way and you saw what happened, people clapped for you" she announced and smiled, I smiled back,
We walked down the street, my hands full of bags, we stopped at a little bar, "thank god for that" I commented, I gave Tula some money we had got exchanged a shop, she went in and ordered,
We sat outside and smoked, "so what did you get then" I asked, "I show you later, "salute" she said and raised her glass.
I asked he what we were going to do for twenty four hours,
"I think we find a nice hotel and relax, then pick up the boat tomorrow and you take me anywhere you want to Rhys" she said and giggled, I sensed the beers going to her head a little,
"Ok boss, let's find a hotel then and get sorted, would like to get a change of clothes for me though" I asked,

"I bought for you already" she replied, "thanks, can I see" I asked? "No, I show you later ok" she put in.

We finished our drinks, Tula talked a lot, she was excited and I was happy too,

We didn't walk too far, "here we go I think" she said and walked up the steps, I followed her and felt like a porter, I chuckled to myself,

Tula talked to the lady behind the desk, she looked at me, "one hundred and fifty pounds British with breakfast" she said, I nodded, "fine" I replied, she paid with the money I gave her earlier on,

We went up to the room, I was thinking what kind of room she had booked, a joining room, or two beds or something, we went to the second floor, Tula swiped the card on the door lock and we went in, the room was big, looked like an apartment, I was very surprised, there was a few doors, I guessed maybe I was in an adjoining room or something, I walked in to the main part of the place, there was a lounge bit with a big tv on the wall, I saw a double bed, I put all the bags on the bed and slumped down,

"wow, I feel knackered" I said and laid back.
Tula, started to pull things out of the bags, I watched!
There was some simple tops and trousers, some sexy knickers and bra's that got my attention, she passed me a pair of shorts and a top too match, I liked it, "thanks mate" I said,
Tula smiled and took out some more cloths on the bed, she was very happy and danced around the room, she went to the mini bar and gave me a beer, I went out to the balcony and had a cigarette and let her get on with her fun,
I could hear her singing away, "Rhys do you want a shower" she shouted!
I went back inside, Tula came over to me and hugged me, she kissed me on the cheek and pulled away, "sit down please" she ordered!
I sat down on the bed,
"I have not been this happy for years, you have changed everything for me, I don't know how to repay you" she said and started to cry, "just be my friend" I told her,

she shouted with joy and jumped on the bed next to me.

Tula was looking into my eyes, "let's go for a swim, there I is a gym and sauna here too" she said and smiled, "no trunks" I replied and smiled back, Tula went to one of the shopping bags and pulled out a pair of shorts, she threw them to me, "ha ha ha" I growled!

"Ok let's do it, then have a good meal and relax for the nigh, could watch a movie or something" I enounced,

Tula went to the bathroom, I was looking around the room, there was a nice sized TV on the wall, a fridge all the normal stuff, only one bed though which was going through my mind, I let it go as I didn't want to upset things, my thoughts for Tula were confusing as all my thoughts usually were for Carmem.

I turned on the TV the news channel came on, I saw a big boat pulling another boat out of the water, a police boat, I recognised where they were, the cove I spent the night and ran into a shore patrol, "Tula, Tula" I shouted! She came in, "what" she asked,

I pointed to the TV, "tell me what they are saying" I demanded!
"They say local police boat has been found sunk in taisa cove, four dead officers were found in the area police are looking into it" she told me, "Rhys what have you done" she asked?
"ok they came into the cove this morning early, they wanted to check me out, things got out of control, I had no choice, you really want me to be your friend, I'm a bad man sometimes" I said to her, Tula looked at me,
"You had no choice, like you said, not sure how you killed four men, you some kind of Rambo, I think I call and see how long boat will be" she announced,
I felt a bit nervous and had a drink, I went onto the balcony and had a cigarette,
It seemed a while I was out there when Tula came out, "will be ok now, you think we should go" she said, I nodded, "ok shame about hotel" she added, "there will be more times I promise you, I just hope I am not dragging you into my problems" I told her,

"My decision, I am a big girl now" she replied and lit a cigarette.

We went back inside and packed up some stuff, I grabbed the hotels bathrobe, "why you want that for" Tula asked, "it's just something I always do sorry" I replied, she laughed, "men" she announced!

We went down to reception and just walked out, nothing was said to us, and we made our way to the boat garage,

it took a good half hour, Tula spoke on her phone, "it ok boat is done, they just left off final coat of varnish spray, it is nothing" she told me,

We met the man who sorted the boat out, Tula spoke in her language and we went inside,

The boat looked good!

"we have to pay more money, he hears the news and says police are looking for a foreign black boat, he say we need to go away from here quickly, he doesn't want to know what happened just as long as he is paid well" she told me, I nodded, the man shook my hand.

"Looks good" I said,

Tula put her arms around me and kissed me on the mouth, she pulled away, "thank you Rhys" she said, and a tear ran down her cheek, she saw the name on the side of the boat, Tula.

I winked at the man and went on board, I found the place where I stashed the money and grabbed a load, I took it to the galley and quickly counted it, and there was a good five thousand British pounds, I took it out side and jumped off the boat, "here you go mate, your payment and a lot more for your troubled" I said, the man was counting the money, Tula translated what I had said, he was smiling and was very happy, he spoke in his language and shook my hand, he hugged me too and kissed both my cheeks,

"With that money here he can sort out his garage, he is very happy, we go now" Tula put in.

We got on the boat and the boatman opened the doors, we pulled out slowly and made our way up the river way to the opening to the sea, I set the sat nav to get us to take us to port Said then down the down the Suez canal, I told Tula,

"Rhys I hear they are strict there going through the port, you have a plan" she asked?

"Not really let's see what happens" I replied,

She looked at me worried, we set off to Port Said, and it wasn't too far.

The port was coming up.

We cruised into the port, a big area, there was a lot of other boats around like us, we sailed through and we weren't stopped, there was a lot of officers around on the dock not paying too much attention,
Tula waved and I saw some men wave back, we went through and into the Nile.
"Bloody el, that was easy" I said, "I heard there was security checks here,
I never been through here before" she told me,
"well my lady we are off, got a long way to go, 81 nautical miles, about three hours ish if we kept a speed of ten knots, that is about 18 miles an hour, could go faster but there was a speed limit on the Suez" I told her,
"I make some food for us,
I bring you up a nice drink ok" she added and went below.
The voyage down the Suez was romantic,

Tula brought me up a glass of something, with a tiny yellow umbrella in it, "salute" she said, I took a swig, "grrrrrrr, that's different" I exclaimed,

"Glad you like it, I wasn't too sure what I was doing to make it, has a bit of everything" she said, she smiled and went below,

I guided the boat down the Suez for about an hour, I could smell nice cooking smells from down below, there were a few boats around, tourists and work vessels, a patrol boat went by slowly having a good look at me, they went away, I was playing around with the radio and found some English speaking channel, they talked of the police boat that was sunk in the cove and the four murdered police men, they thinks it's to do with drugs and are looking for a dark coloured vessel and white persons, that was it, I paid no attention to it and finished my drink, I could hear Tula singing below and I smiled.

We sailed down the Suez for three hours, we saw pyramids and some other nice views,

Tula made some lovely fried beef sandwiches and some nice cocktails, talked and I told some shit jokes that made her laugh, like: "what's the main ingredient you put into gold soup? I had to explain what ingredients mean, "Nine carrots" I told her, she screamed and slapped my back, we had a laugh and smoked some cigarettes, and the end of the Suez was coming up,
We could a large area of water ahead, the gulf of Suez, I calculated we would have enough fuel and supplies to get us across the Red sea and stop off somewhere before we go across the gulf of Eden, could take five days ish depending how fast we go, distance was roughly 1134 nautical miles, we pushed on into the Red sea, it was a bit rough and was starting to get dark now, I spent a lot of time teaching Tula how to navigate the boat, I showed and taught her everything I knew, she took it all in and I was very impressed with her, I told her a lot about myself, never spoke so much for a long long time, she listened and nodded, Tula told me a few things about her, but mainly she wanted to know about me,

she looked shocked with something's I told her, I let her take control and went to where the bags were hidden under the floor decking in the front bunk, I took out a handful of emeralds and went up top, I put the boat on auto pilot and told her to sit down on the small wooden bench,
I moved out of the way the sea charts and passed her a bottle of beer,
"Salute my friend" I said and raised my bottle and took a good gulp,
She did also, I looked at Tula,
 "I have told you things about me that I would never ever tell, I have something for you" I whispered,
Tula gave me a hard stare, "I hope you are not going to get down on your knee or something like that, you're worrying me Rhys, Tula lit a cigarette and watched me put my hand in her pocket,
"Relax I wouldn't let you marry a scumbag like me anyway, I opened the pouch and poured the emeralds out onto the table,
"Oh my god, these are emeralds,

Tula looked at the stones in astonishment.

"I only see these things in expensive shops, they real" she said, "they don't look like much at the moment, these are raw emeralds, they need to be cut up and polished, they are for you, so put in your pocket and say no more, where ever we end up, well get them polished up for you, I recon they are worth about fifty thousand pounds, not too sure" I announced,
Tula just looked at me quiet,
"why you give me" she asked quite sternly,

"they say money can't buy love, don't buy me Rhys, you don't have to, all I want is you to be my friend and look after me, I see in your eyes when I first met you, someone in pain, and a good person, I love what you give to me, thank you, you are here" she said and patted her heart, I grabbed her hand and kissed it, "salute" I said and raised my bottle, we both drank for a while and played with the emeralds on the table. The boat rocked about so I took control, Tula was next to me, she passed me a cigarette, "could be a rough night my deer" I announced, she shrugged her shoulders and went out the back, the wind blew in, "be careful out there, you have no life jacket on, I thought of Carmem, Tula get in here, we hit some big waves, I shouted again, Tula came in, sorry Rhys, I put on life jacket" she replied and put on, new rules on this boat for ladies, oh you're the only lady here, life jacket will be worn at night and if it starts to get rough okeekokee" I growled, "yes captain" she replied and saluted, "now go get a mop and swab the deck sailor" I said, I did the action of mopping up,

she got it and laughed, she came over and kissed me quickly and went down below, I felt too confused, mixed feelings, missing Carmem too much, taking Tula on to hide the pain, I really had feeling for Tula, I wasn't too sure how she felt about me, I had a drink and smoked a cigarette, the boat was rising and falling with the wave, I kept her in control, I heard something smash down below, I shouted to Tula, she said, "all ok, making a desert for you, plate smashed only" I looked out to sea and watched the sat nav, I was thinking what to do through the night, I didn't want to moor up, just wanted to get as far away as possible, I would let Tula navigate for an hour or two, then take over, the red sea at night was very dark, I could see in the distance, lights on boats, it was then I realised we had no lights on, I looked around and found a switch, I flicked it and we had outside lights, I giggled to myself, "fool" I whispered!
"I heard that, you no fool" Tula came up with a bowl of something, she placed it on the table and held onto it.

The weather was calming down a bit, I set the boat to auto pilot and sat down next to her, "looks good" I said,
"Soufflé "she announced, "you amaze me, you made this in that small galley, well done" I announced, she put a spoon into it and passed to me, "for you, I have never made this for anyone" she said, I nodded and tried it, it was great, we finished it all.
"Ok I think you can take control of the boat for a while, I get some rest for a bit and take over" I said, she nodded, I took Tula through a few things and went below, I laid on the bed and went to sleep.
I opened my eyes, there was daylight coming in through the port hole in the bunk, I looked at my watch, 05:30, I thought I was dreaming, I got out of bed and went to the galley, there was some music playing softly, I could smell cigarette smoke, I put a warm top on as there was a cold draft coming in,
I realised what was going on, I heard Tula talking on her mobile phone and laughing, I started to make coffee and toast,

I was a bit annoyed but very impressed with her, I took up the coffee and toast, "hello you, someone been a naughty girl I think" I said, Tula turned round quickly, "I sorry Rhys, I wanted you to rest and I wanted to do this for me, I know we have a long way to go, I want to help you" she replied,
"Thanks mate, good girl, now we have some breakfast and you rest and that's an order lady" I ordered!
Tula nodded, she looked tired, "so how was it then, on your own sailing through the night" I asked, she looked at me, "got scared a few times, nearly called for you, got a bit rough and I went off the sat nav a few times, had to fight the wheel to get back on course, you were snoring in a deep sleep" she told me,
"I am proud of you Tula, I leant to her and went to kiss her, she turned her head so I kissed her cheek, she smiled at me,
"naughty boy" she said and laughed.
We finished breakfast and Tula left me to control the boat, we another two days to go across the red sea.

I was glad we had got far away from Said port, I heard her cleaning up and then there was quiet, I guessed she had gone to sleep, I sailed on, it got a bit rough and then it was good.

I sailed for a good eight hours, I finished my flask and smoked a few fags, I had the stereo playing and sang along when I recognised the music, I heard a noise from below and Tula came up with some sandwiched, "hi, you want something to eat mate" she said and came up, she put the plate on the table and came to me, she gave me a big hug and kissed my cheek, "I sleep too long I think, feel good though" she announced, she kissed my cheek again and sat down, I joined her, the boat was set to auto pilot, "how far to go" she asked? "oh too far yet mate, I think tonight we try and moor, park this thing somewhere and have a nice night and relax" I said, "ye if you can, I can make a nice meal" she replied, I smiled and went back to the controls, Tula cleared up and went below.

I carried on driving the boat for a few more hours, Tula popped up all the time with snacks and drinks, we chatted and had a good time, a few big boats went past and waved at us, we carried on, I checked the charts, there was nowhere to moor so we kept on sailing through the night, we took it in turns to navigate the boat and got to the end of the red sea,

We sailed into the Gulf of Eden, I had made a mistake with my calculations, it would take another two days sailing across the gulf to an island called: Samhah island, I told Tula this and she looked a bit stressed but carried on as normal, food was made, plenty of drinks flowed, we had a good laughs, long chats and took it in turns to navigate the boat, we had spare fuel thank god that we had to use and carried on.

It was getting late, Tula made a good meal that we shared in the bridge, the sea was steady, we had quite a few drinks and I told her some more stories, Tula was dancing around and went below to get some more drinks and snacks, I decided to put the boat on autopilot for the night.

there was nowhere to moor, we drank some more and had a good chat, it was late now, two in the morning, the sea was calm and we cruised on at a modest speed, ten knots, Tula came up wearing a silky nighty, she looked stunning, she had put on extra makeup,

We had a dance to some foreign music and she singed, I told her I had set the boat to autopilot so we could have a good night and relax, "you fancy a shower" she said,

I nodded, "will be nice" I replied,

"With me Rhys" she put in,

I looked at her and nodded with a smile,

I checked the sat nav and everything was in order, I slowed the boat down to ten knots and we went below.

The shower was running and Tula was in there singing and washing and dancing, there was music on the loud speakers,

I quickly got undressed and stood outside the shower with a towel around me, I tapped on the glass door, Tula turned around, she had a fit body, average sized breasts, "wow" I commented, she screamed!, "I not know you come in yet,

come in Rhys" she said, she smiled and I walked in, my towel fell off,
We looked at each other, "what do you think of me Rhys, Tula asked, he body was against mine, I had my hands on her hips, "I have a lot of mixed feelings, I lost my partner, my best friend in the whole world, I met you and did not expect how I much I would think of you as I do, your younger than me, not too much, I know you have feelings for me, ok now I'm talking shit" I said, I kissed Tula, and she responded passionately, our bodies touching each other, I turned the water off and we went to bed.
I awoke to the smell of bacon, I remembered last night and smiled, I could hear Tula singing, I thought to myself, how do I deserve this lady, I am a drunk half of the time, she was beautiful, with a great body and was not shy in the bed, I banged the wall and thought of Carmem and felt guilty, I got dressed and went through to the galley,

"Hello gorgeous, I missed you" I said, "hm, I have little sleep, you noise through night like a bear I think" she laughed after saying it, "sorry if I sleep on my back I snore, you should of pushed me" I replied, "I tried, you like dead dog, no move" she growled, "sorry" I said and gave her a hug, she kissed me on the mouth, "we good together yes, I waited to see if I can trust you, I have been hurt so many times, I see a good man and I take you" Tula said,

I looked at her, I wasn't too sure what to say, I smiled and sat down, the boat was rocking away, I watched her then decided to check the sat nav and went up top, I slapped her bum and kissed her neck as I passed, she giggled and carried on sorting out our breakfast.

It was raining and the surf started to get a bit rough, there was thick fog outside and visibility was poor,

I corrected the boat as we had gone off course a bit, the fog was getting thicker, I was checking the sea charts when Tula came up with bacon and fried egg sandwiches, "yes my favourite darling" I said, "oh dear I can't see anything, is it bad" she put in, "its ok, we follow the sat nav and watch the scope here, no other crafts around us so we are ok, like sailing a bit blind but it will be ok" I told her, she smiled at me and sat down to eat the sandwiches,

We had another days sailing across the red sea, then onto the gulf of Eden,

where we would have to stop off and get fuel and supplies, the sea chart showed a small island called: Socotra,

I called to Tula that the island was coming into view, she came up top with me and massaged my neck, Tula googled it on her phone, "small fishing island, inhabitants around 100, not much news on it" she said, "good a nice quiet place to stop for the night, stretch our legs and maybe sleep on a bed that doesn't rock" I added, she smiled at me.

I sailed around the small island at distance, doing my recce before I closed in and found a good quiet place to moor,

The island reminded me of the isle of white in proportion of size and shape, we closed in.

An old fishing boat sailed past and the crew waved at us, we waved back, I found a place to moor, there was one boat there with an old man on deck moping away,

I waved at him and he waved back, Tula spoke in her own language as I suggested and the old man replied, she asked if was ok to stay here for a while and we need fuel and supplies, "he said its ok and there is a town shop over there" she said.

We secured the boat, Tula gave the old man some money to watch our boat and get us some fuel and we went in search of the shop.

As the old man had said the shop wasn't far, there was about six old stone buildings badly in need of restoration, this was not a wealthy place, a heard of goats came round the corner with an elderly farmer, he spoke in a language I didn't recognise, Tula spoke back!

The farmer pointed to another building and we walked towards it.

Tula walked in, a few people were giving us some hard stares as we walked off the small street,

The door squeaked open and I shut it behind me, it was quite breezy outside.

The shop was full of all sorts of stuff, I felt as if I had gone back in time, tall shelves full of stuff in no order, I recognised a pack of noodles, Tula passed me a basket and we walked around, "what the hell is this" I asked her, I held up a jar with something in oil inside, "It's a sea urchin, it's a delicacy, you forget you are not in your country, there is no burger king here" she replied and smiled, I laughed, someone moved out from behind another shelf, a young lady and spoke in a foreign language, Tula spoke back and they laughed, I smiled and walked around the shop, I found a nice little pen knife with a torch on it and lots more interesting stuff, we filled three baskets and went to a small counter to pay, Tula spent the last of her money paying for all the stuff.

I let Tula pick the food as I didn't recognise much, I picked out some strange sausages and what looked like bacon, I saw a tin of carnation milk, "haven't had this for years" I told her, I filled my basket with man stuff, junk, Tula kept shaking her head I grabbed things and commented on it,

We left the shop with quite a few bags, some small boys ran to us, "let them take the bags Rhys" Tula said to me, the boys took the bags off us and walked ahead, "you will have to pay with your British money now, I don't have anymore, she exclaimed, "shit we have to pay for the fuel" I put in, "I think we might have small problem" Tula replied,

We got to the boat, there was another boat next to our with an a man holding a hose into our fuel tank, "I thought that was locked" I said as we got closer, the man spoke out in Arabic or something and Tula spoke back, she looked at me a bit worried, "he has filled our two tanks and our spare cans at the back, we need to pay Egyptian pounds" she told me,

"Will he take British money" I asked?
Tula spoke to the man again,
"What he say" I asked?
"He say British money no good here, he only wants Egyptian pounds "she announced!
"Well what now" I exclaimed!
Tula shook her head and spoke to the man, he looked annoyed and started to wave his hands around, two younger men climbed off the other boat in front of us and walked towards our boat, the man that gave us fuel was shouting now and pointing to the town we had come from,
The young boys had put our bags on the boat and stood there watching,
Tula had climbed on our boat to talk to the man, I was watching the two approaching lads who were now talking loudly at Tula, I saw an ugly situation coming on so I got onto the boat myself, the man started to shout at me, "Tula ask him if I can pay with some precious stones, the emeralds" I told her, Tula pulled out an emerald from her pocket, I thought good girl,

Tula screamed and fell over, the old man gave her a good slap across the face, he was still shouting and went towards Tula, the two young men had climbed onto the boat and came for me, I saw one of them pull a knife out of his pocket and he came for me. I dodge the blade and grabbed his wrist and twisted as hard as I could, there was a distinctive snapping noise, the other landed a punch on the side of my head, I spun around and gave two blows to his stomach as I dragged the other lad to the floor, the knife was on the floor, Tula screamed! I felt a strong pain in my shoulder and spun around the other lad was standing there with the knife, I realised he had stabbed me in the fight, I kicked the lad on the floor between his legs, he was finished for now, the lad with the knife lunged at me again, I jumped back and fell over the fuel hose pipe, I scrambled backwards over the shopping bags, the young lad jumped towards me, I felt the penknife I had just purchase in the shop under my hand, I clicked the blade out and threw it as hard as I could.

it hit the approaching lad in the chest and he went over the side, his mate was moaning on the floor, I could hear Tula struggling around on the front of the boat and made my way to her, the old man was on top of her, it looked like he was trying to have his way with her, which I couldn't believe, she clawed his face and he slapped her again, he was fumbling around with trousers and between her legs talking in a serious way, I shouted out!

He turned towards me, just in time to catch my foot in his face, the old man rolled over, his penis hanging out, I kicked him again and again as hard as I could, he rolled over the side, Tula laid there crying and holding her ripped dress and top, she growled out in her language!

"You ok" I asked, she nodded, "get below quickly" I ordered!

She did I asked, as I took the fuel pipe out of our boat, I heard Tula scream out so I went back, I grabbed a mooring hook from side and climbed onto the roof,

The other lad with snapped arm had grabbed Tula, she pushed him away as I threw the hook at him, the hook stuck in the lad knocking him off the back of the boat, Tula looked at me and went below quickly, The young lads who had brought our bags had untied the ropes for me, I saw the emerald Tula had on the deck and threw it to one of the boys, he caught it and shouted back, I wondered he knew what that one emerald was worth, I started the boat up and pulled away, I felt a thump on the side of the boat but ignored it, the engine at the rear made a strange noise and I lost power for a second, the boat shuddered and we moved off.

I heard Tula shouting in her own language holding a gun in her hand, I noticed all the sea water behind us was bright red in colour.

We sped off to a good distance, no one followed us so I slowed the boat down, I set the boat to auto pilot heading in a northerly direction and went down to the back of the boat to see Tula.

She just standing there looking out to sea, I put my arms around her and gave a good hug, she cried and hugged me back, "Thank you Rhys" she sobbed,
"was all that red water you're doing" I asked, she shook her head, the motor got him, I was going to shoot anyway" she replied, "I thought so, let's get out of here mate" I exclaimed!
I went to kiss her but she pulled away, "no, I dirty now, I go and wash see you later" she said and went inside, I went back to the wheel house and took control of the boat again, I had a good drink from my flask and thought about what had just happened.
Tula came up after a good few hours, I left her sort things out, a woman's thing, and she was ok, just a bit roughed up,
"I am ok I am stronger than I look" she said and put her arms around me,
we kissed and hugged each other for a while, she pulled away,
"so where to now captain" she asked?

"well my lady, we get across this area and then there's one more stretch to do, I am hoping we won't need to refuel again and go through shit again, I need to change this money into different currencies I think, American dollars, everyone recognises the dollar" I announced Tula nodded, "four days at the most at this speed" I told her, "we have enough food for that, I will make you a traditional Israel meal tonight, you sail I cook, we take turns through the night, get there quicker yes" she exclaimed, "I will miss your warm body against mine though" I commented, she smiled, "plenty of time for that when we get to Thailand" she said I made a moaning noise and looked away playing, she kissed me again passionately and put her hand down the front of my trousers and caressed me, I was hard, she sat on the small stool next to the steering wheel and lifted her dress and pulled me into her, we made love and held each other, I had one hand still on the steering wheel, "see, we can make love and still drive the boat" Tula said.

I smiled and we both started to laugh, we tidied ourselves up and Tula went below, I was still smiling when she came up with two glasses, "cocktail for you" she said and passed me the glass, "salut" she said and we both had a drink, "good, what do you call that one" I asked, "a quickie" she replied, "I do like a good quickie" I replied, "you want another quickie later then" she asked fluttering her eyelids, I made a growling nose and we both laughed.

Tula stayed up top with me for a while, we smoked and enjoyed each other's company. The meal that night was fantastic, the satnav was set and the boat was on auto pilot, what Tula cooked in the small galley was amazing, the different tastes were lovely, she made a desert from the condensed milk that was great too, we cleaned up and went up top to take control of the boat, the sea was calm, Tula was steering the boat, she flicked her cigarette into the sea, I was behind her rubbing myself against her bum, we were both wearing thin clothes so we could both feel each other,

I kissed her neck slowly and massaged her shoulders softly, she leant her head back and smiled, "fancy a quickie" she whispered, I smiled and kissed her neck, I could feel she had no knickers on, nor did I, my hands were now round her front and caressing her breasts, I raised her dress up slowly, she was breathing heavily and still steering the boat, she leant over the small stool, I pushed forward, there was no friction, she wanted me.

We took it in turns to control the boat through the night and carried on the same routine for the next three days, there was plenty of quickies thrown in too, we enjoyed ourselves, Tula cooked some great dishes, we were happy together, but getting tired of all this sailing, I told Tula we should coming into Thai waters soon, she was happy and made us some drinks. We had been lucky with the weather all the way here but now it was getting rough, the boat was bumping around,

the waves were getting big and we rose and fell with them, things in the galley fell out of the cupboards and I heard a few smashing noises, Tula's voice shouted out a few time, she came up to me, "are we in trouble" she asked?
"sat nav's playing up, I'm heading on the last reading from the sat nav, North west towards Phuket, I have heard it is a nice play, not too busy, maybe a few hours, just hope the sat nav sorts its self out" I announced.
I was a bit concerned about the direction I was heading I was not hot with the sea charts and baring's at sea, Moose had taken me through it a few times, I wished I had paid a bit more attention to him a bit more, I knew one thing that before the sat nav went bananas that we were still on the same course as the sat nav indicated, Tula went below and tried to secure things as the rocked about, she came back up with my flask, "I tried to google the weather, no signal" Tula shouted to me and went below, I was fighting with the wheel, speeding up the waves and slowing coming down,

Moose told me that's the best thing to do when in severe weather, I fought on for a good hour, we took on a lot of water, Tula had her life jacket on as ordered my me, I had mine on too, bad memories of people not wearing life jackets and accidents happening then it's too late, I thought if Carmem and fought with the waves, I was glad it wasn't dark, would have been a lot worse.

The bad weather battered us for a good two hours, Tula had to go below as she banged her head, things smashed in the galley and we were taking on a lot of water, we had no sat nav, just sailing on the compass on the last safe heading before things went bananas, the rain was heavy and the sky was a dark grey, we had no network coverage for our phones, nothing, sailing blind, I kept wishing every wave we went up I would see something, there was nothing, just sea, big waves and rain.

I heard Tula scream but I couldn't get down to her, I shouted to her!

I fought with the wheel, it was very hard to steer, I looked at my watch, I remembered what the sat nav said a few hours ago, we should be nearing the coast of Thailand by now, maybe we had gone off course and missed the islands completely, I remember they have tsunami waves here occasionally, it felt like we were riding worse,
Another big wave hit us and I flew against the wall of the bridge, I watched the steering wheel spin around, I tried to get up and was thrown back, I hear Tula scream below!
The boat jerked hard and there was a crashing noise, the windows in the bridge all smashed, Tula screamed again!
I slid across the floor and smashed my head into the door, the boat was all over the place, I dragged myself to the stool next to the steering wheel and pulled myself up, I grabbed the steering wheel and fought with it, there was nothing there, it felt like we had power steering, i wasn't too sure what to do, I guessed we had lost the rudder to the boat so now no one was steering this thing,

I couldn't see anything out of the broken windows because of the rain and the spray coming off the waves, I scrambled my way down below, I was shouting for Tula!

I fell down the steps into the galley, there was stuff everywhere, I shouted for Tula again!

The boat flung sideways with a thud, there was a crashing noise from up top, water was coming in, I shouted for Tula again!, I crawled down the corridor into the front bunk, "Tula" I shouted, I heard her scream from the corner of the room, "come on, we need to get the speed boat sorted, the boat is knackered" I wondered what I just said to her, I knew the speed boat attached to the rear was gone some time ago, I pulled her up, she threw her arms around me, "I love you Rhys" she said when the boat jerked again, we both flew onto the bed, "don't even think about a quickie" I told her, she laughed and fell off the bed as the boat swung to the left, we both made our way to the galley, there was a lot of water in the boat now,

"Are we sinking" Tula asked? I nodded at her and pulled her forward with me.
The boat came to a sharp stop, fell forward and Tula fell on top of me, "what now" I shouted, the boat was filling with water, the boat tilted to the left, things smashed!
I got myself out to the back of the boat.
We were on top of rocks, the waves were smashing into us and knocking us about, I went back below,
I told Tula to stay in the galley as I went forward to the front bunk and pushed the bed aside, I pulled up the floor boards and grabbed the holdalls, "I need a hand mate" I shouted!
Tula showed her face, there was blood on her cheek, "What" she replied, I passed her one of the bags, and "take it to the back of the boat" I commanded!
I grabbed the rest of the bags and two rifles and started to make my way to the back of the boat.
I heard Tula scream, the boat tilted over, I fell over against the side of the wall, water was coming in fast now, I had no strength, I sat there and thought to myself,

"game over my friend" I whispered, I thought of Carmem, "see you soon mate" I said and sat there in the cold water, the boat rocked over and I fell over again, a rifle fell into my lap, I looked at it.
"This is not the last post" I growled!
I got up and slung the rifle over my shoulder I dragged two of the holdall bags with me as I made my way through the galley, I shouted to Tula, there was no reply, I got up to the back of the boat, the weather was starting to get a bit better, the rain had stopped,
I got myself outside, there was no sign of Tula, the bag I gave her was next to the bench, I shouted for her!
The boat had smashed onto some rocks at the base of a large cliff, the boat moved again,

I pulled the bags out with me and quickly tied some life jackets to the carry handles of the bags, I shouted again for Tula!
There was no reply, the rain stopped and the waves stopped banging the side of the boat, it got brighter and the bad weather just went away, so unreal I thought to myself.
I sat there looking into space, water all around my legs, I saw my silver flask and grabbed it and had a drink.
I don't know how long I sat there for, when I heard someone shouting!
I got up and saw Tula standing on the beach waving at me.
She was shouting in her language, I sensed she was swearing at me and I was right as she was shaking her fists at me!
"Hello darling, fancy a quickie" I shouted, bad move, she shouted back in her language!
I threw the bags off the boat and stuck some guns in the other bags, the front of the boat was completely smashed up, "thank you mam" I said and saluted the boat, Tula was still shouting at me!

She came over to me limping, I pushed the bags over the side of the boat and fell over with them as the boat rocked.

I laid on the rocks, looking up at the now clear sky, I thought I was in a bad dream, I thought of Carmem.

"Rhys, rhys" I heard someone calling out! I tried to talk but I couldn't, everything went black.

I opened my eyes, my head was hurting, I ached all over, there was a fan spinning above my head, I could see a window with rain hitting it, I was on a bed, there was a tube coming from my arm with a solution being pumped into me, I pulled the needle out and blood went everywhere for a minute,

I closed my eyes and tried to remember what had happened.

I remember helping Tula to get off the boat before we got smashed up on the rocks, we had the bags off the boat and Tula was pulling them further up the rocks with difficulty,

After that I remember nothing, my head was aching and I laid on the bed,
The door opened and a nurse came in, "what has happened here" she screamed!
"Where am I" I asked, "you are in hospital, you had a bad knock to your head sir" she said.
"Who brought me here" I added?
"Young lady call for help from the beach, your boat is destroyed, you are lucky to get off it, you were trapped, lady not able to get you off the boat, she get help for you, she save your life, you stay her for three days, in concussion, I think you ok now, I need to do checks on you before doctor comes, you in mess now, why you pull out needle, it just to help you get energy back" she told me and started to clean me up.
I let her get on with it, the door opened a gain and Tula walked in, she saw me and smiled, "you awake now, fantastic, I worry too much for you" she said and came over and hugged me,
"So you saved me then" I said,
She nodded at me and cried.

"I go for help, you got trapped on the boat, a door was on your leg and you bang your head bad, you pass out, I not strong enough to pull you off the boat, I went for help, they get you off boat just in time before it went under the water" she told me, "you're a good girl Tula, I owe you so much" I replied.
"You owe me nothing Rhys, I am just so happy to see you ok" she put in, she started to cry, "Hey no tears now, did you get things off the boat" I asked and winked at her, she nodded and gave me the thumbs up sign,
"I have a hotel for us not far from here, when you are ready to leave the hospital" she announced.
The nurse left us,
"Tula the bags with the money and the weapons, where are they" I asked quietly,
"I sorry Rhys I lost them" she said and smiled,
"Oh well, easy come easy go, never mind" I said and looked really disappointed,

"I joke with you, I get them off boat and hide in a small cave in the rocks while you were being saved, I do not know how I did it, I was exhausted, I make sure no one see me, I check every day, they are still there, hard to get to, the water is strong there, I show you when you are better" she added,
"I'm better already" I announced, I got out of bed instantly, "we need to get those bags where we can keep our own eyes on them, too much to lose" I announced!
"Ok ok, I think we need to wait for doctor to come like the nurse said, then we leave with no problems ok" Tula exclaimed,
I nodded and got dressed, Tula had brought me some fresh cloths,
"Thanks, good taste, my size too" I told her,
"I think I know everything about you know Rhys and more" she added and smiled,
"I smiled back, "you dirty girl, fancy a quickie" I said, "stop it" she said and helped me get dressed,
The door opened and a doctor came in,
"Mr Evans, you are looking much better, than when you came to us, I am thinking you can leave us as long as you feel ok",

"No strong headaches you have" he asked, "no doc, I feel great sir, thanks for looking after me, how much we owe you" I asked, "no pay here, we are a charity hospital, Miss Tula has made a very nice contribution already, thank you very much, now look after yourself, if you start to feel dizzy and get strong headaches please come back ok" the doc said and walked out, me and Tula packed what little I had in the room and left, there was a jeep outside, "you want to drive" she asked and pointed to the jeep, I looked at her and smiled, "why not, you seem to have everything in control, I like this a lot, me and you are going to do well together" I told her,

We jumped into the jeep and pulled off, Tula told me where to go, the track to the beach was rough and very bumpy, I started to get a headache, Tula told me to stop, so I did, we walked round climbed round the rocks, the waves were splashing strong, she pointed to what was left of a boat, "that's our boat" I exclaimed, there was nothing left, bits and pieces all over the rocks, "shit" I put in, "we have some climbing to do, don't ask me how I got the bags in there, panic, shock, I don't know, I just did it and helped the men get you out of that boat" she told me, I pulled her to me and gave her a big kiss, she kissed me back strongly, "come on before the water gets high and strong again, she announced!

I followed Tula across the rocks and to a narrow gap in the rocks, "in here" she said and went in, she went to the back of the small cave and pulled a bag from behind some rocks, "here you go captain, your treasures are here for you, I borrowed some and changed at the bank to pay for things, I came down here every day in swimming cloths and snorkel to look as if I was trying to salvage things from our boat, I stayed on the beach the first night to watch, I nearly froze to death" she exclaimed, "you just keep on amazing me mate" I told her,

Tula went to the jeep and took out my flask, "here big boy I think you deserve this" she said and poured me a drink,

She took a swig first then handed me the cup, I knocked it back, it burnt my throat but warmed me up, I had been off the booze for three days, no wonder I was feeling wonky, Tula could see it, she said I seemed different, I wasn't too sure if that was a good thing but ignored it, We lit two cigarettes and enjoyed the moment.

We got the bags loaded onto the jeep, it was hard work getting over the rocks with the waves smashing in, I don't know how Tula did it on her own, I thought to myself, "So what now" I asked her? "I have booked a nice hotel you will like it" she said, I asked her she minded to drive back as I had a pounding headache, Tula noticed I was in stress, "you want to go see the doctor" she asked, I just told her to get some strong painkillers and I will be fine, we set off.

It didn't take long to get to the hotel and we took the bags in, a boy helped us and we tipped him, we got to our room on the first floor and dumped the bags on the bed.

"we need to split the money up, I think, find a bank and set up an account" I said, "I already did it in my name, hope you don't mind,

I had to sort things out whilst you were in hospital" she told me, "do you mind if I fall in love with you madam" I announced, Tula laughed, "fancy a quickie" she said with a smile, "what do you think" I answered!
We jumped on the bed and made love, I laid on the bed and Tula gave me a massage and I fell asleep, my headache had gone, I was happy, I dreamt of Carmem.
I heard Tula's voice, "sleepy head, you ok" she called out, I saw her come out of the shower, and she looked sexy,
"Sorry I fell asleep, you made me feel so relaxed" I replied,
"No problem, I know you are still on the mend" she said and laid on the bed next to me, chatted and cuddled,
"so what now" I asked, "I don't know Rhys, we stay here for a while, see what happens, maybe, we can buy a property or something, I don't know" she said, I laid back on the bed and thought about things, Tula got up and went to the fridge, she passed me a beer, "here you go, drink that and tell me what we do next, you are the boss" she said,

"No bosses with you and me ok and I mean that, we do things together and decide together ok" I out in, Tula smiled and went to the small kitchen and potted around.
I thought of Carmem again.
"ok, we go out and see what's going on with this island, I don't fancy going to the main land of Thailand, too busy, too much corruption, I like the idea of an island for now, I think, wow, what do I think, what do you think" I said, "has that beer gone to your head already" Tula asked, "not too sure baby, let's get dressed and have a look around" I told her, "I have already looked around, the main town is a busy place, lots of bars with girls for rent, massage parlours, hotels, there is a shooting range on the island somewhere, there are diving schools and boat trips, I have heard the police are not very strict her, there is a gang who looks after most of the bars and girls, there is a lot of private villas rented by foreign people with a Thai partner, for a small island there is a lot going on" she told me,
"Wow, you have been busy, well done on the recce mate" I exclaimed.

We sorted ourselves out and hid the bags of cash and weapons, I pulled the wardrobe away from the wall and did my tricks, with the help of my pen knife, and went out.
It was hot and humid as we went outside, we jumped into the hired jeep and I drove off, Tula directed me, we drove down the main strip, it was early so there wasn't too much going on, lots of bars with people of all ages drinking and chatting with the bar girls, young boys ran to us wanting to clean the jeep or our shoes etc., we drove on slowly,
"what if we had a bar, crazy idea yes" I said, "never thought about working a bar" Tula replied, we drove on, "I have qualifications for scuba diving, could run my own school, you could to trips around the island by boat, I don't know, I need a drink" I said, "ok" Tula replied and we pulled over next to a bar we found on a road close to the sea out of town.
We jumped out of the jeep and went to the bar.

The bar was quiet, there was two standing there looking bored, when they saw us they called us over and was all happy and giggly, me and Tula sat on stools by the bar under a sun canopy, I asked for two beers and was given them, they were cold,

"lovely" I said as I took a swig, there was a pool table at the back of the bar that was looking at, "you want to play" one of the bar girls asked in broken English, I saw Tula's eyes on me, the two girls at the bar were wearing not too much, they were young and flirty, asking too many questions and that, just being friendly to us, one of the girls brought a game to us, she showed Tula how to play, a dice game, the other girl wanted me to go and play pool with her, "go one then, I'm watching you mate" she said!

I got up and went to the pool table with the young lady, I saw Tula watching me, she smiled, and "you want another beer dear" she called out! "Yes please dear" I replied and smiled at her, the young girl set up the balls on the table.

I broke off and potted a red and carried on, I potted another four balls then it was her turn, she laughed and giggled round me, as I went past her to take my shot her hand brushed my leg, I looked at Tula, she didn't see it, we carried on playing the game when Tula came through, she passed me a bottle of beer, "who's winning then" she asked, "he very good" the young girl announced, "I'll give you a game next mate" Tula put in and waited for us to finish,
"ok game on, loser gets the drinks in" I told her, she smiled and passed to me the balls from the pockets, the young girl went back to the bar, Tula had asked for some light snacks, she came close to me, "I think the other girl out there is a lesbian, she was getting too friendly with me, kept touching my hand yuk" Tula announced,
"Wow" I muttered!
We played pool together and had a few more beers, the bar snacks arrived so we went and sat down outside under an umbrella,

We had little pieces of smoked pork on sticks and crab, some king prawns and some sticky rice, it was nice,
We heard someone bang the bar with their hand, I turned around and saw a man standing at the bar pointing his hand at the girls, talking in their language, he waved his hands around and pointed to me and Tula, "I think I should see what's going on here" I whispered, Tula held my hand, "nothing to do with us Rhys" she said, I stayed where I was, the man sat at the bar and read a paper, the girls cleaned up around the place, one of them came over to us to ask if we were ok and if we had finished, I said it was great, I pointed to the man at the bar and put my thumb up, I assumed she understood me, she whispered: "boss of bar, not happy, we always quiet here, we are too far from town on our own here, there is another bar just round the corner, they the same, most people use bars in town, he not happy, he want me and my friend to excite people to come here, or we have no more job" she told us quietly and took our plates away,

I looked at Tula, "too much information" I whispered, Tula nodded, we smoked a cigarette each and went to the bar, the bar was in a square shape, reasonable size, I could see through to the kitchen behind the room where we played pool, I saw a dart board on the wall,

"fancy a game" I asked Tula, "I don't know this game" she replied, the bar girl gave us the darts, I showed Tula what to do and threw my three darts at the board, Tula came forward and threw her first dart, it missed the board and hit the wall with a thud, "sorry" I said to the bar girl, Tula threw her second dart, it went straight into the bulls eye, she screamed out!, the bar girls clapped their hand, the man at the bar looked over,

Tula threw her last dart, it hit the metal on the board and bounced back, Tula jumped out of the as the dart flew into the wooden bar next to the man there, it just missed his leg, we both looked shocked at the man, he pulled the dart from the bar and stood up, "here we go" I whispered,

I went to put my hand out to say sorry when the man threw the dart at the board, the dart went straight into the top double twenty slot, he smiled, "nice shot" I commented, "you want play me for money" he asked, I nodded, "we play for thousand baht, that was about ten pounds, "why not" I replied, he told me this was his bar, he passed me a bottle of beer from the bar, he spoke to the girls and they turned the music up as two young men sat down on the other side of the bar, looks like they were on their way back to town from the beach, I threw first, one twenty, one triple eighteen with a fluke and another twenty, Tula was getting some more beer from the bar, she watched us, the bar girl was opposite her on the other side of the bar, talking to her, they played a game as I carried on playing darts with the manager.

The boss of the bar thrashed me at the darts game, I lost four thousand baht to him, maybe fifty quid or something, "you play pool with me" he asked, I told him in a bit after I had a chat with Tula,

I sat next to her and I saw the young girl leaning over the bar, her breasts on show as there was no bra and her top was loose, the reached out and touched my hand, "you have a very beautiful lady here, I hope you look after her" she said in bad English, "I know, thank you very much young lady" I said, "I not too young Mr" she replied and touched Tula's hand again, "help" Tula said and smiled, we were getting a bit tipsy, we had another beer and the boss of the bar walked past, "you want to play pool now" he asked? I knew there would be money involved, "ok, let's have a game, just one though before the missus gets jealous" I told him, "no worry bar lady take care and keep her company, I have more girls come here later, they dance and have fun with you" he said, I nodded and looked at Tula, it was all harmless fun, I hoped, Tula was playing with the girl too.

I went over to the pool table with the boss, he offered me one of his cigars, it was strong but I didn't mind as the beer had put me in a good mood,

He wanted to play for ten thousand Bhat, "that's getting a bit serious, you sure" I asked?

He nodded, "no problem my friend, we can go higher if you want to" he said, I looked at him, I knew I was good at pool, been playing the game for a long time, learnt in the army long time ago and always beat the other lads when paying for cash, I told him to hang on and went to speak with Tula, she didn't mind as she was drinking a cocktail and dancing with the young bar girl, she looked sexy, they both did, she was having fun, I went back to the boss,

"Ok, let's make it interesting, three games for one hundred thousand Bhat" I said, the bar manager looked at me sternly, "ok Mr English, I play you for that" he agreed.

I shot first and broke the balls up on the table and potted one in the pocket, put another two balls down and snookered him, he came to the table and took a shot and fouled, I had a free shot and put another three balls down, he was looking a bit concerned now, I finished my beer and got another one and one for him too,

He potted four balls next and I took my turn, I cleared up and put the black ball down, I had to say which pocket it was going in, so I won the first game.
We set the balls up for the second game and he broke off.
He potted five of his own balls and it was my turn, I put one down and fouled giving him a free shot, all his balls went down but he missed on the black, I cleared up and was on the black too, I couldn't put it down, he took a shot and it went into the pocket he nominated.
We set up the last game after we smoked a cigarette and had another beer, I was concerned about driving back into town later after all the beers, he said no problem, we could leave the jeep here over night, the bar was open twenty four hours, the girls will watch it, he said we could stay here to if we wanted to, there was room out the back, he was showing off a bit I sensed, he said he could get anything that we wanted and winked at me, "really, anything" I said and winked back, "for sure, we talk later on I think" he put in,

I nodded and broke the balls up, none of my balls went down so he took his go and potted three of his red balls and smiled at me, "you play good English" he said, I told him I was a Welshman and had to explain where Wales was, we carried on with the game, we ended up with both of us to put the black ball to win, I missed and he wasted his free ball.

It was a hard shot for me, I named the pocket but I had to bounce the black ball off the other side of the table and bring it back into the centre pocket, "I don't think you can do that" he said, with that I took the shot and it bounced off the other side of the table and went straight into the pocket I said,

He looked at me and squinted his eyes, "you play well, I owe you too much" he said and finished his bottle of beer, "I tell you what, we forget about what you owe me and I buy your bar" I told him, "cost you too much I think" he replied, "how much" I asked?

"Two million Bhat" he said and smiled, I played with my phone and worked it out, "that's just over forty thousand British pounds, ok" I said, he looked shocked and sat down, "I think you play with me" he said quietly, I sat down at the table and looked at him, "I am not playing" I told him, "you are not allowed a business here, you have to either be married to someone who owns a business or be a silent partner, or something" he said, "I become your silent partner, or you hand over to one of your bar girls, by the books, I marry her and Bobs your uncle" I replied, "what is bobs uncle" he asked, "just a bit of slang, means job done, by the books, you get a percentage maybe, depends how we work this deal out" I told him, "we have triad gangs on the island, not as bad as the main land but they are here, I have to pay every month to them so they look out for us, we never see them, they tend to stay in the busy parts of the island, in the main town" he told me,

"So I think we have something to eat and make a night of it" I said and shook his hand,

"I am seeing when you wake up that you think you make a mistake and not go through with this my friend" he announced,

"I promise you something, however drunk I get, when I make a deal I make a deal, once we have shook hands the deal is done, tomorrow we will sort out the money for you and finalise the deal, I need to know what you want to do" I told him,

He said did not want to have any interest with the bar after the sale, he wanted to move from the island and go further inland and help his parents out on their farm, he told me that he would talk to his best bar girl and arrange something, the bar would be in her name and there would be a lot of money in it for her to marry me just on paper and run the bar for me, I took all this in, we shook hands again and played another game of pool, he beat me this time.

I went to the bar whilst he answered his phone, "hey there gorgeous" I said to Tula, "how much did you lose this time" she said dancing with the pretty bar girl, I sat on the stool and pulled her to me, I kissed her on the lips, the bar girl gave me a dirty look and went back behind the bar, "you want more beer sir" she asked? I nodded,

Tula looked at me, "you look serious what's wrong" she asked,

"Ok I lost the game and a lot of money, however I bought this bar whoops" I said, Tula looked at me with open eyes, "ha ha very funny, I think you drink too much" she said,

"I am serious I bought the bar for forty five thousand pounds, a bargain or what" I told her, "you are serious yes, I see your eyes, ok I never ever thought I would be working a bar, sounds good to me" she replied,

"There are complications to sort out but it will be sorted out and this will be our bar, need to think of a good name and how we can change things" I told her,

I felt excited and Tula was too, we got up and danced.

The boss of the bar came over and I introduced Tula to him, "tonight all drinks and anything else are on me pretty lady" he said and kissed her hand,

"I go now and sort things out, tomorrow we meet here and sort things out ok" he said, I agreed and he left.

As soon as he drove off the bar girls were happy and danced around and partied,

"So this bar is ours now" Tula asked? "Yes darling, soon" I replied, "can do a lot of changes and make a nice home I think" she said,

I didn't tell her that I would have to marry one of the bar girls yet,
I thought of Carmem, I lit a cigarette and thought to myself.
Tula pulled me to her and gave me a big kiss, "so what are we doing now" she said, "let's stay here have dinner, the boss says there are rooms out the back that we can stay in, the bar is open all night, its ok here" I put in, "yes, the girl said that there are more girls coming for the night shift, I can have a good massage she said, I would like it" Tula said, "me too" I told her, "I watch you big man" she said, I laughed, "you are my girl, I don't need anyone else" I replied, Tula smiled and asked for some food, three more bar girls pulled up on a moped and went behind the bar, there was now more bar staff than customers, "this bar needs a change, happy hour, boat trips, pool competitions and darts, karaoke night, got lots of ideas, seventy and eighties night, cocktail challenges, barbeque night and more" I told Tula, she smiled at me, "you are really excited aren't you" she said, "oh yes, I see a new start for us" I put in,

"I just want to be with you, whatever comes extra I will take it on with pleasure" Tula replied,
"we will see, nothing to lose, see what happens tomorrow when everyone is soba, let's have a good night and stay here" I announced, "fine with me" Tula said and winked at me,
Our food was brought to us by a young girl, "enjoy" she said and went back to the kitchen,
"Smells nice, bon appetite" I said, "looks lovely" Tula replied,
We had crab claws in a soup,
There was another plate with prawns and crispy squid,
We both tucked in,
It was great.
It was getting late now, the sun was going down,
We enjoyed each other's company.
The sea view was amazing I had to shake my head to make sure I wasn't in some dream.

From the bar we had a good view of the sea, I think the bar was the last one on the road to one of the many smaller beaches on the island,

There was a few more beaches down on the beach, small huts converted into bars,
The road was quiet as the main tourist beaches were on the other side of the island, that is why the boss of the bar was complaining to the girls,

Money was not being made here to cover the costs of the bar, it was just about ticking over I was told by one of the bar girls who was now talking to me trying hard to befriend Tula,

The bar wasn't busy at all, maybe seven customers, I did notice the menu only did light bar food, no main meals, the music was a little too loud at times, the bar girls cloths were basic and cheap, I was getting lots of ideas already,

Tula got up to dance with the young lady again, actually she was dragged to the floor, I liked it to see it, actually turned me on a bit, I went to the bar and asked for a beer, a girl came over, one of the new ones, she started to flirt with me instantly, we ended up playing a bar game with dice, loser pays for the beer, that's another thing I would change, the bar girls would not drink alcohol, as I could clearly hear and see one bar girl playing pool with a guy and getting drunk, the girl who served me was pretty, I noticed a few bruises on her arms that were covered in makeup.

I asked her what happened, she looked around, "boss get mad some time, if we quiet, he take us for himself sometimes, he pay bad, too low, no good for us, he say if we leave his bar the triads will be watching for us and give us trouble if we work in town" she told me, I looked at her, "I have heard you want to buy bar from him, will be hard for you and good for us I think, good luck" she added and put her hand on mine, I looked into her eyes, she must have been seventeen, eighteen, that's it, very pretty, but her clothes were a bit shabby, I would have all the girls in a basic uniform, I looked at Tula, I could not see her and got a bit worried, I got up and looked around, I asked i=one of the bar girls if she had seen her, she pointed to the toilet, I relaxed and went back to the table where I was talking to the young lady, I heard Tula laughing, I turned around and saw her come out of the toilet with the young girl who had been chasing her all night, I felt a bit shocked and got up, I walked over to her, "you ok" I asked her, "I am very ok" she replied and looked at the young girl who was smiling, "how about a game of pool love" I asked? "love to sexy" she replied, we went past the bar to the other room where the pool table was, the bar girl gave us two beers as we went past, I started to set up the balls, "you look like your enjoying yourself with your new friend" I put to her, she looked at me, "you too with the young bar girl" she replied, "I am getting information off her, she says the boss is a bully and takes them when he pleases and tells the girls if they leave the bar the triad gang will give them trouble" I told her, we both looked at each other and laughed, "we both drunk I think" Tula said and took a shot, she potted a ball and carried on, four more balls went down, "hey you, be gentle" I exclaimed!

I had my go and potted two balls and snookered Tula, I saw her eyes, her friend was next to her and touching her leg, she took a shot and potted her ball and the remaining balls, she had the black ball to pot, I had five balls left to put down, she looked at the young bar girl, they kissed and she took the shot, the black ball went down,

Tula and the bar girl both screamed with delight and kissed again, Tula looked at me, "another game English" she said,
"I am not English and you know this madam, I am impressed, more beer I think, game on, let's have a bet on this one" I said, "ok darling" she replied"
Tula came over to me and gave me a hug, "I am so happy Rhys tonight, let's stay here, will be safer than driving back to our hotel" she asked me?
"yes fine by me my princess, set them up, I'll get some more beer" I told her and went to the bar, the girl I was talking to earlier was at the bar on her own as it was quiet, she passed me a bottle, I told her to have one for herself and she smiled, she followed me to the pool table, Tula looked at me, "so what is the bet then" she asked?
I looked at her, "ok, you win, we stay here with your friend together and me, I win we stay here together with your friend and mine together, all together all night" I said, Tula gave me a hard look, "ok" she replied, she smiled and drank some beer from her bottle,

"Let's let the girls play as well" I added, "yes I like this" Tula announced,
I took the first shot and nothing went down, Tula had her shot and potted two of her balls, my bar girlfriend took a shot and potted nothing,
"I think we are in trouble mate" I said to the bar girl, she shrugged her shoulders and smiled at me,
I took my shot and potted one, Tula's friend potted three balls and put us in a snooker,
"Bloody hell girls, be gentle, two games ok" I announced and went to the table, we all laughed,
I took a shot and fouled, I hit one of Tula's balls by mistake, "bollocks, more beer I think" I asked, the bar girl called out to the bar and some more beers were brought to us,
Tula cleared up and potted the black.
She stood at the table smiling, "one to the girls I think" she said,
I looked at the bar girl with me, "if we lose we sleep in the jeep tonight" I told her, she laughed, "I think not, too many mosquitos"

she told me, she went to the table and broke up the balls, two of our colours went down, "Good shot mate" I shouted! She came to me and hugged me, Tula gave me some eyes and smiled, Tula's friend took a shot and potted another two more balls, we were all happy, we took a break and smoked cigarettes, Tula was very friendly with her friend and she knew I saw this, I knew she was showing off, "ok folks, after this game whatever the result we have all had a good night, loads of fun, I think we have some food and go to bed for the night, I would live a massage, make me feel better for a good night's sleep and then sort a deal out with the boss tomorrow" I announced, everyone looked at each other, I know I was drunk and slurred a bit, "we have nice room here, I give good massage to both of you, professional" the bar girl said, "I give good massage too" Tula's friend put in, Tula looked at me, "I think we are both in trouble" she said and laughed.

Tula started to dance with her young friend, the bar girl with me grabbed my arm and pulled me to her, we danced too.

The music changed song and we went back to the pool table,

"So girls, who will win then" I said, "the girls of course" Tula replied and laughed. "I'm all on my own here" I put in and smiled, Tula's friend too her shot and potted a ball and that was it, my bar girl took her shot and potted all of our balls and the black, "hey, look at that, the bar girl was very happy and came to me and kisses me on the mouth, I saw Tula's eyes, she wasn't too much bothered with it, "so it one game each then" I announced,

"let's have some food and talk, enjoy tonight, massage sounds good later" Tula said and looked at her friend, I nodded, my friend spoke in her language at the other bar girl for some food, we went and sat outside and smoked and danced, more beer was brought to us, the food came and we sat down,

Another bar girl came over very friendly and placed some plates on the table, she spoke in Thai to her friends and left smiling,

We had had what we had had earlier on in the day, the bar's basic snacks that were very nice, fried prawns, crab claws, sticky rice and some dips, we all enjoyed it, some more was brought to us and it was all eaten,

"Well that was lovely" I announced,

"Shall we grab some beers and go to our room" Tula asked?

"Yes, sounds good to me" I replied, the two girls laughed and spoke in their language, we all went got up and went to the back of the bar, my bar girl opened the door to a room and we went inside,

the room was average size, a double bed was in there, Tula's friend turned on the fan and went to the bathroom, "what is going on here mate" I asked her, "I am not too sure, let's have a nice massage and see what happens" she said to me,

I growled and jumped on the bed, the young bar girl came next to me and started to cuddle me,
Two Thai girls, me and Tula on the same bed, I felt nervous,

I thought it was part of the massage, one of the Thai girls pulled me to her and kissed me on the mouth, I responded,

Tula cane over and kissed me too and the bar girls, hands were going everywhere and boobs were out, the girl who went to the bathroom got on the bed in her knickers, things calmed down and me and Tula laid on the bed whilst the girls gave us both a fantastic massage for nearly an hour, we turned over, the bar girl looked at me, "I massage for you sir" she asked, Tula looks at me and leant over and put my willy into her mouth,

I noticed the other girls head between Tula's legs, Tula laid back and closed her eyes, my bar girl took my penis in to her mouth and did what she did, I think we both orgasmed at the same time, we were holding each other's hands and looked at each other smiling, "well what can I say, never expected this from you my dear" I whispered, Tula smiled, "me too" she replied,

The two girls took off their clothes completely and washed us then they stated to kiss us both, I was very turned on, my bar girl pushed me onto Tula and guided me into her, Tula moaned in ecstasy, the other bar girl was rubbing her private parts over Tula's face, I pulled out of Tula as my girl had climbed onto Tula, her bum was in front of me, she pushed back and I entered her, then entered Tula, we all changed positions and I ended up with Tula's girl and my girl was between Tula's legs, we all made love to each other for a good while and had our orgasms, we all laid on the bed and smoked cigarettes.

The two bar girls fell asleep, so me and Tula got up and washed ourselves and put our cloths on, we went through to the bar, it was after twelve at night, the music from the bar was not too loud, we went through and sat down at the bar, there was a hand full of men at the bar, two was watching the tv, another old guy was playing a bar game with one of the girls, a bar girl and an oldish man were playing pool, a girl came to us with a big smile on her face, "you want some beers" she asked, Tula asked for a pims and I had a large whisky, she brought our drinks over, "you have good time, you have to pay for girls to leave the bar, that is the rule here" she put to us,

"Ok I just thought, actually I am not too sure what I thought, how much" I said, "two thousand baht each sir, they will stay in room all night for you when you ready to relax" she replied, I paid the girl and me and Tula had a chat.

We decided to go for a walk down to the beach, we took some beers with us, one of the bar girls warned us to take care, some people had some trouble down there at night before, I thanked her and we walked off.

There wasn't any lighting on the road to the beach, just the moon light, we drank from our bottles and smoked a cigarette each, there was lights on the beach as we approached, there was some music playing, a moped passed us with three girls on it, "you want good time with us" one of the girls shouted!

"had it already" I shouted back and put my arm around Tula, "I am still in shock what happened, I hope this doesn't change anything with us" I said to her, Tula looked at me,

"nothing change Rhys, we both enjoy yes, so no problem,
we can do whatever we want to, but I want us to do it together though" she replied" "of course, you fancy a swim with me" I asked her, she nodded and we walked onto the sand, the sand was warm and we went down to the water, tiny waves came in, the view was fantastic, I heard a voice, "you want a drink, I get for you, I watch your stuff if you want to swim" a young boy said, I nodded and gave some money to him, he ran off to the bar that I could see. Tula took her top off and her wrap, she had a bikini underneath and looked very pretty, The boy came back with two beers and a bowl of nuts, "I watch your stuff for you yes, I trusted here" he told us, Tula said thank you and we went into the sea, it was still warm from the days sun, I was watching the young lad next to our stuff, he smoked a cigarette and talked on his phone, me and Tula was playing with each other , the water was up to my chest, Tula rapped her legs around me,

"I love you Rhys" she said, "I love you too you sexy thing" I replied, we kissed and made love,

Tula pushed away and swam in the sea, I went towards the shore, I was a bit concerned about our stuff, the young lad was walking around, "hello sir, you want more drinks" he said, "yes sure, thanks mate" I replied, I passed him a few notes, "too much" he said, "keep it mate, I am in such a good mood, I sat down on the sand and watched Tula swim, she shouted to me to come and join her, I waved back and lit a cigarette, the boy came back with more drinks and a bowl of crisps, "I go now ok, take care" he said and walked off, the lights on the bar behind us went out, there was more people on the beach further down having a party, there was one light next to the trees so it wasn't too dark, I checked my waist bag, I wasn't too sure how money I had in there but I sensed some was missing, I laughed to myself, I heard Tula calling to me, I waved at her, I finished my beer and had another cigarette, I laid on the sand watching Tula swimming, she came out and came to me, "come in and swim with me, good fitness" she said, I passed her a beer, she lit a cigarette and sat next to me, "I am so happy, thank you Rhys, we will have a good time here, I hope all goes well with the bar, I can cook good meals for the customers, I look forward to it, she kissed me and flicked her cigarette away, I watched her finish her beer, "one more quick swim then we go back to our bar ok" she said and walked back into the sea, I watched her, I drank the other bottle of beer and had another cigarette.

I opened my eyes, the beach was quiet, I must of dozed off, I looked for Tula, I wasn't too sure how long I had been dozing for but I felt a bit chilly, there was no sign of anyone on the beach now, I went to look at my watch, it wasn't there on my wrist, I thought I might of left it back at the bar, I looked for my mobile phone, it wasn't here, my waist bag was missing too, I called out to Tula!

I went to the water and looked around and called her name again, my heart was pounding, I looked around, there was no one anywhere, the moon was bright in the sky, I called Tula's name again, I went into the sea, there was no sign of Tula, I went back to where our stuff was, Tula's bag was missing too, I picked up a bottle of beer and finished it, I lit a cigarette and walked about, I felt dizzy, what was going on, I thought to myself, I walked up and down the beach calling Tula's name out for ages, it was starting to get light now, I saw something on the beach further down and made my way to it, as I got closer it looked like a body, I ran to it and threw up. I found Tula lying there in the sand, her head was face down, o hoped it wasn't her but it was, there was blood on the sand, I knelt next to her and turned her around, I was shocked to see her face a mess, blood everywhere, I checked her pulse, nothing, she was stone cold, I couldn't make any sense what had happened her, I held her in my arms, I heard someone calling out, I looked and saw a man coming over, "you ok my friend" he said, he looked at Tula, "what happen, I call ambulance and he ran off, the water was around us,

Blood was everywhere, I looked at Tula, her wounds were too much, her back was cut to bits, she had an arm missing, I cried and held her.

I heard a siren and saw flashing blue lights over by the beach bar, two men ran over to me, "what happened" one of the medics called out, the other medic pulled Tula away from me and checked her, I didn't want to let go of her, the other medic pulled me away, "sir we have to check her, what happened here" he asked again, I looked at him, "I don't know, I fell asleep she went swimming, I found her like this" I replied, "I think she hit by a boat, injuries too much, had no chance, I sorry we must take her to hospital, you come with us please" he said to me, two police officers came running onto the beach and spoke with the medics, "sir I need to take some details from you ok" the officer asked!

I just sat on the sand looking at Tula, "my fault, I fell asleep, stupid" I shouted and thumped the sand, "you have to come with us sir, we need to know who she is" the other officer told me,

I was pulled to my feet and walked back to the road, I got into the back of the ambulance and we headed to the local hospital.
I had to fill in a lot of forms at the hospital, they wanted to see my passport and Tula's, I told them I would get it as they were in the hotel, I left the hospital and took a taxi to our hotel, I went to our room and sat on the bed, I lit a cigarette and tried to think what was going on, I went to the mini bar and drank a small bottle of whiskey,
The room telephone rang!
I answered the phone, "Mr Rhys police want to talk to you sir" a lady said, I told her I would be down soon and hung up, I thought to myself about a few not too good things coming of this situation, I quickly thought about things, I got all the money into a bag and the emeralds also a few small weapons, I threw in some cloths and went to the window, I was getting rather nervous, we were on the second floor, two high, I opened the door to the room, I prayed there wasn't an officer there, there wasn't,

I made my way down the corridor and went down the fire escape.
I went into the rear garden and found a back gate, the lock was old and broke easily, I went out onto the back road and walked away from the hotel, I wanted to go to the bar that I was supposed to buy but left it, I had no reason to go there now, I walked for a good ten minutes, a taxi pulled up, "I take you somewhere mr" a man said, "yes I would like to go to the main land by boat" I said, "I take you to port sir" he replied, I jumped in and sat back, the taxi pulled off, I looked out of the window thinking about Tula.
It didn't take too long to get to the port, the taxi stopped, "ok, next boat in half hour" the taxi driver said, I thanked him and paid him and got out, I made my way to the port office, a small stone building, quiet as well, I went inside and went to the kiosk window,
There was a young girl there, "can I help you" she asked, I told her I would like to go to Pitaya for a week and return, she booked me a return ticket and I paid her.

I was expecting a lot more, like my passport, a stamp, where was I staying bla bla bla, I was happy about it easy, too easy I thought to myself, there was no customs, just an old security guard sitting in the terminal, I saw a bar and made my way to it, there was a few other tourists about, some were quite rowdy and two security officers had to sort things out, I went to the bar and sat down, I put my bag next to my feet, a young lady came to me, "what would you like before your journey sir" she asked, "I cold beer please" I replied,

I lit a cigarette, my drink was brought to me, "where you go sir" the bar girl asked, I told her, "it very busy there not like here, be careful there" she advised me, I thanked her,

She offered to play a game with me, roll the dice in the box and flip over discs that corresponded with the dice, I bought her a drink and we chatted, "you want short time with me" she whispered and put her hand on mine, I looked at her, "I would live to, but have no time, sorry" I replies,

"You can take next boat, I make you feel so good" she said, I heard a noise from a boat, "my boat is here, I have to go" I told her, I tipped her well, she smiled and she waved good bye to me.

I grabbed my bag and went to the boat and got on, a man took my ticket and showed me where to go, I had bought some beer bottles from the bar that were in a plastic bag and a big packet of crisps and some Thai cigarettes, I sat down and looked out the window, more people came on board. The boat sounded the horn and we sailed out to see, I went up deck and looked back at the port, I saw a police bike stop at the port I and thought about things, I was a bit concerned about me carrying weapons in my bag so I dumped them over board, I lit a cigarette and had a beer, it was a bit choppy, I thought of Tula then Carmem came to my mind, I looked out to sea and sat down.

The journey took two hours, I could see the main island approaching, there was police there, I thought I was in bother,

The boat stopped and people got off, I followed them,

I walked past the police and got to the high street, it was busy, aa lot of traffic and loads of bars, tall hotels everywhere, I walked down the high street sweating,
I found a hotel and went in to the front desk.
"hello" the hotel girl said, "can I book in for two weeks please" I asked, the girl asked for my passport, I explained I had lost it at Phuket, she was ok, I had to fill in some forms, I paid for the room and went to find it,
The room was nice, a double, I went straight to the mini bar and had a strong drink, I took it to the balcony and lit a cigarette and looked about, there was an open bar below, there was a lot of bar girls there, one looked up, "he mister, you want massage" she called to me, I nodded, "what room you in" she asked, I told her, I emptied my bag and hid most of the money behind the wardrobe, I had to force it away from the wall and pushed it back into place, I freshened up and covered myself in deodorant, I had another drink from the minibar and sat on the bed,

I felt tired and turned on the TV, I found a movie channel and relaxed,
There was a knock at the door,
I got off the bed and opened the door, there was a small young lady standing there,
"hello, you call me from the bar outside" she said, "oh yes, come in gorgeous" I said to her,
I closed the door and laid on the bed,
The young lady took her clothes off and stood there in a tight top and her knickers,
She climbed on the bed and started to massage me,
She massaged all of me,
I had extras and felt totally relaxed,
She asked me if I would see her later,
I told her yes, I paid her and she left,
I ordered some food and watched a film, the food came and I ate it, burger and chips,
I drank some beer and fell asleep.
I woke up to the noise of birds on my balcony, it was early,
I turned on the TV to find out the time,
I found the news channel,

It was nine o clock, I got showered and had a shave and went out with a load of money, I walked around and found a safety deposit box shop, and I paid for a box and put the bag in it,

I was asked for my passport and explained I had lost it, more forms to fill,

I left the shop,

"hey mate come have a drink" I heard someone call, I looked and saw a small bar, it was still early in the day so I ordered a coffee and some fries, I sat at the bar looking at the TV, a girl at the bar passed me an English paper, "bloody ell, the Sun" I said and started to read it.

My coffee and fries came and I dug in.

I spent most of the day at the bar, played pool with some of the girls and had lunch, I went to the local bar and exchanged my British pounds for their currency, and I went to my hotel and hid a lot of the money and went back out.

The bar I was at earlier was a bit busy when I got there, a lot of men at the bar, all ages talking to the bar ladies,

I found a space and sat down, a young girl came to me,
"hi, you come back" she said,
I recognised her from earlier on,
She got me a drink and we chatted and played some games,
I bought her a few drinks and joked and had a good chat,
I had had a few drinks and I told her my sob stories,
She look really concerned and comforted me, her name was Sulay, and I ended up taking her out that night,
She took me to a bowling alley and we had a god time, we had a nice meal in a restaurant and went on to a night club,
We got drunk and went to my hotel, we went to the pool bar that was about to close as it was late,
We had a drink and got into the pool, Sulay was all over me,
I had spent quite a lot of money through the day on her, she was happy, we made love in the pool and went to my room and slept.
I spent the next two weeks with Sulay,

I bought her cloths and she took me to where her parents lived,
I was upset as they lived in a squat,
I gave them money and we left, she took me to a racing track and we both drove go carts around the course, we had a great time, she looked after me,
I heard news about Phuket Island and about a lady found dead on the beach, the police were investigating into it,
Sulay stayed with me every night and I told her a lot of stories,
She looked very happy with me but I sensed how many other times she had done this,
Sulay took me all over the island,
I hired a jeep and bought her gold pendants and spoiled her.

CHAPTER 5:
Thailand tragedy:

"Come on Mr Rhys are you going to go with pretty lady, she love you long time" someone said to me in an oriental accent!
I opened my eyes and saw Sulay looking at me from behind the bar,

She told me she had to go to her mother as she wasn't too well, I gave her money, a lot and let her go.

Sulay never came back to the bar, I asked her friends at the bar where she was every day, they told me she go to another island to look after her family, and I never saw her again,

I made my way to the bar, still drunk from the night before, weeks had passed and all I did every day was get up and get rid of the girl I spent the night with and go get a massage, then spend some money on rubbish, my hotel room was full of crap stuff that I had bought.

I made my way to the bar,

I could hear a strange trumpeting noise from somewhere!

I recognised the tune and remembered!

Army bugle call, the Last Post!

My head was slumped into my arms on the bar,,

I raised my head up and looked around,

My vision was blurry,

There was a big fat man who I had seen too many time at the bar sat close to me half on a stool and leaning at the bar, he was running his hands all over a young girl, she wasn't too happy with him doing it,

I saw the television above the bar, CBN news was on, something about British soldiers killed in Afghanistan and the coffins were being brought of the Air force Hercules plane,

The bugle call of the last post was being played!

"what the hell is this crap, you see what happens when governments mess with other countries they don't even understand about, they shouldn't of been in there interfering man, let them sort out their own troubles, them soldiers got what they deserved"

The fat man interrupted the news cast loudly,

I heard other people at the bar call him stupid and a few other things!

The fat man slammed his hand on the bar, "hey you, where's my drink gone, I never finished it, now you goanna make me buy another one, you bars are all the same" he growled at the young girl behind the bar,

I turned and looked at the fat middle aged man sat next to the bar with a very young lady on his lap,

The fat man growled and banged the bar again the girl on his lap laughed but looked worried!

I looked at the fat man who was sat next to me,

"That was the last post bugle call mate, show some respect for the soldiers that have died doing their jobs and serving their country" I put in!

"Listen mate, you've been snoring next to me for the last half hour: the fat man slurred!

I went to raise my hand and protest when someone pulled my hand down,

"Mr Rhys I think, take you back to your hotel, look after you" I heard a woman's voice say to me,

I turned my head to see a young lady dressed in a crop top and wearing tight shorts, lots of makeup on her face, very pretty!

She had oriental eyes,

"Hey pall take my advice and let her take you back to your hotel my friend" the fat man next to me said and laughed out loud!

He got up with a struggle and pushed the young girl who was sat on his leg aside, "fucking cheap whore! He slurred! And waddled towards the toilet,

" I served in the German special forces, a professional army not like all the other armies that fuck things up" the fat man added" he pushed another man off his stool, "what you going to do about it" he growled!

I looked at the girl who was sat on the fat man's lap,

"You can do a lot better than him young lady" I mentioned to her,

She nodded, "he is a pig, but he keeps buying me out of the bar every night so lady boss: mamma san say I have to make him happy whilst at the bar, he make me sick" she whispered to me, "he cannot do anything just make me dance for him then he fall asleep" she added!

The other girl who wanted to take me back to my hotel pulled my arm, "so you want two girls now" she exclaimed!

I looked at her, "hey, I didn't mean that" I told her, "for sure" she replied angrily and stormed off!

I looked at the young girl who was sat on the fat man who went to the toilet,

"I need shit paper in here now" the fat man bellowed from the toilet!

The bar girls all looked at each other nervously,

Mams san came out,

"Mr Rhys you still here, what is all the shouting about" she demanded!

The bar girls told her what had happened,

"He is stupid fat German, no good to my girls and owes me too much money" Mama san complained!

"Mama san give me some toilet paper" I said to her and smiled,

Mama san smiled back and threw me a roll of toilet paper,

"He is a bad man Mr Rhys, he messes with my young girls, they hate him, and he makes them do bad things, I want rid of him" Mamma San said quietly,

"If I don't get some shit paper in the next ten seconds I'm going to wipe my arse on the fucking dirty towel in here! The fat man bellowed!

People started to leave the bar quickly,

"This happen all the time, police do nothing"

Mama san winged!

I stood up with the roll of toilet roll in my hand,

"Ok, let's teach fat boy some respect I think" I growled!

"Mr Rhys, I don't want trouble, you both come here long time, you good man him bad man" she pleaded!

I cut her off!

"I'll be gentle, you know me" I told her and walked to the toilet,

"Be careful you moaw" she said to me meaning I'm drunk,

I knew I was drunk, I had been for the last eight months!

Someone called my name but I was on a mission now,

I went into the small toilet and said in a girlish voice,

"I have your toilet roll for you, you naughty man, say please and I will put it underneath the door for you sir"

"See I drink your shit beer and eat your crap food and get a bad stomach you fucking whores" the fat German shouted!

The door to the cubicle he was sat in was pushed open,

"What the fuck are you doing here boy, you queer or what" he bellowed!

I just stood there holding the toilet roll,

"Would sir like me to wipe one's bottom for him sir" I announced!

"just pass me the shit roll you drunk before I get off this seat and shit down your scrawny cowardly neck boy" he exclaimed!

I flew forward and stuffed the toilet roll into his mouth and pulled him forward onto the floor,

He hit the floor hard,

I jumped onto his back and got his arms pulled behind him with a struggle,

The fat man cried out! There was a rather disgusting noise from his behind!

Then the smell of shit was in there air,

"Jesus Christ man, you just shit everywhere" I commented!

"I'm not well man, you caused this jumping on me like this" the fat boy yelled out!

"You should show some respect to those who have fought for their country and died doing it" I growled!

"You starting that crap again boy, fuck you and all your fake comrades" fat boy announced and started to struggle with me,

"When I get my hands on you I will show you how we German Special Forces do things, you yellow coward" he added!

I saw red big time,

"Ok fat boy" I whispered and swung him around and pushed his face into his own faeces,

"No one calls me a coward, ever, you know nothing what I've been through" I whispered again,

The fat man was coughing and spluttering, I rolled him over and spun him round again on the floor, he was covered in his own shit,

I had it all over my hands too,

I gave him two good kidney punches and left him groaning on the floor, I washed my hands and arms,

"ok mate let's have you up and out, pay the bar bill and clear off before Mamma San calls the police, she's told me all about you" I growled!

The fat man started to cry, "I'm sorry please help me I need a doctor" he moaned!

"Get up you pig" I warned him and stepped forward,

"He saw me move towards him, "ok ok, no more" fat boy moaned!

The fat man pulled himself up, "you really hurt me boy, I'll be pissing blood tomorrow" he coughed out!

I pointed to the exit door to the bar, "go now before I really get annoyed, you've just messed with an ex SAS trooper boyo" I told him!

He looked worried as he held himself up, he pushed the door to the bar open and staggered out,

The smell was terrible, I was retching as I followed him out,

The fat German fell into a table and knocked a chair over, "sorry Mamma San, here" the fat man threw a wad of notes on the floor, "I am so sorry, I go now, I won't come here again" he slurred!

The fat man stumbled onto the street, people in the bar were shouting at him, women were screaming as he was in such a mess and the smell was terrible!

I walked to the bar and sat down on a stool,

"Beer please, actually I'll have a large jack" I asked smoothly,

All the girls behind the bar looked at me, in fact I felt everyone staring at me,

"Shows over here ladies and gentlemen" I announced!

I drank my large drink in one go and stood up,

"Mamma San sorry for the mess in the toilet, this should cover it" I exclaimed,

I put a wad of notes on the bar and walked into the street,

"No problem Mr Rhys, you good man, Always welcome here, thank you, see you tomorrow" Mamma San announced!

I heard a lot of clapping as I walked away,

I gave a thumbs up and carried on walking,

"Wait, Mr Rhys" I heard someone call out!

I turned to see the young girl who was with the fat German run up to me,

"Thank you, you sort fat man out, he bad man to me, you nice guy, let me take care of you please sir" she asked,

"You don't have to call me sir young lady" I told her,

"I am not too young, I look young, I am twenty two" she exclaimed,

"See my ID card" she said taking out a card from her pocket,

"You look about eighteen girl, ok walk me home, I need a shower then we get some food, you hungry" I asked her?

She smiled and nodded and went to hold my hand, I pushed her hand away, "need shower I am stinking of that fat man's shit" I told her, she laughed and we walked down the street.

We got to my hotel, it was really late, I looked at my watch, three thirty in the morning I saw,

There was a night guard on the front desk half asleep, he greeted me,

"Mr Rhys, you ok, pretty lady take care of you" he said,

"Just a friend mate, going to have a quick shower the go and get some food" I said to him,

The night guard smiled and nodded,

"I get food for you and some drinks, bring to your room, its late now, you stay here rest sir" the night guard said,

I looked at him and looked at the young lady, she smiled at me and nodded,

"Ok mate, sounds good to me" I replied,

"What you fancy to eat princess" I asked her,

I felt really drunk,

"I think we have rice and prawns, very nice, make you sleep" she said softly,

"Bring a bottle of whisky my friend" I told the night guard,

"Ok Mr Rhys" he said and closed the front door and left,

Me and the young lady went up the stairs, I stumbled a little, she grabbed my arm, I laughed and she did too!

"Here we go" I said as we got to my room,

I opened the door with a struggle and pushed the door open, the cold air hit me in the face as I walked in,

"Shit I left the air con on brrrrrrrr" I said and laughed,

"It's nice, too hot outside" she replied,

The hotel I was staying in was nice, bit expensive but safe, I needed a safe place after what I had been through not so long ago,

"Nice hotel, I never been to this one before, too expensive" she said,

The lights came on automatically by sensor and I went straight to the mini bar, "want a drink" I asked her,

"Ok, can I have a whiskey" she said and smiled,

"You want a whiskey, why not girl" I announced and laughed, I turned the TV on to a movie channel,

"You choose, I'm off to take a shower, I stink" I said, I opened two miniature bottles of whiskey and passed her a bottle and a glass,

I downed mine in one go, "grrrrrrrrrrrrr that hit the spot" I growled!

The young lady laughed and changed the channel on the TV.

I walked to the shower,

I was getting undressed when I realised I didn't even know her name,

"What's your name, I'm sorry I should have asked, how rude I am" I shouted!

There was no answer,

I climbed into the shower and turned the water on, the water was nice and warm on me, and sobered me up a bit,

I could hear music coming from the main room and heard her singing,

I was visualizing her robbing my wallet so I walked into the lounge with a towel around me,

I couldn't see her, the TV was on, I smelt smoke, I looked out onto the balcony, she was there, sat on a chair smoking a cigarette and holding her drink,

I went out to the balcony,

"Hey girl, you ok" I asked

"I fine, I think I do wrong sometimes, you good man, I am happy here with you, and you are not like other men, you different" she said,

"I actually thought you were going to rob me, I am sorry, what's your name" I asked feeling embarrassed,

"Tinoy" she whispered and took a drink,

I lit a cigarette and sat down, we smoked in silence, and I was thinking all sorts of things,

"You look troubled Mr Rhys, what is wrong" she asked me?

"Lady you would not believe what troubles me, maybe I will tell you later, shower time" I announced!

I put my cigarette out and headed to the shower,

The water on my face felt nice, I washed myself well,

I could hear the young lady singing,

I got out and dried myself, I gave myself a good blasting with body deodorant, Lynx,

Brushed my teeth and that was that,

I was looking in the mirror wondering why the hell I have just done all that and no flaked out on the bed as usual, I felt something strange about this young lady,

I threw on a white bath robe that was hanging on the back of the bathroom door and went into the lounge,

"Something smells nice" I said, a side table was all set up and the meal was all laid out nicely,

Tinoy was out on the balcony again smoking and drinking from a glass, I went out to her,

"You ok" I asked?

"I am fine Mr Rhys, let's eat, can I go and wash quickly please" she replied and smiled,

"Of course, I have a spare toothbrush and there's another bath robe in the bathroom if you want it pretty lady" I said to her,

She smiled and went to the bathroom.

All the food had lids on top to keep the heat, I went and got another drink from the mini bar,

I could hear her singing in the shower, I was tempted to go in there but didn't!

Tinoy wasn't very long and came out wearing the spare white rob and smelled nice, all her makeup was gone off her face and her hair was hanging down, she looked very young!

"Do you need a hair dryer" I asked?

"It's ok, I like to let dry natural, and I look ugly now" she said,

"You look very pretty Tinoy my guest for tonight, let's eat" I announced!

We ate the meal, it was very tasty, the last few weeks I had been eating crap food, I really enjoyed it,

"Fancy another drink my lady" I asked?

"Mr Rhys you want me for your lady" she asked and smiled,

"I didn't mean it like that, just my daft sense of hum or, joking, you are my guest tonight, make yourself at home, you can do whatever you want, I have a spare bed room through there, you can stay, no pressure" I said,

Tinoy looked at me firmly, "you not like me, I never been called a guest and I have never slept alone, I scare to sleep alone Mr Rhys, she growled!

"ok from now on no more Mr Rhys, just call me Rhys ok, you can sleep were you want to, I'm going to have a drink and smoke out there for a while" I announced!

"I come out too when I clear away food Rhys, you go, I come out soon and smoke too" she replied, I took another bottle from the fridge and went on to the balcony,

I must have been out on the balcony for maybe ten minutes when Tinoy came out,

"I drink and smoke with you Rhys out here, it ok" she asked?

"you are very welcome, I would love to sit down and have a good long talk with you, you tell me all your troubles and what has happened in your life, then I will tell you what I have done, tomorrow if you want to" I said softly,

Tinoy looked at me sadly, "I have bad life, I know think you want to know about me, nobody ever wants to know about me Rhys, you are different from other men's I feel safe with you, this is good, I never feel safe for so long" she whispered,

"You're ok with me mate, I pushed her on the shoulder as a joke, she cried in pain,

"Sorry, too strong for my own good" I said,

"No it not you", she said and pulled the bath robe off her shoulders, I was shocked to see a lot of bruises and bite marks around her shoulders,

"Jesus Christ, what happened to you" I asked in shock!

Tinoy started to cry, "hey hey hey, I have some medical stuff to put on those bruises, hang on" I announced and went straight to the bathroom, I had some savlon and spray for strained limbs I grabbed some co-codomol tablets for pain and strained muscles,

I came back into the lounge, "ok first I will rub in this cream on your shoulders then add some spray and you need to take these tablets, won't really work to well because you've been drinking, but in the morning you can have some more and then I take you to the doctor and get this sorted, I don't want to know who did this now, but tomorrow after we have breakfast I want you to tell me please" I insisted"

Tinoy wiped her tears away and let me rub in the cream,

She was shaking.

"You don't need to shake young lady, I take care of you, relax have another drink, smoke, relax" I added,

Tinoy looked at me and smiled, "you good man Rhys" she whispered.

"Ok, that should do, need more cream later and a doctor madam ok" I announced and pointed my finger at her,

I went to get another miniature bottle of whisky, "you want some more" I asked her,

Tinoy nodded and smiled, she was changing the channels on the TV and found a music channel, she started to sing to a Whitney Houston song, it was nice, I passed her drink and went on to the balcony for a cigarette,

Tinoy came out and stood close to me,

I could feel her leg touching my leg,

"What a lovely view, such a peaceful night Tinoy" I said to her,

"I think you have too much problems too like me, I see you in bar long time, you not notice me, I too busy with stupid German man, I see you look at nothing for long time, I see you thinking too much, I sorry for your hurt" she said to me,

I looked at Tinoy, "I do not know what to do with you" I said and pulled towards me so softly and hugged her,

I kissed her on her shoulder, "you will be ok I promise you mate" I whispered to her,

"Thank you Rhys" she replied and hugged me back,

"Ok girl, let's go inside, I'm dead tired" I told her, she slapped me on my back,

"Me too" she replied,

We went inside, I closed the balcony door, and Tinoy walked towards the other bedroom and looked at me,

"No you don't, you sleep here tonight" I said pointing to my bed,

She smiled and got onto the bed,

I turned off the lights and got onto the bed next to her,

"Night night mate" I whispered,

"Night night Rhys" she replied,

I laid on the bed looking out the window,

"Sweet dreams mate" she said and hugged me,

I heard her start to snore quietly, I felt relaxed and smiled.

I awoke to the smell of coffee.

I went straight to the fridge and drank two miniatures of Brandy, I opened a bottle of beer and sat on the bed and passed out.

The next few days were the same, as the last few weeks, drunk most of the time, Tinoy looked after me, I was sick a lot and would always be in a mess when she would return to the hotel with more booze, we would watch a movie, she would give me a massage, I would give her money and she would go out and buy stuff for her, we would get drunk and fall asleep.

I went out one night with her and we went to the cinema, I got too drunk and caused a lot of trouble, we were thrown out, I fell into the street and threw up, Tinoy managed to get me back to my hotel and put me to bed.

I could hear water running somewhere,

I got out of bed feeling really uneasy, I saw Tinoy, I tried to talk but slurred, my head was spinning, my feet hurt and so did my hands, I looked at my hands, there was black spots on my fingertips,

I checked my feet and saw more black spots, I ignored it, I called for Tinoy, "I am here, you not look to good, I put you to bed last night, you keep going to toilet and be sick, I was going to call doctor, you stop me and pass out again" she said to me, I got up and went to the toilet,

I threw up blood and looked in the mirror and didn't see myself, I saw a blur, I went back in the bedroom and went to the mini bar in the room and had a whisky, and I fell back on the bed and laughed,

Tinoy shouted at me, " I think you want to kill yourself, you drink till you die, what for, you tell me what has happened with you, you want a new start you say, this is the wrong way to go Rhys" she shouted at me!

I pushed her away and she fell on the floor and banged her head, I looked at her and told her to go, Tinoy started to cry, "I love you Rhys" she said, "you just love my money you thieving whore, now get out and go and rob someone who gives a damn" I shouted!, she came towards me, I shouted at her, "go now" I growled, she left and slammed the door shut, I went to the mini bar and opened a bottle of whiskey, I started to walk to the balcony, my feet were in a lot of pain, my fingers were so sore too, I sat on the lounge chair on the balcony and looked at my feet, the black dots on my toes were slightly bigger, and my fingertips were worse,

I wasn't too bothered, I heard a voice from down below,

Tinoy was standing outside the bar,

"Rhys you need help, let me call a doctor for you, I come up and get the rest of my stuff and leave ok" she shouted,

I put my fingers to my lips and told her to shhhhhh! I sat back down and smoked a cigarette,

I heard the door shut and here Tinoy,

"I take stuff and go, give no problem to you, you know where I am if you want to see me, can I have some money please" she asked, "you know where my wallet is, send me some food later please" I told her,

Tinoy put her head through the mosquito net that was on the balcony,

"I go now ok, you take care"

She touched my shoulder and left, I lit another cigarette and swallowed down the rest of the bottle,

I looked at the cigarette in my fingers, I wanted to take a smoke, I could not get my hand to come up, things were all blurry, I thought I was drunk again I laid there on the chair on the balcony and went to sleep.

Someone was shaking me,

"Mr Rhys, Mr Rhys"

I could hear someone call out,

I looked up but my head just fell back down, I was being moved around,

I kept hearing my name, everything was blurry, there was a blue flashing light in my eyes, "Mr Rhys, Mr Rhys" I kept hearing someone call, "Rhys what you do" I heard a voice call out, I recognised it,

I tried to pick my head up but couldn't,

I opened my eyes and saw a blurry figure, I felt someone holding my hand,

"Please take care of him" I heard her say,

I could feel straps going across my chest and I was being bumped around,

A siren was shrieking loudly,

I closed my eyes.

CHAPTER 8:

My Carmem.

My mouth was so dry, my eyes were open but I couldn't see anything, something was over my eyes, I could see shapes through the cover, my hands were strapped down and so was my legs, something was in my mouth, like a big tube, it went down my throat as well, I tried to swallow and could feel the tube,

I needed a drink so badly,

I laid there and tried to think what had happened, I couldn't, things didn't make any sense to me, I saw a shadow in front of me and tried to talk, all I could say was errr, errrr! I heard a voice talking in Thai, my eye cover was taken off my eyes, "Mr Rhys, you wake, good, you very sick, in hospital now, you need to rest, your body shut down" I heard the nurse say, I couldn't see her properly, I tried to move my hands but the were tied down, I got one free and put my hand to my mouth, I felt the tube there, "Mr Rhys no you must leave that there, the doctor coming soon to see you" the nurse said, my hand was strapped back down I had no strength to fight, "water" I managed to moan out, "ok ok" she said, I felt a little bit of water on my lips and that was it, I could see a tube in each of my arms and the was a machine next to me making a beeping noise, I closed my eyes.

"Mr Rhys are you awake" I heard a man's voice, I opened my eyes and the was a small man looking at me, he was wearing a white coat like a doctor, there was two nurses next to me, I tried to talk but the tube stopped me, the doctor spoke in their own language, one of the nurses came close to me, "you must keep still now and do not swallow, I take tube from your throat for you" she said,

I was a very uncomfortable feeling when they took the tube out of my throat, I coughed once it was out, I tried to talk but could only whisper, I wanted to go to the toilet, I whispered to the nurse, "need to pee pee", she looked at me and smiled, "you have a catheter in, you can pee pee" she said back to me, I looked down and saw the tube coming out of the sheets, I moved my feet, they ached, my hands ached, there was stitches in my left upper arm, I had ivi drips in both arms, "what happened" I whispered,

"Mr Rhys you are very ill still, you were found in your hotel unconscious after drinking too much alcohol, you caught Menninger cockle septicaemia, a bad form of meningitis, your body shut down, you were eighty percent dead, we fight to keep you alive, you fight too, well done, you had a sexual disease too, too much alcohol, your liver is in a bad way and you have jaundice sir" the doctor told me, I just looked at him, "will I be ok" I asked, the doctor nodded.

The nurses did their checks and gave me some water, they explained I would talk like a frog for a few says because they had to rush and get the oxygen tube down my throat, it would of scratched my Larynx, the cut on my arm was done to get another tube into my main vein with medicine, my body had shut down so everything was done quickly, I was lucky to be alive, I was told, the nurses gave me a wash and some water, no food yet, my intravenous bags were changed and my catheter bad too,

I laid there and went to sleep, I was given morphine for the pain I was still in.

I dreamt of Carmem and Tula, Tinoy was there too, all sorts going on, dead bodies everywhere, we were all being chased around the world on a big boat.

I heard my name being called out, there was a nurse standing there,

"Mr Rhys, time you get out of bed now I think, your catheter has been taken out, did it whilst you were asleep, less discomfort for you, you have wet the bed in your sleep, not your fault, you go to toilet now, you just have one tube in your left arm now, use the walker to help you walk, the tube is attached to it" she said, I realised I had wet the bed "well look at that, a big boy like me peeing the bed, where's my diaper" I said, the nurse laughed and pulled me up, my head started to spin, I was dizzy, "take time, no rush, you been in bed for over two weeks, legs will be weak, no rush, you on the mend, you lucky man" she put in,

I got up with her help and steadied myself, I shuffled forward and got to the toilet, I looked I the mirror and was shocked to see myself, a sober me, my face was skinny and pale, I needed a shave, I sat down and tried to pee.

I think I was in the toilet for ages, I could hear my name being called out!

I wasn't too sure if I had a pee or not, I think I dosed off, I went out of the toilet and was met by a nurse who took me to my bed,

I was in a room on my own as I had been quarantined whilst the doctors were working out what I was suffering from, they thought I had come from Cambodia and caught some nasty disease there.

I was moved to a bigger ward, most of the time I was under the influence of the morphine I was taking, where the septicaemia had had taken its toll on my fingers, elbow's, knees and toes I was in a lot of pain,

The doctor told me this would be a long time healing, I could be affected by arthritis for the rest of my life in the limbs affected, I had my morphine tablets and laid there in a haze,

A nurse came with my lunch, I was starving, I had been on liquid food for two weeks.

I must of lost two stone, the food was Thai, all cooked with spices, all I could eat was the rice, the nurse had to feed me as my fingers were too sensitive to hold a spoon,

"you must eat more to get strength, I shave you later, make you look better" she said, I asked for some morphine and she said later, the doctor said I was too higher dose and wanted to bring the dosage down as I had come dependent to it.

I complained to the nurse that the pain was too much and she went away, she returned with some tablets, "take quickly now, no tell" she whispered, I swallowed down the pills and instantly had no pain, I laid back and fell into a dream.

Another week went past, the doctor said I would be going to phisio therapy treatment, he was also concerned of the high bill I was now owing the hospital, the hospital had contacted the hotel I was at and gained access to my room to find any id, they found my passport and other stuff, the doctor told me he had to contact the British embassy as he was concerned how long I was going to be here without any payment, I told the doctor I had money to pay and would pay when I was able to get the money, I knew he didn't believe me, he kept asking me to let one of the hospital staff go and get the money for him, why wasn't the money in a bank account, where was the payment, I was getting very bored with him,

"Mr Rhys, we need a payment for your medicine, if no payment soon we will have to discharge you to normal Thai hospital, facilities low there" the doctor told me,

That's when I discovered I was actually in a semi private hospital.

One of the nurses who had befriended me for quite a while now told me that if I had gone to a normal hospital I would not of survived, she said I owed about 15 thousand pounds, she brought me chocolate from time to time, I could feed myself now with a strain, the nurse took me to phisio therapy where they really put me through a strenuous session, I had become unfit and had lost a lot of weight, my phisio staff were hard on me for my own good, I was told I had a uphill battle to fight, it was going to take a long time before I recover from the virus.

I had three hours a day in phisio for another week.

"Mr Rhys" I heard someone call out, I opened my eyes and sat up on my bed, there was a man and a woman dressed in military uniform standing there.

I recognised the uniform, British army,

"Hello there Rhys" the lady said and smiled.

"the British embassy contacted us, they were contacted by the hospital because you have a very large bill and have no money to pay for it, they checked your passport and found out that you could possibly be connected to another person who was still classed as AWOL from the army" the man told me, "

"yes we did a deeper investigation into you and there are too many branches to check, if you are Rhys Evans alias Dean Davies, still reported absent without leave from her Majesties British armed forces for over fifteen years now, I think you could very well be in some bother, there is a trail of disaster behind you, certain intelligent agencies would like a good chat with you" the lady put in, I laid there and stared at them, the nurse was still there I made a hand gesture and she knew what I wanted,

She returned with some tablets that I took straight away,

I could hear the man in army uniform talking but I wasn't listening, the tablets took effect and I felt a bit drunk again,

I laid there smiling,

"I really don't think this is something to smile about" the lady said, "so what name do we call you" she added?

"Rhys will do", I laughed, and "24707494 sir" I said out loud and laughed again,

"Take a note of that number please" the man said to the woman,

"We appreciate how sick you are and we are talking of getting you transferred to a military hospital for your own good,

We will take care of the bill for the time being until we can officially identify you" the man said,

"I can see you have been through hell and back and heard some other stories, you are lucky man to survive this virus" she announced, I stared at her and closed my eyes.

I must of dozed off when I felt a hand holding my hand, I opened my eyes and saw the friendly nurse, gave me some chocolate and some tablets, "no take now, I talk to you" she whispered, "I take you for wash ok" she added, she had done this before a few times over the weeks I had been there and given me special washes too!

Pin was her name and she spoiled me from time to time, I had promised to give her a lot of money when I was better when she started to get me extra tablets for the pain I was in,

We got to the shower toilet and she closed the door and locked it,

"Rhys I hear too many stories about you, I like you and don't want to see you in trouble,

The doctor wanted to call the Thai police and put you in the jail what the call the monkey house.

Pin told me a lot more that was being planned for me,

I trusted her and told her about the money I had hidden, I said she needed to get me to the hotel when I was supposed to be in the phisio for three hours tomorrow, she nodded and washed me sexually.

I woke to see another nurse standing next to me, "Mr Rhys I take you to doctor ok" she said, I nodded and slowly got out of bed, there was a wheel chair for me and she pushed me out of the ward and down the corridor, we went through a few more doors and she stopped, the was a doctor standing there and they both spoke in their own language,

"Mr Rhys I am doctor chin, I have been asked to do a phyciatrict analysis on you" the doctor announced,

The nurse left us and closed the door behind her, I sat there looking at him.

"I understand you have been very sick and are now on the mend, I am told you have a dependency for morphine now, the British embassy and other authorities want to know exactly how you are feeling, you have had a few meetings now and you are showing signs that there is something else wrong with you" the doctor told me,

"You better believe it sir, so they think I am whako now do they, unfucking believable" I growled and banged the desk, I really hurt my hand then, the doctor stood up shocked at my outburst, another doctor came in and spoke in Thai,

"This is so bollocks, I need a piss" I shouted!

I was wheeled out of the office and back down the corridor, we went round a corner and stopped at a nurse's desk, I didn't recognise this part of the hospital,

I saw a white man being wheeled towards me,

"ya mate where are we dude" I called to him as he passed me, he looked at me, "mental ward mate" he said and laughed, he was wheeled away, the nurse who wheeled me here was talking on the phone, I looked through a window into a large room, the walls were padded and I could see a few ladies in there, two was just walking around in circles, one lady was in a wheel chair playing with her fingers, I was about to look away and think I am not going to end up in here when a lady caught my eye, I looked harder, this woman had pale skin no Thai look, I thought I recognised her, I pushed myself closer to the window, she looked like Carmem, impossible I thought to myself, I banged on the window, it was plastic, I shouted her name out, there was no response, she was just looking out of the other window into space,

I banged the window again,

I got out of the wheel chair and went to the door to this communal day room, the door was locked, the nurse on the phone called out to me to get back in the chair, I banged the door, no one inside looked at me, "Carmem Davies" I shouted!

The woman turned to me.

"Carmem" I shouted again!

Another nurse pushed me into the chair, whilst the other one put a strap around me, I struggled with him, "Carmem Davies" I shouted, and the woman looked at me and put her hand up and looked away.

I kept calling her name, I saw one of the nurses do a gesture with his hands, as if I was going bonkers,

I felt a sharp pain in my arm and looked, the nurse stepped back with a syringe in his hand, "you sneaky bastard" I growled, I looked about the area and tried to memorise what part of the hospital I was in before I passed out.

I had seen Carmem, I was not going crazy, or was i!

I was visualizing images in my mind of my Carmem, it was her,

"Mr Rhys" I heard my name, I opened my eyes and realised I was strapped in my bed, the young nurse was there,

"Pin what's going on" I asked,

"You cause big problem today, hospital doctors not happy with you, you go to shyciactric ward tomorrow maybe Your country pay bill and want to take you to military hospital once the doctors have made an examination on your mental health state",

She paused and I stared at her.

"the army has been here twice today, you were not with it because of the tablets I give you, I am upset with myself for giving you the tablets, I am sorry,

the army people said you were getting worse mentally and left after having an argument with one of the doctor's here" Pin told me,

"Pin listen to me, I have seen someone today I recognise from some time ago, someone who was very special to me, she is in the mental ward, her name is Carmem, I need to see her" I told her, she looked at me, "I cannot get there, there is a key code on the doors in that department" she said.

"I need to get to my hotel and get the money, I need you to help me, we must get this woman out of here too and then disappear, you come with us, and I take care of you" I told her,

Pin looked at me hard, "who is this lady" she asked? "She's my Carmem" I replied, I felt a tear role down my cheek,

Pin wiped it away, "ok I help you, I will be in big trouble, you look after me" she said, I nodded, "you know I will Pin" I replied.

"Mr Rhys" I heard my name, I looked over to see the lady from before in the army uniform, she came over to my bed and sat on a seat, she looked at my straps, "I hear you have been causing a fuss in here, and not to worry, we will have you out of here tomorrow and we will take better care of you than these lot" she lowered her voice,

I looked at her, "she went into her brief case, "I need you to sign some paperwork for me for your release from Thai government medical administration over to the British military medical board, red tape to cut, you are very special to us Trooper, many people want to talk to you" she announced,

"You mean crucify me" I told her,

"Listen to me Rhys, if they find out who you really are and what you have done in the past",

"We will never be able to get you out of Thailand, they will lock you up and throw away the keys mate" she added! "We will get you out of here and there will be some heavy investigations, things will be sorted out I promise" she exclaimed to me, "How can I refuse a sexy lady like you, I suppose a blow job is out of the question, what you think" I told her and started to laugh, "yes keep playing the game Rhys, the more insane they think you are the faster we can transfer you, oh by the way, I will have to get to know you a lot better before I give you a blow job trooper" she told me and smiled, she walked away after tapping my leg.

My head was spinning with thoughts, a doctor came over to me and talked to me about me being transferred to the military clinic, he asked me if I was happy with it, he said I would see another doctor later to have a good long chat about how I feel,

I knew where I was going, down to the nut house again, I thought about Carmem and laid back on the bed, the doctor walked away,

Pin came over, I have some news for you, I take to toilet and for cigarette ok" she pushed me to the toilet in the wheel chair.

We went outside to the smoking area and she lit a cigarette for me,

"The lady you ask about, was brought her by some Russian sailors, she was found floating in the sea, she was nearly dead with dehydration, no details on her, she doesn't talk, she said something one day to a doctor like ajuda" Pin told me, "yes ajuda means help in Portuguese," I told her, she hasn't said a word to nobody in five weeks, the hospital has contacted different governments but nobody knows who she is or where she comes from, we hold her in the phyciatrict dept under the mental health act" Pin said,

"Pin I am supposed to go to phisio later on, do you think we can get out of here for a while and go to my hotel" I asked her?

I think we go at night, I am on night shift, I should be sleeping now, come sleep with me if you want" I said, she smiled and smoked some of my cigarette, "I see you later, I take you to phisio and we go see this woman ok somehow, I know who to talk to" Pin told me, "good girl" I replied.

Pin wheeled me back to my bed and gave me some tablets, I took them and relaxed and went to sleep.

My arm was being moved and I opened one eye sarcastically, there was the man from before in his army uniform,

"Hello again Rhys, I need you to sign some forms to finalise the transfer" he asked,

"Bloody comie bastards" I shouted out!

"They'll put me in Battersea dogs home after thieve chopped my bollocks off" I added! And closed my one open eye,

"yes he gets worse, I take him too mental care dept now to see doctor, I think you come back tomorrow" I heard Pin tell him, "he really is going bonkers, I will have to think about things, thank you nurse" he added and marched off,

I opened my eyes and smiled at Pin

"You bad boy, you make me want to laugh" she said and rubbed my leg,

"We go and see the lady" she said and I got into the chair once my straps were taken off me.

Pin wheeled me down the corridor.

We came to a door that had a key code, Pin tapped on the window and waved, the door was opened and we went in, I saw Pin give the other nurse money as they spoke in their own language, it was quiet in this part of the hospital,

Pin wheeled me to where I had seen Carmem, she wasn't in the room, there was other women there but not who I had seen before, Pin spoke to the nurse at the desk and she pointed down the corridor, Pin wheeled me down the corridor there was a few more doors, there was a clicking noise, the nurse had opened the door remotely from her desk, we went in, there was three beds and I saw a woman sat on the end bed looking out of the window,

"Carmem" I called to her, she didn't turn around, "Carmem Emilia Lopes Davies, god damn you woman it's me Rhys" I growled, she turned around and smiled and waved at me, "that is all she does all day smile at you and wave, the doctor said it's to do with her waving so much for help when she was in the sea, she had a nasty bump to the head that has caused amnesia and messed her brain up, the doctors do not know what to do with her, I got out of the chair and went to her, I sat on the bed next to Carmem and had a good look at her, she was thin in the face and the sun and sea water had changed the colour of her hair, her eyes were still green and brown, she looked into my eyes, "do I know you" she asked, "Carmem, I love you sweetheart, I thought you was dead, I am so sorry" I told her and went to put my arm around her, she pushed me away, "do I know you" she said again and waved her hand, I stood up, "you are my Carmem and that is that, don't worry my love I will fix you" I told her, she looked out of the window, I want to Pin, "I want to talk to the nurse out there" I told her, "why" she asked, "find out what medication she is on, she's spaced out" I put in, Pin wheeled me out, "chee vego depoise linda. ew chee amore kereeda parra semprees" I said loudly to her in Portuguese, I used to say it all the time to her, Carmem turned around and stared at me, she put her hands to her face and cried, she looked at me again, "what has happened to me Rhys" she said quietly, I got out of the chair and went to her,

We hugged and I kissed her, I was holding her up as she went limp, I laid her back on the bed,

"Be careful Rhys too much shock for her to take" pin said as she came to my side, she pressed the buzzer and the other nurse came in, Pin and the nurse spoke in their language,

"This is great news, she not talk for five weeks, I must tell the doctor and run tests move her from this ward" she said in a panic mood,

"wo there lightning lets calm down, Pin tell her I am taking her from here today for ever, I will pay her well if she says nothing" I said,

Pin spoke fast to the nurse, the nurse looked at me and nodded, I asked Pin how much money she could get as soon as possible, she told me about twenty thousand Baht, I told her to get it I would pay her back later, it was about a thousand British pounds, a hell of a lot to Thai people, "It is all my savings for a long time Rhys" Pin told me, please get it and give to your friend for her help" I said to her, she nodded, "I go now, be back in twenty minutes, Malo the other nurse will look after you" Pin announced and went off, she kissed me on the cheek,

The other nurse went out and did her checks and came back, Carmem laid on her bed, I had been talking to her but she didn't respond to me,

"So what rubbish you been giving her then, I explained what I meant,

"Doctor give her strong medication to relax her" she said,

"Relax her, turn her into a cabbage" I growled! I continued to talk to Carmem but there was nothing, she just looked out of the window, I pointed to a scar on her head to the nurse, "she had a bad knock to her head" the nurse told me, "it's time for her medication, the doctor will be doing his rounds soon",

"He walks round with a security guard as some of the patients here can get violent" the nurse told me,

Pin came in breathing heavy, she spoke to the nurse and handed her a wad of money, she spoke in Thai, "thank you for your help" I said The nurse came to me and kissed my cheek., "She knew here, temporary, she not like it, with this money she go to mother's farm and help out, plenty money for her" she said, "tell her if she helps more I give her a lot more" I said to Pin, Pin spoke to Malo in their language and she nodded,

"Ok so we need to get out of here now" I said.

"We have cloths for her, I get her changed" Malo announced and went off,

I talked to Carmem and said the same thing I said earlier on that she responded to,

Carmem looked at me,

"I called to you, you left me in the water, you disappeared and I float for days on my own" she said, tears rolled down my face,

"I am so sorry, I didn't even know you had fallen off the boat my love" I whispered to her,

"You left me" Carmem said, a tear rolled down her face,

"You come back for me now and rescue me please Rhys" she added,

"I am here now sweetheart your safe now" I replied and we hugged each other.

Carmem had her cloths changed so she didn't look like a patient, the plan was I was to be wheeled out of the rear of the hospital to the smoking area, we had a two hour window where I should be at the phisio, Malo would push me, Carmem would be there as a visitor and Pin would go to her ward and see if things were ok.

Off we went.

Malo pushed me through swing doors, she had to help Carmem too, Malo put Carmem's hand on the handle of my wheel chair and we went out the back and waited for Pin,

I lit a cigarette and so did Malo, Carmem watched us,

"Can I have one" she asked, Malo lit one for her, Carmem smoked the cigarette and coughed, we carried on smoking.

Pin came out and took the cigarette off me and took a long suck on it and blew out the smoke, she spoke fast in her language and looked very nervous, she passed me a bag and I looked inside, there was cloths for me to put on, Pin took off her nurses jacket to reveal a nice thin outfit,

"We need to go now, the phisio people told the doctor you did not turn up for your treatment" she told us, she passed me a bottle of pills,

"These are yours to take, they are not the other ones" she added I knew what she was talking about, Malo took her white jacket off and threw it in the bin,

"We go now" Pin said and we all walked off.

We made our way out of the hospital grounds, someone shouted to us, I turned to look back, a security officer spoke in Thai,

Pin spoke back in Thai and he officer looked hard at her and walked away,

"What was all that about" I asked?

"They look for you, I tell the officer I see him right later, he knows me a long time, I help him to get job, he owes me favour,

We walked out of the hospital grounds,

Malo flagged a taxi down and we all climbed into the back and drove off,

I told Pin the name of the hotel and she told the driver, Carmem looked tired and stared onto space, I put her hand on the side rail and she held on,

We got to the hotel and went inside, there was a bar and we sat down, and Pin ordered some drinks,

The drinks came and we chatted,

I told Pin to go to reception and ask to book a room, I told her my number, and she went off after drinking down half her bottle of beer,

We watched her talking to the girl at the reception, she came back with a room key.

"Your room is taken Rhys we have room next to it" she said,

"Shit" I moaned, "me and Pin will go to the room looking like a normal couple, Malo you bring Carmem up in half hour ok" I told everyone, we all nodded, I drank my bottle of beer and felt a bit drunk,

Me and Pin stood up and went towards the stairs, just as we were about to go up someone called my name,

"Mr Rhys, you gone long time" a young lady said, I remembered her, we had a few drinks together before and other stuff, "we pack up your room and store your stuff for you, you go to hospital, they keep ringing here to ask for your money to pay for medicine, the manager refused to give the money you have in our security box" she said with a smile, Carmem stared at her and looked at me, the young girl took me to a locked room and opened the door, she showed me my rucksack and some cloths.

I thanked her and told her I would pay her later, she locked the door as we went out with my stuff, me and Pin went up the stairs and got to the room, we went in, I went to the balcony and opened the door, we were on the first floor, I wanted to climb onto my old rooms balcony, Pin told me not to as it was to light and I would be seen,

I went to my bag and looked through my stuff, I shook my cloths and a card fell out,

"Yes, bloody yes" I announced,

"Swipe card for next door" I added and smiled,

I told Pin I was going to talk to the girl who gave me my bag back and pay her, see if I can get some information on who was in my old room, offer her some more money or something, Pin nodded her head and sat on the bed, "I take shower" she said and went to the bathroom, I left the room and went down to reception, I put my baseball hat on and my sunglasses that was in my bag and looked around for the young girl, she wasn't at reception, I asked the girl about my security box, I told her I had lost my key, she asked for my passport and I told her I had lost it too, she checked my name on the computer, "do you remember the memorable word sir you told us for security" she asked?

"the last post" I told her, she smiled and went to the back room, she came back with the box and gave me a small key, I thanked her and opened it, there was a pile of money in there that I took out, I passed the box back to the girl and gave her a few thousand Bhat, I gestured to her: Shhh! She smiled and nodded to me, I walked around and saw the young lady, I remembered her name and called her, she came to me,

"Hello Rhys you ok" she asked, "I am now I have seen you, can we talk somewhere quiet" I asked her, she nodded and took me to a small locked office.

I gave her a wad of money, "this is for you and I need some your help" I said to her, she looked at the money I had given to her before she put it in her pocket, she locked the door and came to me, her arms went round my neck and she kissed me very passionately, I kissed her back, she was after more as her hand went down my shorts,

I told her to hang on, plenty of time for that later I told her, she stopped and listened,

I asked her who was in my old room how long are they there for, she asked me why, I told her a story that I had hidden more money for safety behind the wardrobe and I needed it, she went to the computer and logged in, I watched her type away,

Mr and Mrs Smith, English, here for two weeks, they have gone out on a cruise round island they won't be back till tomorrow" she told me,

"Bloody great, good girl, now come here you" I told her.

I got back to my room, Carmem and Malo was there sat on the bed watching the TV, Pin I need some help, come on,

I and Pin went out and I swiped the card on my old room's door, the lock clicked and I pushed the door open, we went inside

I went straight to the wardrobe and pulled hard, it came away from the wall,

I pulled some more and reached behind, I felt the hole in the wall I had made to stuff the bags into, I reached and felt the bags, I pulled them out and threw them on the bed, I pulled out the weapons as well, Pin's eyes went very big, "why you have those things Rhys" she asked, "long story, tell you later, I pushed the wardrobe back into place, we cleaned up the mess and took the stuff back to our room,

I opened the bags, piles of money wrapped up in bundles, there was another bag I opened and poured out all the emeralds,

"Remember this lot" I asked Carmem, she looked at me, "you came back for me, thank you" she said and looked at the stones

"She needs time Rhys and a lot of patience" Malo said, I have her medication, I look after her" she exclaimed,

"ok we get another hotel before the hospital starts snooping around, I need to convert the British money in to Bhat, I want to buy a boat and we get out of here" I said,

"Malo, Pin you can come with us if you want to, you are both very welcome, I will look after you, they both nodded,

We all had a drink.

I gave Pin a lot of money to change at the bank and Hula too, I was taking a gamble that they may not return and we all left,

Pin and myself went out first and then Malo came out with Carmem, "Mr Rhys" I heard my name being called,

The hotel manager was stood there.

I remembered him from when I first booked in at the hotel,

"Please come with me" he said and walked to his office,

I told Pin to wait at a bar round the corner and she went off, I followed the hotel manager into his office,

"Take a seat" he said and pointed to the chair, I sat down, he locked the door, and I got up instantly,

"What the fuck you do that for faggot, the only thing going up your arse id my boot" I growled, I knew he was gay,

"I sorry I have to hold you here till the police come, hospital call police, you not pay the bill, I am sorry" he announced,

I pulled him towards me and gave him a sturdy head but, he went down like a sack of spuds, I found some tape in the draw and bound and gagged him, I left the office and snapped the key in the lock and left the hotel.

It was hot and sweaty as I walked down the side street, I saw the girls sat under an umbrella with some drinks, and Carmem was eating some crisps.

"What happened" Pin asked?

"All sorted out, but we have a problem I have been told that the police are coming to the hotel for me" I told them,

"We go to hotel on other side of island, I know where to go, can get boat there, I have an uncle who works for a boat company there" Malo announced,

We finished our drinks and jumped in a taxi, Malo spoke to the driver and paid him and we set off, we passed the hotel as two police motor bikes pulled up, the officers took out their hand guns and walked in,

"That was close" I commented,

Carmem looked at me, "you came back for me" she said and looked out the back,

Malo looked at me.

It took half an hour to get to another town resort, we stopped off at money exchange place where I exchanged some money, Pin bought a few pay as you go mobile phones and we sorted them out on the remain of the journey, there was hotels everywhere and bars, the taxi stopped and we got off the back,

Pin paid the driver and he drove off, we walked for five minutes, Malo pointed to a hotel and we went inside, Pin and Malo checked in with no problem, they acted to be a bit drunk, me and Carmem waited in the bar outside, Malo came out and told us they have a big room for two days, me and Carmem followed her in, I was singing as I went past the reception and had my arm around Carmem, she went to push it off and we went into the lift, Carmem gave me a dirty look, "why you do that" she asked?

"ew chee amore linda, para sempree" I spoke in Portuguese, she smiled, "you come back for me" she said again, I left it at that, we got out of the lift and went into the room.

"so Malo you take me to get some more money changed, Pin you take Carmem out and do some shopping, spoil her for a while, talk to her, we meet back here later and eat" I exclaimed, we all had a mobile phone with each other's numbers stored on speed dial, I put a phone in Carmem's pocket, I told Pin to buy her a nice hand bag and make up, sexy under ware and stuff, the stuff that makes women happy, she understood what I was talking about, Malo looked at me,

"Don't worry, we can do shopping once we sort this boat out" I said and she smiled, we all left the hotel.

Malo took me down to a marina and we looked about, there was for sale signs on the boats, there was some nice medium sized cruisers here, we walked past them all and went further down,

"Here we go" she said and pointed to another smaller marina, there was some nice boats for sale here too,

"Malo" someone called out, we turned around as an elderly gentleman approached us, she screamed and ran to him, they hugged and laughed, they both spoke quickly in Thai,

Malo looked at me as she took out a wad of money I had given her, I nodded and she stuffed it into the old man's pocket, he looked at me did the prayer sign with his hands,

The old man walked through the gates of the front of the marina, we followed, I could see a row of boats in the water tied to their moorings, and the old man pointed to the boats and spoke in Thai,

"He said any one of those are for sale" Malo said, I went closer to have a good look,

"How much for this one" I asked pointing to a nice one,

She spoke to her uncle, "two million" he says.

I worked it out on my phone, that's about forty thousand pounds, not too bad, let's have good look around, I told Malo that whatever one I buy I wanted a new name put on the boat, she told him and he agreed.

We looked around the other boats and I found one that I liked, the old man wanted a bit more for this one, he had to make a telephone call to the owner of the marina to make sure it was ok, the boat was nice, not too sporty, an average size, plenty of room for four persons.

The old man came out of the office and nodded, he spoke in Thai to Malo,

Malo looked at me, "ok now you pay and he will get the new name for the boat sorted out, she said, we all went into the office and made arrangements of the payment.

I could pay it all today, a good chunk in Thai baht and the rest in British pounds, fifty pound notes, the old man cleared this with the owner on the phone again, Malo asked if she could stay with her uncle for a while, I went to have another look at the boat and phoned Pin, I told her I had the boat was on my way back to the hotel, she asked if I could come down to the main shops and help, she said Carmem was talking and buying stuff, it was amazing, I told Malo that I was going to the shops and would see her later at the hotel, she was happy to stay with her uncle, I reminded her about the name of the boat.

CARMEM.

I flagged a taxi down and jumped in, the driver spoke to me, I just pointed forward and he drove on, I had Pin on the phone, she said she saw me so stop the taxi, I did and got off, Pin paid the driver,

"come Rhys you must see this" she said, I followed into a ladies cloths shop, and saw Carmem wearing a pretty dress, her hair was done and she had makeup on, she looked beautiful,

I walked slowly up to her, she was talking to the girl in the shop in Portuguese, the young girl understood, "Carmem" I called out and she turned around, "is it too much, what you think" she said and winked at me, I fell to my knees and tears rolled down my cheek, "thank you lord for this glorious moment" I said and stood up, Carmem looked at me, "you been drinking again Mr" she growled, "she's back" I shouted and went to her, I gave her a big hug, I went to kiss her and stopped, I looked into her eyes, they were different, we kissed, "I could murder a drink mate, this shopping just wipes me out, have some nice stuff to show you, Pin has been so nice to me, I was sat in the chair and girls were doing my nails and my hair, Pin was talking to me, everything came at once into my head, I thought I was going to pass out, I remember too much you scumbag, oh and have I got a bone to pick with you later" she growled and slapped my face, I smiled, "I love you" I said,

"I know, now give me a hand with these bags, us girls have got some drinking to do, oh pay for the dress too please darling" she said and winked at me, "yesh my lady" I said like the thunder birds butler says to lady Penelopy,

I followed them out and we found a nice bar, I got the drinks in, three beers, "what is that, me and Pin want some cocktails, how about a screaming orgasm" Carmem asked Pin, Pin smiled, "I haven't had one of those in a while" she replied, "nor have I, got some catching up to do" Carmem added,

Looking at me and nodding her head.

"I don't understand, one minute Carmem doesn't remember a thing and is in kuku land the next instance she is back to normal" I asked Pin as Carmem had gone to the loo,

"It happens, triggers, things she has missed, I have seen it before, it's amazing and lovely, she is a beautiful woman, I am jealous by the way Rhys" Pin exclaimed, it has been great, I owe you so much the way you looked after me in hospital, friends for life" I told her, she leaned over and kissed me, "our last kiss" she said and pulled away, "and don't you think I won't tell Carmem one day how you took advantage of an innocent young nurse just doing her duties you bad boy" she said and laughed, "you're not that innocent" I commented, I saw Carmem walking over, she looked like a new woman, she started to dance to the music and a young man walked towards her, I made my move and nudged him away, "sorry mate, she's taken, I put my arm round Carmem's waist and we danced,

Malo came into the bar, Pin had called her on the phone, Pin and Malo came up and danced with us, the young man came over again, "sorry mate all three girls are taken" he looked a bit shocked and walked away, we all laughed and had a good time, we had some more drinks and had a nice meal and went back to the hotel,

Malo's phone rang and she answered it, "the boat is ready when you are ready, it has full fuel tanks with spare, there are supplies on board and she is ready to go" she said, "ok I have a plan, let's get to the hotel, pack up and spend the night on her" I said, "spend the night on what" Carmem asked, "surprise my darling" I replied, "I hate your surprises, I need another drink" Carmem said and walked off, we laughed,

We got to the hotel and packed up, we walked towards the marina, "there she is" I announced and pointed to a boat by the water.

"Oh my god, another boat" Carmem announced.

She saw the name on the side:

"Carmem" she said,

She looked at me, "I love you Rhys, you came back for me" she announced and kissed me hard on the lips,

"Ok people let's see what this baby can do shall we" I announced and we all climbed on, Malo's uncle untied the ropes and I took her slowly out of the marina.

We bounced around as I opened her up and got out to sea, I wasn't too sure where we were going, just well away from Thailand, too many people wanting to talk to me,

We sailed for a good two hours and slowed right down, I saw a small island in the distance and decided to go there for the night, auto pilot was set in the direction of the island and we cruised along, the girls were on the front of the boat all wearing life jackets, my rule, I joined them with a drink and danced along,

We made our way to the back of the boat and sat round a small table, Pin brought up some nice cocktails, I had a large whisky,

Carmem saw my drink, and shook her head, "I hope something works later on boyo" she informed me, Pin and Malo laughed,

"I want to make a toast, to Carmem" I said, we all stood up and said Carmem, we had some cigarettes and plenty more drinks, Malo and Pin made some nice food they brought up whilst me and Carmem had a good chat about what had happened, the night went on, we were close to the island, I pulled up and we secured the boat to a wooden jetty, a man met us there and Pin paid him to stay the night,

We ate the food and had some more drinks, I set up the rifles on the front of the boat and let the girl's fire off a few bullets at some floating target I had made, they loved it.

It started to get dark, me and Carmem were dancing together, and she kissed me,

Pin was dancing Malo and I saw them kiss, I had been noticing them getting closer for a while now,

We all sat down, it was starting to get windy,

Pin passed out some cigarettes and we smoked, "

"Tonight we all sleep together" Carmem announced and kissed Pin on the mouth, then Malo, I looked shocked, "hello I am jealous here" I exclaimed!

"Easy tiger, you got three women to look after tonight" she said to me,

I looked at Carmem and then to the other girls, they winked at me,

"I blew out some smoke from the cigarette,

"Oh dear, be gentle ladies" I commented,

We all laughed and went inside for the night, everyone was in the front bunk in their knickers and bra's we had some more drinks and smoked cigarettes till the early hours, we talked about all sorts, I told the girls of my adventures with Carmem and what had happened,

I remember Pin kissing me and Carmem kissing Malo and that was that.

I awoke to the boat rocking,

I made my way to the bridge and started the engines up,

I set the sat nav to the next island that was over a day's sailing away, I heard the girls moving around,

Carmem came up with some coffee, "Drink for the captain" she said, and passed me a cup of coffee,

I took a swig and winked at her, there was a little bit of something else in it,

"Sleep well" she asked,

"Wow you girls snore too much, at one point I actually got scared, thought I was sleeping with a pack of wolves" I told her,

She laughed, you remember what happened last night you naughty boy" Carmem asked, "bits and pieces" I told her,

I really wasn't too sure what had happened but I had an idea but thought no way did I do that, the girls came up with coffee dressed in their night cloths still looking at me, "naughty boy" Pin said to me,

I saw Malo nodded her head and wink,

"So where are we going captain" they all asked as we pulled off,

I took a swig from my cup and flicked my cigarette out to sea,

"Not sure, but I know a mate in Africa, Midnight we used to call him in the army, the biggest black man I ever saw and dam honoured to of served with him, he runs a small security group in the diamond mines, trying to stop the workers taking the diamonds for themselves, over the years he has kept a load himself, he needs help to get them out of the Country, hey ho another adventure" I shouted!, Carmem looked at me and winked, I pushed the throttle forward and off we went.